The Heatwave

KATE RIORDAN

PENGUIN BOOKS

PENGUIN BOOKS

UK | USA | Canada | Ireland | Australia
India | New Zealand | South Africa

Penguin Books is part of the Penguin Random House group of companies
whose addresses can be found at global.penguinrandomhouse.com.

First published 2020
001

Set in 12.5/14.75 pt Garamond MT Std
Typeset by Jouve (UK), Milton Keynes
Printed and bound in Great Britain by Clays Ltd, Elcograf S.p.A.

A CIP catalogue record for this book is available from the British Library

ISBN: 978–1–405–92262–3

www.greenpenguin.co.uk

For my mum, of course

You fit into me
like a hook into an eye

a fish hook
an open eye

— Margaret Atwood

PART ONE

July 1993

The letter is there when I get home from work. I know it's French immediately. The handwritten number 7 in the postcode gives it away: crossed and curled, so un-English. La Rêverie is finally calling me back.

The summer sun is relentless in the place I come from. There, the hard earth absorbs all the heat it can, leaving the rest to hang in the air, heavy as swaddling. On the hottest nights, I would lie awake in damp sheets, the windows and shutters flung back, and listen to the cicadas whirring and the frogs belching and the thunder rolling around the hills, like marbles in a bowl.

I didn't miss France when we left. I was grateful the two of us could hide away in north London, safe among the streets of red-brick houses and trees that lift the paving stones. I don't even mind that I've become a permanent foreigner, despite my excellent English, the accent always giving me away. 'Oh, you're French,' people say, smiling. 'All that lovely wine and cheese.'

I think in English now. I even dream in my adopted language. But as I put down the letter and begin to digest what it means, I do so in my native tongue. It happens automatically – the old language so easy to inhabit that it's like a shirt you no longer want but still fits better than anything else.

At the telephone in the hall, I open the address book to G. I still don't know your father's number in Paris by heart.

'*Oui?*'

His accent is good, better than when we were still married, when I would tease him, saying, 'Greg, it's not "wee". You have to move your mouth with French. Use your lips.'

'I'll use my lips, all right,' he always said, pantomime-raucously, and then he would kiss me. We were forever kissing in the early days. Kissing and laughing. We always spoke English together, despite living in France – and not just because my grasp of his language was so much surer than his of mine, but because it balanced things, somehow. A house full of English with the whole of France outside.

'Oh, Sylvie, it's you,' he says. His voice, low and slightly hoarse, is still capable of piercing the softest parts of me. 'Is Emma all right?'

'Emma is fine.'

I can picture him as if he's standing in front of me, the hand that isn't holding the phone turning over a crumpled pack of Gitanes, a soft chambray shirt, ironed by someone else now, impatience in the deep groove between his eyebrows.

I swallow, wishing I'd thought about what I would

say before I'd rung. 'Look, I need you to take Emma for a few days, maybe a week.'

'We talked about the end of August, didn't we?'

'Yes, but I need you to have her now. As soon as possible.'

'What? Why? Where are you going? The schools haven't even broken up yet, have they?'

I can see the letter on the table from where I'm standing, its sharp white corners.

'They break up on Friday. She'll only miss a few days. I can drop her off in Paris on my way south.'

'South? Sylvie, what's going on?'

'Something happened at the house. The solicitor wrote to me about it. There was – there's been some damage.'

'What sort of damage?'

'A small fire. It was probably accidental, but it's going to cost. The house has been standing empty for ten years now and this kind of thing is only going to crop up more. It needs to be sold and I have to go there in person, sign some papers. You know how it is in France, how complicated they make these things.'

'Well, we'd love to see Emma, of course. But I don't think it'll work.'

'You know I don't want her going back there. Besides, I'll be stuck with the solicitors half the time.'

'Sylvie, I've got a buying trip and Nicole is taking the boys to her mother's in Normandy. It's all arranged.'

I don't reply. I had known, really, that he would say no. In the silence that follows, both of us lost in our own thoughts, the line hums between us.

'So you're finally going back,' he says eventually, and takes a long drag of his cigarette.

*

Though it's early when we leave the flat and begin the journey south to Dover, the day is almost gone by the time we drive off the ferry in Calais, the men waving us impatiently down the ramp, neon jackets garish against the sky that's always grey and brooding here. You're quiet beside me, but a mounting excitement is leaking out of you, like the noise from the Discman earphones you're hardly without these days.

I follow the car in front of us into the right-hand lane, blue motorway signs flashing overhead. As we drive on, deeper and deeper into the darkening mass of France, the voice in my head that hasn't paused since I got the letter grows louder, more insistent. I find I'm gripping the wheel so tightly that it's slippery with sweat.

I glance at the dashboard clock. It's late. Up ahead, the sign for a budget hotel glows out of the dark. I let out a breath I didn't know I'd been holding and pull off the road. In the fluorescent-lit reception area, silent except for the hum of a vending machine, it doesn't feel like the country I left behind – the sleepy France of my childhood or the place where we were once a normal family. No, that's disingenuous. Whatever we were, we were never normal, not even from the start.

*

In the morning, I pour you a second cup of *chocolat chaud* in the breakfast room and gesture to the packets of dry *biscottes* piled high on the buffet table, the round pats of pale Normandy butter.

'Have some more, darling,' I entreat, smiling to make up for the strain in my voice. 'It'll be a long day.'

But you're much hungrier for the scene's foreignness than your breakfast: not just the deep bowls of coffee and thin slices of cheese layered in ripped-open croissants but the children with their perfect table manners, their brightly coloured spectacles.

You lean forward and drop your voice conspiratorially: 'There's a man over there who keeps looking at you.'

'No, there isn't.' But my eyes are already searching the room because it's impossible not to.

You're grinning, which makes me smile too.

'He just did it again,' you say. 'He's so obvious. Over by the window in the green shirt. He's on his own. He's probably divorced too. You should go and say *bonjour*.'

'For God's sake, Emma!' though I'm laughing now.

'You're really good for your age, Mum.'

'Ah, I love a backhanded compliment.'

You roll your eyes. 'No, but you are. You're really pretty. Men always look at you. That Nick who asked you out at work was basically obsessed with you.'

I spot my admirer then, our eyes meeting for an instant. There's something of Greg about him: the way he holds his knife and the unconscious flick of his head because his fringe is too long. I used to cut Greg's hair for him when we were married, newspaper spread under the stool in the kitchen.

I stand, my chair scraping on the hard floor. One of the children has begun to sing-song, *'Maman! Maman!'* and I don't know how much longer I can stand it.

*

We follow the slower, narrower D roads after Lyon, sunlight slanting through long lines of poplars. I'd forgotten the meticulous commitment to signposting every minor village and hamlet, not just when you enter but when you leave too, the name slashed through with red. The countryside around us feels endless after London: age-softened farmhouses and the occasional shuttered restaurant marooned at the margins of vast fields. I glance over at you, drinking it all in. It must be so exotic to you, yet it's where you spent your first four years.

The sun climbs as we drive, the car growing steadily hotter. You fiddle with the radio, snorting with derision at the terrible French pop songs but stopping when you find a station playing Edith Piaf. I wind down the window and, in the first blast of air, I smell the past. It's indescribable. The closest I can get to it is hot stone, lavender and a distant note of something like panic.

Half a mile from the house, we almost get lost, which seems absurd given that I've lived more of my life in this part of the world than any other. A petrol station has appeared on a corner once occupied by a peach stall we used to stop at, and this throws me enough to miss first the turn and then the sign. It's only when we're suddenly in the heart of the old village – the dappled shade of the plane trees, the café's round silver tables and the dusty awning of the *boulangerie* all utterly unchanged – that I realize where we are.

I turn the car around with a screech, not yet ready to be seen by anyone who might know me, and soon we're bumping down the dirt road to La Rêverie.

Quite abruptly, more quickly than is comfortable, we reach the rutted track that winds down to the ramshackle barn where logs for winter fires were stored, along with the rusting rollers and ancient farm tools my father pointlessly hoarded. I don't look at it, driving round to the front of the house instead.

I turn off the engine. You're silent next to me. I reach out to tuck a loose strand of hair behind your ear: English mouse and a little ragged at the ends because you're always trying to grow it longer. You've made me promise you can have it streaked when you turn sixteen. *I want it blonder,* you've been saying all spring. *Not this nothingy colour.*

'Mum, I don't think I remember this,' you say now, your voice high and young. 'I thought I did, when we turned off, but . . .'

'It might come back,' I say, hoping it won't, that everything from that time has been permanently erased. You were so young when we left, and I tell myself, as I have so many times, that that's why you've apparently forgotten everything.

We get out and the ticking under the car's bonnet echoes the cicadas that fill the bushes around us. Their

9

cries will get faster and more frenzied as the day wears on, the sun steadily climbing, the temperature rising. '*Écoute, chérie. Écoute les cigales*,' my mother used to say when I was little, in a bid to stop me running outside and getting overheated. *They'll tell you if it's too hot to go out today.* I'd forgotten that.

The house is exactly as a foreigner would picture a *maison de maître* in the South of France: thick grey stone and a steeply pitched roof, tall symmetrical windows concealed by mauve-blue shutters, the paint powdery with age and the ferocity of the sun. The garden that surrounds it is walled at the front and topped with railings. I push back the metal gate, whose letter box still bears my maiden name in faded letters, and it swings in easily, as if used every day.

Inside, the bougainvillaea spills over the grass and the lavender bushes have gone woody and sparse, but it isn't as unkempt as I imagined a garden abandoned for a decade would be. It still looks like the place I remember. Weeds grow up through the path to the door, but the dense column of cypress that casts one side of the house into deep shadow always needed cutting back, even in my earliest memories. I glance up at the furthest bedroom window, the one most obscured by the cypress's deep shade, and see that one of the shutters has slipped its hinges.

By my side, you crackle with something: anticipation, mostly, but also a little fear. Perhaps you've caught it from me.

'Was that her room?' you ask.

I look sharply at you. 'That's right. Do you remember?'

'Just a guess.'

You look at it hungrily then, as if the braver part of you wants to believe someone is up there now, watching you through the gaps in the shutters. The cicadas have stopped, and the silence is unnerving. Then, in miraculous unison, they start up again, even louder than before, and I stride determinedly towards the front door, fumbling in my bag for the key, knowing that if I don't go in right now, I might drag you back to the car and drive straight home.

The church-cool air of the darkened hallway smells of mingled damp and smoke from the recent fire. Beneath them, faint but bone-deep familiar, I can just discern La Rêverie's older scents: beeswax, butter-softened garlic and my mother's olive soap.

I'm so struck by this that it takes me a while to notice that your breathing has changed. I scrabble in the inside pocket of my handbag, praying that the inhaler I carry from habit rather than necessity is still there. At last my hand closes around plastic. I pull it out and shake it.

You're fine after a couple of puffs, though your hands are already beginning to shake – a side-effect of the drug seeping into your muscles.

'Okay now, darling?'

You nod, just once.

'It must be all the dust and damp,' I say, and you nod again, though both of us know that your asthma is triggered by stress and not by allergies.

While you're unpacking, I wander around the house, methodically opening each door, except the one I'm not yet ready for. The shutters scream as I push them back, revealing fat black flies in sinister piles on the window-sills. As the light floods in, dust swarms.

Last of all, I steel myself to go and look at the fire damage. I know it's in the scullery off the kitchen – *la souillarde* – a small space housing little more than a sink, draining board and a couple of curtain-fronted cupboards that remains dark and cool however stifling it gets outside. Its window is no bigger than a sheet of paper, with chicken wire instead of glass in the frame.

Though the smells of fresh damage are strong when I open the door, it's not as bad as I've been imagining since I received the letter. Two of the whitewashed walls are now marbled with black. In places, the marks are as high as my head. It's hard to tell what is scorched and what is mould, the evidence mingling darkly. But whatever happened here, water must swiftly have followed fire. Otherwise the whole house would have gone up.

*

As evening begins to thicken around the house, you ask if we can go and eat in the village. We walk the ten minutes in, the tarmac soft under our feet, legs shiny with insect repellent in preparation for the evening's emerging mosquitoes. The sun has already dipped behind the hills by the time we sit down at a table outside a pizzeria that wasn't here before. We're overlooking the tree-shaded patch of earth where the old men always played *boules* in their caps and braces, and doubtless still do, though they're not out for the evening yet.

You ask me to ask the waitress for a Coke, too shy to try speaking in French, and I order a beer instead of my usual wine. When it comes, so cold that droplets of condensation have formed on the glass, I gulp it down like water and gesture for a second.

I catch your disapproving look and smile. 'I saw that, my little puritan. It's not like I've got to drive.'

'It must be strange being back,' you say cautiously, when you've finished your food. You're swirling a plastic stirrer around your Coke glass.

I nod, though the second beer has made it less so.

'Do you miss it now that you're here?'

I look up, surprised at your perceptiveness. On leaving for London when you were four, I bundled everything into a deep drawer marked 'France' and slammed it shut, forgetting there was so much to love about home.

'I'm sorry I've kept you from the house for so long. You were born here too. It's as much yours as mine.'

You glow. 'It is?'

I smile and squeeze your hand.

'Mum, are you sure there's no way of keeping the house? It's such an amazing place. We could come here every summer. We could.'

I bat away a moth as it dances close to my eyes. 'It's impossible, *chérie*. I would need to buy out your aunt Camille and I can't afford it. You know what she's like.'

You frown, pulling your hand away, and for a split second you remind me of your sister. 'I don't think you'd do it even if you did have the money.' And then, as if you've heard my thoughts. 'It's because of her, isn't it?'

I dig my fingernails into the table edge. 'Emma, do you have any idea how hard it is for me to be back here?' The alcohol makes the words sharp and I regret them immediately. 'Look, let's not argue. I'm sorry I didn't bring you before, but we're here now, aren't we?'

You don't reply but after a while you nudge my hand in apology. Quite suddenly, I want to cry.

The walk back from the village is dark. No, not dark: pitch-black. The stars have been blotted out so thoroughly by clouds that it takes until we reach the turn-off before I can distinguish the shadowed bulk of the hills from the sky.

Despite the lack of visible moon, La Rêverie seems to stand in its own dim pool of light as we approach. Or perhaps it's just our eyes, still adjusting to the country-side after years of London's perpetually thrumming glow. It looks bigger by night, a monster of a house rising out of its dark moat of garden. I don't look at the windows as we go up the path, keeping my head down, pretending to hunt in my bag for the key I'm already clutching.

Earlier in the afternoon, I had shaken out my mother's soft old linen, only a little musty, and made us up a bed each: the creaking mahogany double Greg and I once shared, which was my parents' before us, and one of the narrow twins in the bedroom next to it for you. Your old room has only its small cot-bed and I don't want you in there anyway.

'I remember this,' you exclaim, in the room that's been a spare my whole life, pointing to the faded blue *toile de Jouy* wallpaper, which, in one corner, has begun to peel. 'I used to sit on the floor and make up stories about the people.' You go closer, tracing a finger across the men in stockings, the ladies with their pompadours and fans. 'I remember them.'

*

I wake at exactly three in the morning, the dimly glowing hands of my travel clock a perfect L. Downstairs, at the very edge of my hearing, I hear the ormolu clock in the salon as it chimes the hour. The bright, metallic ting is a sound older than memory to me, one that marked a benign passage through all the nights of my childhood, and I turn over, comforted. I'm just slipping into a dream of my mother winding it when I sit up, the bed groaning with the suddenness of the movement. I haven't wound the clock.

*

The next morning I find you at the bottom of the terrace steps, barefoot in the long grass. I shade my eyes against the startling glare of the sun, my head tight from lack of sleep.

15

'I found the swimming pool,' you call up to me, full of glee. 'I didn't know there was one. It's so cool.'

You don't remember it from before. I try to smile: this is a good thing.

'Perhaps we can see about filling it, if the pump's still working,' I make myself say. You're a strong swimmer; I've made sure of that. I paid for years of lessons at an over-chlorinated municipal pool near our flat in London.

You look at me oddly. 'It's already filled.'

I know it was emptied ten years ago, when we left for good. Neither Camille nor I have touched it since.

But of course you're right. The water glimmers mysteriously through the row of parasol pines my conservative father planted in the fifties for the sake of his daughters' modesty. It isn't the blinding turquoise of resort swimming pools but deep, darkling jade. On overcast days I always thought it looked like green ink.

I kneel at the edge and dip my hand in. Hardly yet warmed by the sun, the water runs like chilled silk through my fingers. There are only a few leaves and insects floating on the surface, clustered at the far end. Someone has cleared it recently.

I wonder if Olivier Lagarde arranged it. Perhaps he wound the clock in the salon too. I have the strangest sense that these things are simply the house welcoming us back. And perhaps trying to keep us here.

I glance at my bare wrist. 'What time is it?'

'About half ten, I think.'

I get to my feet. 'I have to meet the solicitor at eleven, in the village.'

'I'm staying here.'

I pause. 'I thought you wanted to go to the hypermarket. You'll have to come with me if you do. I'm going there on the way back.'

You grumble as we walk to the house but I know you don't mind, really. You've never been the sort to put up much of a fight. My lovely biddable girl.

*

Only one other table is occupied at the café in the village – a couple, Dutch most likely: all long legs and hiking equipment.

'Darling, why don't you go and look in the *tabac* over there?' I hand you a crisp ten-franc note. 'Buy some postcards. The solicitor and I will be speaking in French.'

You blink, slightly stung, but go anyway, just as the waiter arrives.

Olivier Lagarde turns up just as you disappear into the shop across the square. He's much handsomer than I'd expected from my dim memory of his father. It's already hot and he's rolled up the sleeves of his shirt, his arms burnished against blinding white cotton and the chrome of his watch. His grip when he shakes my hand is firm and warm. As he sits down, the Dutch woman's eyes rake over him and I feel a little jolt that she might assume we're together.

'Madame Winters, thank you for meeting me today.' He smiles easily, appreciatively, his eyes intent when I meet them.

'Please, call me Sylvie,' I say, looking away first. 'And it's Durand again, actually. I'm divorced.'

'Bien sûr. Sylvie, then. You've seen the damage now, I gather, and that it's really quite superficial. I hope that was clear in my letter. I didn't want to worry you unduly. You were lucky, though. It could have been . . .' He spreads his hands. There's no need to say how it might have turned out.

'Do the police know who did it?'

He shrugs. 'Kids with nothing to do, who else? It happens all the time in the countryside. Especially when people know a house is standing empty.'

'Have they arrested anyone?'

He shakes his head. 'To them it's a small thing. They couldn't find any signs of forced entry. I'm sorry, Mada— Sylvie, but they weren't very interested. One of them said it was probably the Gattaz boys.'

I nod. It's a name I haven't thought of since childhood. That and the French that comes so effortlessly is both liberating and rooting. No, confining. I wonder if this is how it's going to be: the inexorable descent into the past; the years in England flickering and fading at the horizon.

I take a sip of my coffee: tiny, bitter and delicious. 'I don't remember you. From growing up round here, I mean.'

'No, I went to school in Avignon. Stayed with my aunt during the week. My father insisted, but look how it turned out.' He smiles wryly. 'I ended up here anyway.'

'Monsieur Lagarde,' I begin.

'Please, if I'm to call you Sylvie, you must call me Olivier.' He smiles again, as though we've shared something intimate.

It occurs to me that he might be flirting but I'm so rusty I can't be sure.

'*D'accord,*' I say, inclining my head. '*Olivier. I said to you on the phone that it might be time we sold La Rêverie. We've been putting it off, my sister and I, and I'm not sure why any more. Maybe what happened is a sign that we should get on with it.*'

'*I can help you sell, if that's what you want. I can put you in touch with someone at Century 21. Martine. She's good. But you should know that it's a sluggish market. The old Pelletier farm has been empty for two years now.*'

He catches the waiter's eye, then looks back at me. '*Stay for another?*'

I find myself nodding and he holds up two fingers.

'*It's the best time of year for the tourists, at least,*' he continues easily. '*There's a chance someone like them*' – he nods at the couple in walking gear – '*might decide they want their own piece of France. Five good-sized bedrooms, a big garden with a pool: it would make an excellent holiday home for a family. Though we're slightly off the beaten track here, of course. Now, if it was an hour closer to the coast things would be easier . . . I said the same thing to your sister when we spoke.*'

The sun has moved so it's beating down on my head. I shift slightly towards Olivier to escape its glare and knock against the table. He puts out a hand to steady it.

'*Désolée,*' I murmur, aware of the heat rising in my cheeks.

Absurdly, I find myself wondering whom he would judge to be the more attractive of Camille and me. Your aunt was the archetypal Parisienne even before she was one. She always looked down on the ageing housewives

19

in the village for their thickened waists and badly dyed hair. I hadn't seen her without an immaculately made-up face since she was eighteen. I run my hand through my own unbrushed hair, then make myself stop.

Across the square, you sidle out of the *tabac* and stop to turn a carousel of postcards.

'*May I say, Sylvie?*'

I wait, hoping he isn't going to say what I think he is.

He looks uncertain for the first time. '*I just wanted to say how sorry I was for your . . . loss. I hope you don't mind me saying this, but after what's happened at the house, I felt it would be strange not to.*'

This is why I hadn't wanted to see anyone who knew me from before. Though it feels like Olivier is coming from a place of genuine concern, I know what people in this village are like. Always hungry for more gossip, they're perfectly capable of filling in any gaps with speculation and guesswork. I wonder what they came up with about us, which rumours persisted, and firmed up over time into hard truth.

'*Thank you, it's kind of you to say so,*' I say. '*Though . . .*' I pause '*. . . I would prefer you not to mention anything about it in front of my daughter. In front of Emma. She doesn't know every-thing about . . . what happened here. About the fire – the old fire.*'

He nods and we finish our coffee in silence. I'm glad when you come sauntering over, hair shining in the sun, a paper bag in one hand and a chocolate ice-cream in the other.

'It's not even midday,' I exclaim in English. Olivier laughs, probably grateful the tension has been broken. I smile at him and, just like that, the awkwardness melts away. I can't help it, I like him.

'I love it here,' you say, eyes bright and imploring. 'I hope the house stuff takes ages.'

Olivier grins at you. *'Pas de problème, Mademoiselle.'* He switches to heavily accented English. 'In France, these things always do.'

*

Drained by the sheer size of the *hypermarché*, the two of us are lying prone next to the pool by two o'clock. The sun is fierce, like a physical weight pressing down, its effect almost like a sickness. I know I need to get on with things but my limbs have turned watery. I feel as if my hope to leave by the end of the week is spooling away, out of reach.

I drag over the only working parasol so it covers you and pull my own lounger into the dappled shade of the oleander tree. When I shut my eyes, patches of brightness bloom pale red through the lids. I'm just drifting into sleep when I hear screaming. I leap up and towards you without conscious thought, heart galloping, but you haven't moved. You're still sleeping, the headphones clamped over your head continuing to buzz.

I must have imagined it, teetering on the brink of dreams. I lie down again but can't settle, the echo of that phantom noise still reverberating in the heavy air. I recognize that scream. It's the same voice that murmured in my ear as I drove south. A girlish voice, melodic but threaded through with steel.

I go back to the house and find my eyes drawn to the *souillarde* door. Behind it, the cold tiles under my bare feet are a shock after the sultry garden. The air is like wading through river water, my arms goose-pimpling as I inspect the mould again, as if I might find clues written in its patterns.

I'm sure it's got worse overnight, the black marks beginning to spread around the small window like a dark, blurred-leaf creeper. I bought a spray that should bleach it away but I don't want to be in here. There's a prickling at the back of my neck, the kind that says you're no longer alone, though I know I am.

I'm just pulling the door shut behind me when I catch movement through the window. It's so brief that it's not even a shape, more a shift in the pattern of light out there by the barn.

An old gate is tucked into the overgrown hedge at the side of the lawn. It's rusted shut when I get to it, white paint blistered, and it screeches as I wrench it open. It doesn't look like anyone's used it since we left, which should be reassuring but isn't. It only adds to the dream-like strangeness I can't shake, of a place simultaneously abandoned and alive, like pockets of heat and cold in the sea.

The patch of earth between the house and the barn is palpably hotter and drier than the garden. I don't go into the barn. I already know what the damage looks like in there.

I shade my eyes to check the path snaking away towards the drive. There are no footprints but, further away, something has raised a cloud of ochre dust. Out on the main road, the wasp drone of a moped engine fades out of hearing. Once the air clears, everything is still, baking in the afternoon glare. The only movement is the heat shimmer that warps the distant blue hills.

*

The garden is losing its colour to the dusk. We've just finished eating a drawn-out supper of tomatoes, cheese and bread. Someone spying on the scene would see a mother and daughter relaxing into their holiday, but my shoulders are stiff with tension.

Fortunately, you seem not to have noticed. Or perhaps you have, because you stretch your arms and yawn noisily. 'I could get used to this,' you say, in the old-man voice that always makes me laugh. 'What do you think, love? Shall we stay?'

It's a favourite game of ours, this pretence we're a long-retired couple who take pleasure in small things; we do it in the flat while I'm making dinner. You've been less willing lately, and I've missed it, an eccentric side you don't reveal to anyone else.

'If you like it here, dearie, then so do I,' I say, trying not to sound too eager.

'You're a good girl. I couldn't have asked for a better wife all these years.'

We get the giggles then, made abruptly helpless in the intense way that veers close to tears. I pull down

23

my sleeve to wipe my eyes as we lapse into an easy silence.

'Do you believe in ghosts?' you suddenly ask, and the switch in mood pulls me out of my happiness like a slap. I reach for the pale Bandol rosé I've been drinking since this afternoon. I only drink occasionally in London.

'Ghosts?' My voice quavers slightly. 'No, I don't think so. Why, have you seen one?' I intend this to sound light-hearted but it doesn't quite succeed, the question mark too loud.

'No, I just wondered.'

'Did you hear a funny noise? Remember, it's an old house and it's summer now, too. When the temperature changes, everything creaks.'

'It's not that.'

'What, then?'

You shrug. 'Just some places are . . . I don't know. Like this place is. It's old and stuff but it's not just that. Our flat's Victorian but I can't imagine seeing anything there.'

'And you can here.'

You shrug again.

'Are you going to start sorting out our old things tomorrow?' you ask after a while. 'I can help if you want.'

'You're good to offer, sweetheart, but it'll be boring and dusty, I expect. I thought you wanted to get a tan.' I keep my voice casual because I don't want you going through everything. I don't know what you might stumble across, or how to answer your questions if you do.

You poke at your arm. 'This pasty skin will never go brown. It's already pink, like Dad's.' You look straight at me. 'Don't you want me to help?'

You're testing me, which is so unlike you. By unspoken agreement, we only talk about her obliquely. I've caught you enough times, though, gazing at that photograph in the hall at home, the only one of your sister that's on display. I presume you keep quiet because you don't want to make me sad, and I've let you believe it's as simple as that. Here, though, things might be different. Perhaps this is the beginning, tectonic plates shifting just enough to trigger the first tremor.

'You can help if you want to,' I say woodenly.

'Is there much left that was hers?'

You aren't looking at me but off into the darkening garden. You've poured yourself a dribble of the rosé, I don't know when.

'I – I'm not sure,' I say honestly. I can't remember exactly what was cleared and what wasn't. While so many of my memories from ten years ago are pin-sharp, others have blurred.

'I know you don't like talking about her, Mum,' you say, drinking your unasked-for inch of wine in a single gulp. 'But I don't see how we can't. It would just be weird, wouldn't it, now we're here? She was my sister but I know barely anything about her. She died, you and Dad split up and we moved to London. That's it.'

I don't reply. I can't think straight because my blood is suddenly loud in my ears.

You get up and put your arms round me. 'Please don't

be upset,' you say, breath hot in my ear. 'You can tell me things, you know. I'm older now.'

'You're not an adult, though, are you?' I say, more abruptly than I mean to. What I really want to say is, *You're still my little girl. Your sister at thirteen was so much older than you.*

You straighten up, offended, and pull your hand away when I try to take it.

I know I should explain everything properly. People always assume there'll be a better time and then it's too late. But I don't think I'm capable of it, not right now.

Neither of us says anything for a while and I listen to the small sounds of the garden preparing for night.

You consider me for a moment, your finger circling the rim of your glass. 'Do you think her ghost might be here, at La Rêverie?'

The loosed words swirl in the gloom, bright and unearthly, like phosphorescence. Around us, only perceptible if you know it as I do, the garden lets out a soft sigh.

1968

I conceive her in Paris, in the middle of the student riots: the glorious chaos of *Mai 68*. Her father says that our first child will be all fire and spark, forged as she was in the bonfire of old, conservative France.

We are students ourselves, or at least we were until recently, the two of us renting rooms on the fourth-floor of a house in the sixth *arrondissement*, plaster peeling from its belle-époque bones. Greg has already graduated with a 2:2 in political science while I have given up my studies in London to be here with him, persuaded that a degree doesn't really matter. It's just a piece of paper, he says, when I worry about it, his long pianist's fingers circling my navel, just another way the Establishment makes people buckle down to a conventional half-existence. What matters is this. He gestures towards the city beyond our tall, dust-streaked windows. *Real life*.

We came to Paris ostensibly for him to see more of my homeland. He'd enjoyed French at A level and had gone on holidays to France as a child: bracing weeks on the beaches of northern Brittany where he'd had his first erotic experience. I think about her sometimes, that long-ago Madeleine who bewitched a teenaged Greg in the early sixties. She instilled in him a weakness for French girls that steered him unerringly towards me as I sat sipping a half of mild in the union bar one winter-dark afternoon, trying to pretend I wasn't cold and homesick in London, that I liked English beer. Without Madeleine, he might have walked straight past and gone on to marry an English girl instead. And me? I might have gone home and married a nice boy from my village, London washing off me as easily as grime in the shower. When I think about this, about Fate and its vagaries, and how we might have missed each other by inches, I feel dizzy.

Greg wanted to come to Paris partly because of the growing unrest. He'd heard about Nanterre, which had been shut down after trouble between the university authorities and the students. I tease him for trying to shake off his suburban background, be something more dangerous than he is. His poor parents are horrified that their clever son has gone off the rails, has run off to Paris with his foreign girlfriend.

Soon it's July, and the city begins to swell with the usual tourists, to swelter with heat, and the riots run their course. We give up our digs and catch a train south so he can meet my parents. My mouth tastes of old coins as we rattle through the vastness of my country's interior because I am almost three months pregnant. I reach out for my new husband's hand, our fingers entwining. We have been married for twenty-two hours. I was surprised he suggested we marry when I fell pregnant. I'd expected him to say that such conventions didn't apply to us.

I'm surprised again when he loves La Rêverie, the village, even my parents. I'd feared he would think them staid, conformist. I was secretly dreading that he would argue over dinner with my father about Catholicism. But he doesn't, their exoticism, like the gentle enchantment of the house, seducing him effortlessly.

The months roll placidly by, and our return to Paris or London isn't discussed. Instead, we stay on in my childhood home. As silver streaks my swelling abdomen and islets of darker skin rise on my cheekbones, I am in a sort of heaven, idling quietly through the days, a cotton-wadded, rainbow-glinting life. My mother knits tiny clothes from the softest wool and I paint jungle animals on the wall of the room that will be the nursery.

As summer fades to autumn and then winter, I can't wait to meet her. I know without question that she will be a girl. When she kicks, I pull up my blouse and watch her heels rippling my skin. Excitement eddies through me at the thought that I will soon be able to weigh those tiny feet in my palms.

There is no apprehension, only anticipation. One night, too uncomfortable to sleep, I wish for her to be beautiful and clever, my fingers crossed under the covers. In the morning, I turn to Greg in the bed beside me, press my lips against his bare shoulder. 'I've thought of a name for her,' I say, stroking his long fringe out of his eyes. 'I dreamt it. We'll call her Élodie.'

1993

Perhaps it's what you said about ghosts that lures me to her room after dinner. I've drunk too much today and, as I climb the stairs, I feel slightly off-balance. Butterflies take flight in my stomach as I reach the landing.

I've found an old cache of bulbs in the kitchen and replace the one in the hall that's blown without mishap, light blazing from the bedrooms so I can see what I'm doing. It occurs to me that I should wait until morning to do the one that's gone in Élodie's room but I can't keep away any longer, the alcohol spurring me on.

I carry in a chair as though it's a chore I do every day, humming while I clamber onto it because I'm nervous now, one hand groping in the gloom for the fitting. When my hand brushes against the old Bakelite and it begins to swing, I jump, and in trying to catch it again I touch an uninsulated section of cable, just for a fraction of a second. I feel it as a violent jolt inside me, a huge interior bang.

When I open my eyes, I'm lying on my back on the floor, the light fitting swinging above me and faint music playing from below. I'm just wondering if my electrocuted brain has manufactured it when you turn the volume right up. Of course it must be you, though for a moment I wonder.

I know this song like the angles of my own face, though I haven't heard it in years. The plaintive opening verse of 'Good Vibrations'. Sunlight and hair and perfume. I never listen to this one – I once walked out of a shop mid-purchase when it came on. It reminds me too painfully of her, she who loved it best of all. Now, when I'm hearing it for the first time in so long, the harmonies rise and entwine, like spirits wheedling to be let in. I run down the stairs and, in my rush to lift the needle, make it screech across the vinyl.

'Mum, what are you doing?' You're caught between surprise and exasperation.

'Sorry. I just –'

The telephone saves me. Its shrill ringing makes me jump. As I pick it up, my hand is shaking, my head beginning to pound. I'm hoping to hear Olivier's mellow tones or even Camille, whose familiar brusqueness might shake me out of myself. But it's your father, and he has never been very reassuring in a crisis.

'What's wrong?' he says. 'You sound a bit drunk.'

'I just fell, actually. I was trying to change a light bulb.'

He laughs. 'There's a joke in there somewhere.'

'Did you ring up just to imply I'm an idiot?'

'No,' he replies, stung. 'I rang to see why you hadn't been in touch. You said you would be when you arrived, which was two days ago now.'

Two days? It feels like weeks. 'I'm sorry,' I make myself say. 'We've been busy. I meant to.'

'So,' he says, carefully. 'How is it?'

'It's just as it was.'

'And is it all bad memories, or have you managed to dredge up some good ones?'

I glance around but you've wandered into the kitchen. 'You say that as though I only wanted the bad ones.'

'That's sometimes how it felt.'

'It wasn't us, Greg,' I say softly. 'We didn't make any of it happen.'

I hear him pull in a long breath and I think he's going to sigh with impatience but then I hear the tremor that means he's close to tears.

'Look, why don't you have a word with your daughter?' I say. 'She's here.'

There's a beat of silence, and I know he thinks for a split second that I mean Élodie. I think that's why I said 'daughter' rather than your name: a desire to transmit a tiny bit of what I'm feeling in this house down the telephone line, to hiss in his ear.

You take the phone from me. 'Not much,' I hear you say, as I wander over to the double doors that stand ajar, admitting a cool ribbon of night air. 'Just lying by the pool, really.'

The garden, as I step out into it, smells of oleander flowers and hot dust. There's a new moon, a narrow paring that makes me think of the scar that curved over Élodie's right eyebrow.

I did my best, I say to your father in my head, where the conversation we've had so many times is continuing to play out, the old script unchanged.

I sit down on the third step and my fingers go automatically to the small bloodstain that no one else would ever notice. How many other places here are inhabited by difficult memories? So many tiny hauntings that you can't help treading on them, splinters of glass working their way under the skin.

Moonlight scatters across the swimming pool when I get there. I don't look into the void under the oleander tree. Something of her is here, too, or has been very lately. The after-burn of a presence hangs like cordite in the air. 'Élodie,' I whisper. 'Have you come back?'

The cicadas, which have been silent, begin to roar.

1969

She slips out of me, like a fish, after just five hours. Before I have time to absorb her arrival, she is borne away screaming, fists clenched so tightly they shake, and I fall into a padded black hole of sleep.

On French maternity wards, routine is everything. Babies are fed at set times and then whisked away, so that the mother can recover and get used to the fact that life has utterly changed. For eight days and nights, I am a model patient, doing exactly as the nurses order. I don't beg for extra feeds or longer holds with my baby. I eat all the food I am given and sleep the rest of the time. Ironically, it's like being a cosseted child.

They are pleased with me. '*Such a sensible one*,' the sister says to Greg, when he comes to collect us. During the journey home, I sit on the back seat and watch her sleeping. I am a mother, I think. How is it possible? She is so perfectly contained, her shell-pink eyelids so unmoving that I lean in to check she's still breathing.

'Do babies dream?' I whisper to Greg, in the front, and he smiles.

Although my joy is laced with fear, it's the kind every parent feels, the kind that hurts your heart and makes the world seem as amazing as it is hazardous.

I am a mother.

You creep into my bed just after two. As you cuddle in closer, cold feet twining around mine, I notice the wind has picked up. Somewhere, a loose shutter is creaking. It's the one in the room at the end of the hall.

'I had a nightmare,' you whisper, 'and then I couldn't get back to sleep. It's so dark here.'

I put my arms around you. Your skin is cool and smells slightly of the musty sheets. 'It was only a dream,' I say, hoping you won't want to tell me about it.

The shutter bangs and you jump. 'I think that's what woke me up.'

'I'll go and fix it.' I push back the bedclothes and the air of the room feels chilled. It will rain soon. I used to love it as a child when the temperature abruptly dipped like this, in the deepest trench of night. The rain always cleared the air, the sky the next morning a dazzling crystalline blue, the garden bristling with new vigour.

I try the light in the hall, but it doesn't work, despite the new bulb. The whole house probably needs rewiring – it hasn't been touched since the fifties. Feeling my way along, I experience another attack of déjà vu. It's like being tipped headlong into the past, the waxed boards under my feet and the precise angle of the black stairwell to my right so utterly familiar that I feel as if I've invented the years in between.

I hesitate on the threshold of her room and the shutter bangs again. The door creaks loudly as I open it. The only light comes from the storm outside, flashing intermittently as the shutter swings back and forth. In the distance, thunder rolls.

At the window, I twist the handle and a sudden gust shoves the frame hard into me, thin glass shuddering in loose putty. I have to lean right out to get hold of the shutter, trusting the wooden bar across to take my weight. I've almost grabbed it when some base instinct makes me rear back into the room and away from the drop, convinced that someone is behind me.

On the second attempt, I grab the shutter's catch as it blows back in, breathing hard as my fingers fumble to fasten it. As I push the windows together and turn the handle to lock them again, the rain is coming down harder, the thunder answering, louder now. I hear you call me from the other end of the house and I rush out, eyes averted from the shadows where the bed stands.

'What is it, *chérie*?' I say, when I get back to you, trying not to show I'm out of breath. You're over by the window. Outside, the rain ratchets up another notch, a hiss rising from the stone terrace. Lightning flashes for a blinding moment.

You turn to me, eyes wide. 'There's someone out there. I saw them.'

The garden is full of swaying movement: water and wind pummelling leaves, bending branches. I peer hard into the dark voids between the shrubs and trees, but there's nothing.'

'It's okay, it's just the storm. No one's there.'

I turn back to the window just as a perfect, pink-tinged fork of lightning illuminates the scene, like someone taking a photograph with a powerful flash. As the thunder cracks over us, directly above the house now, I think of the camera Greg bought for her when you were born, and the last film developed from it. Those horrible photographs, the same small face featured in every one, pinprick pupils red from the flash. The single word that had crept into my mind: *proof.*

The storm moves on, the gaps between the lightning and thunder stretching out until I lose count of the seconds. You've already fallen asleep, and I'm drifting away myself when I hear it – the revving of moped engines, four or five at least, all overlapping, as though competing. The noise, amplified by the wet road, gets louder and quieter, then louder again, and at first I think the wind is buffeting it to and fro. But the wind has dropped away to nothing. I understand that they're riding up and down the same short stretch of road.

I tiptoe to a window facing that way and, as if they know I'm watching, one of the bikes peels off the road and on to the drive that leads to the house. Leads to us. I can't move as it approaches slowly, frozen in place. At the moment it looks as though it will surely collide with our car, it veers away, accelerating back towards the others with a roar. I don't know how long I stand there, the cold white light of their headlamps strafing again and again over the dark fields, over the house, over my hands, still clutching the windowsill.

Although we are living with my parents, the three of us – mother, father and child – might as well be the last people on earth. We are inseparable, even at night: Greg has brought her cot into our bedroom. My mother disapproves of this in her gentle way, says we are making a rod for our own backs, but we simply smile. We know best, is what Greg and I secretly think.

There is so much love inside me that I feel permanently replete. I have to remind myself to eat, to drink a long glass of water after I've expressed my milk. If there is a single tiny cloud on the horizon, it is this: I can't seem to feed Élodie on the breast. She won't latch on. She turns her face away, even when her tiny stomach is fizzing with hunger. I've wept about this in Greg's arms a couple of times, and he hushes and rocks me as though I am the baby. He reminds me that it's still my milk, even if she'll only accept it from a bottle.

I watch him when he's with our child and, though I would never say for fear of offending him, I'm surprised by how good a father he is. I knew he'd love her but assumed he would do it from arm's length. I've seen it with friends of his who have had children: these sixties men with their hair long over their collars, their radical ideas, who insist they're nothing like their own fathers, until it comes to doing anything domestic.

But he's not like that. He's fallen in love with her, I suppose. I never thought I could bear for him to love anyone as much as me, but it's her so I don't mind at all.

When I wake the next morning the bed is empty beside me, a single long hair coiled on the pillow. I sit up and turn the clock round. It's late again.

Outside, the weather is glorious, a few dead branches on the grass the only traces of the storm. Everything seems revitalized, the garden virtually humming with life. I remember the mopeds but the menace of them in the night, like encircling wolves, feels diminished in the sunshine. They become bored teenage boys again.

I can hear you talking as I head towards the pool and it throws me because no one but us is here. For an uncomfortable moment, it takes me back to our first months in London, when one afternoon a supply teacher had beckoned me into the classroom. 'Emma has an imaginary friend she speaks to,' she said, as we sat awkwardly together at a child-sized table. 'She says her name is Élodie.' I had to explain there'd been an older sister and the poor woman had flushed to her roots.

As I approach the swimming pool now, I see you're talking to a boy. Both of you have your backs to me and he's armed with a net on a long pole. He's taller than you by a head and, though lean, he's obviously older: probably eighteen or nineteen. Sensing my presence, he turns round, his face strikingly familiar.

'*Je suis Luc*,' he says as I stand there mutely. '*Luc Martin*.' He pushes his hair out of his eyes and steps forward to shake my hand the British way.

'It was Luc who did the pool,' you say jubilantly. 'His English is really good.' You glance furtively at him to see if he's gratified, but he's still studying me. I wonder what he's been told about the neighbour who left her house abandoned for so long.

'*Luc. Of course. You're grown up now. You were a little boy last time I saw you.*'

He smiles, slightly abashed, and you look from me to him, trying to work out what I've said.

'*It was very good of you to do the pool, but how did you know we were coming?*'

His smile slips. '*Oh, it was my dad*,' he says, after a pause. I notice for the first time that his hair is damp, his shorts too. He must have been swimming before you got down here. I don't know whether I mind about that or not.

'*Yeah, it was him*,' he says, more definitely. '*He heard you were coming back. He thought we should get it cleared out and filled up.*' He ruffles his hair, and the gesture is so like Laurent at the same age that I inwardly sway, thrown out of time again.

'*I should give you something for doing it.*'

He shakes his head, relaxed again now. '*It's fine, I like coming here. And Papa wouldn't let you anyway. If I wasn't here, he'd have me working in the fields and I'd much rather be doing this.'*

'Well, all right, if you're sure. Thank you. How is Laurent? And your mother, of course.'

Annette Martin had never liked me. When we were young and at school together, she was jealous that Laurent preferred me, that I was his childhood sweetheart – she wanted him even then. Later I think it was because I went off to London and found myself an Englishman, as though I considered myself something special, too good for the men at home. We all tried to be friends for a time: when Élodie was small your father and I must have crossed the field that separated our properties half a dozen times, Élodie in a sling across Greg's back, the sun canted low over the neat rows of vines.

One night, trying to make small-talk, I confided in her that I was exhausted from the nights of broken sleep that came with a small baby. She and Laurent didn't have any children then – Luc came along later. She was unsympathetic. *'Did you assume you would be different from every other woman with a newborn, then?'* she said, as she brushed past me on her way to the dining room where the men were sitting. She had spoken too quietly for them to catch it. She flirted shamelessly with Greg that night, though it was obvious he found it embarrassing.

I blink, back in the present, and see that Luc is regarding me with an appraising eye. Normally you'd be embarrassed by how distracted I seem but you're too busy gazing at him to notice. I can't blame you: he's beautiful in that way boys sometimes are, just for a year or two before they coarsen into manhood.

I think he'll probably be your first proper crush and don't know how that makes me feel. Mainly nostalgic, I think – for your babyhood; for the me I was when I felt like that about Laurent; for the time before Greg and I lost our way. Before any of it.

1969

Her eyes were a dark foggy blue when she was born. There was nothing unusual in that, quite the opposite, but I didn't know any babies and so that colour was new to me. It made me think of the word 'unfathomable', not only in the way of oceans deep beyond calculation, but the other, more abstract meaning, too. Unknowable. An enigma.

While she spun and swooped inside me, I knew she was tethered; an extension of myself. Now she's been out in the world for a few months, I understand that she's an entirely separate person, even if she does rely on me for her survival. Lately, I have had the strangest sense that she resents me for this dependence, though she can't yet lift the weight of her own head.

In many ways, motherhood remains as mysterious and elusive a state as it was before I entered it. I had assumed I would be her everything: the hazy figure her eyes searched for, the voice that instantly soothed her. I had thought instinct would take over, that it would be all joy and exhaustion and fierce protectiveness for someone so helpless. And there is all that. I just hadn't anticipated the force of her, the self-contained strength of her presence. Sometimes I feel I have to court her, win her approval.

A couple of weeks ago, her left iris began to change. A speck of amber, like a coin winking from a well, has spread until there's no newborn blue remaining. The other is stubbornly unchanged, though I check it every day. Regardless of colour, there's never any expression in them. They seem unable to latch on to me or anything else that moves. I worry about this so much that I take her back to the hospital to get her sight checked.

'*They're absolutely fine,*' says the doctor I've waited two hours to see, the receptionists shooting me disapproving looks because I haven't done things in the proper order. '*Nothing to worry about. Although . . .*' He tails off, his head on one side.

'*What?*' I say too quickly, trying to decipher his expression.

Élodie is lying on her back, on a small foam mattress dotted with pictures of sailboats. The doctor doesn't reply and we both watch her in silence, though I don't know what we're waiting for.

After an interminable minute, he picks up one of Élodie's tiny feet. '*Babies are always moving. Have you noticed? They're always on the go. It's part of the reason they need so much sleep, so many feeds.*' He lets the foot drop. '*I've never seen a baby so still.*'

'*Is that bad?*' I say, resisting the urge to pull at his sleeve when he pauses again.

'*I'm sure it's nothing,*' he says eventually, with a glance at his watch I don't miss. '*She's probably just a bit behind.*'

Did she come early?' He moves away to his desk to check her notes.

'*No, she was two days late.*' I pick her up to put her back in her pram and she's heavy, inert, boneless, not like something so newly brought to life. '*Could there be something wrong with her development, do you think? Is that what you mean?*'

Another look at the watch. He closes her folder. '*Madame Winters, it's natural for new mothers to worry. Your baby is perfectly healthy. Her sight is excellent. Go home and ask your husband to run you a nice hot bath. Have a glass of wine.*' He smiles and we're dismissed.

'*Do you think I'm an hysteric?*' I ask Camille that night, on the phone. Greg is not there to run me a bath. I've taken to ringing my sister every few days.

'*Of course not,*' she says, as wearily as I'd hoped she would. Unlike the deep discussions Greg and I have about parenthood late into the night, I find her dismissiveness comforting. '*You need to do less thinking and sleep more. You need to get out, too. Bring her to Paris for a few days.*'

But I don't go. I tell myself that I haven't the energy but it's not that. I don't want to witness something of my own unease creep into my sister's face. In a strange way, I'd rather think it was just me.

1993

I'm in the study when you find me, sorting through old books, most of them yellowing paperbacks I can't imagine reading again. Dust motes drift and turn on invisible currents in the air. I've been here all afternoon: my father's old correspondence alone has taken me hours to sift through and stuff into bin bags.

'Mum?'

I clutch my chest. 'God, you made me jump. I was miles away.'

You scratch at a mosquito bite, your face preoccupied. 'Can we go for a walk or something?'

I look up at the window and see it's already evening. I realize I've been squinting to read the spines of the books.

'Is everything okay? You must have been bored today, on your own.' I follow you into the kitchen where the ancient fridge is humming loudly. 'Em?'

'No, I just . . .' You tail off, your fingernails pressing hard into the bite. I pull them gently away and resist the urge to take your chin and tip it up to the overhead light, to ask again if you're all right, if you've remembered something.

The atmosphere between us or around us, I'm not sure which, lightens as soon as we leave the garden behind. The fields that border the house once belonged to La Rêverie but my father sold the last one just before he died. It's been Laurent's for more than twenty years now, and the Carignan grapes he planted in the late seventies hang heavy with good health. Just as in my memory, the low sun has turned the rows into broad, curving ribbons of brown and green.

'You brought your sketchbook, didn't you?'

'Yeah, why?'

'I was just thinking that you could do some drawing out here, or in the garden. There's a nice view towards the house from over there.' I point, embarrassed by the effort in my voice. You don't look up. For the last couple of years, I haven't known which version of you I'm going to get from one minute to the next, whether I'll need to wheedle or cajole you.

'Maybe,' you say.

'I was thinking, if you're interested, we could look into some proper art lessons when we get back.'

You take this in, then flash me a brilliant smile; the sun coming out again. 'Really? That would be cool. Laura goes to this class on Tuesday nights. Could I go to that one?'

'If it's not too expensive.'

'Can I ring her later? I can ask how much it is then.'

I nod and you push your arm through mine.

'So, why did you want to come out, *chérie*?' I venture,

after a while. 'I don't think you've ever volunteered for a walk. What have you done with my daughter?'

The joke doesn't quite land and you ignore it, pulling away, turning inward again.

'Emma?'

'I dunno. I just felt weird this afternoon. Like when I was lying by the pool with my music on, I kept thinking someone was talking to me but then I'd turn it off and . . .' You scuff your toes into the earth as I lead us around the perimeter of the field.

I touch your arm lightly. 'It's probably because we were talking about ghosts yesterday. You're like I was when I was a girl. I was always getting funny feelings about things. Camille used to roll her eyes, say I was so dramatic.'

In the far corner of the field, a pale blur transforms itself into Laurent as we get closer. His beard is flecked with salt and pepper and there's a small paunch straining at his shirt, giving him a bearish air.

'*You look good, Sylvie,*' he mutters in my ear, as we embrace. '*I was hoping you'd come over. I didn't want to intrude.*' His eyes haven't changed, and I'd forgotten that uneasy blend of affection and guilt they always inspired in me.

I smile. '*I'm sorry I didn't before. I —*'

'*It doesn't matter.*'

I put my arm round you. You're frowning slightly, evidently feeling left out of the conversation.

'And this is my Emma,' I say in English.

He takes your hand between his large ones and pats

it. 'You are a Durand, certainly,' he says, accent heavy. 'The same . . .' He gestures at his mouth.

'Smile?' I say.

In fact, you don't look like my side of the family. With your freckles and tendency to flush, you look like your dad. It was Élodie and I who were alike, with our heart-shaped faces, though my features were rendered much more exquisitely in her, with their almost eerie symmetry. The only thing that wasn't symmetrical was the dimple in her left cheek, just like mine. A flaw that people thought was pretty.

'She must be the same age her sister was when –'

'*Thank you so much for getting Luc to sort out the pool for us,*' I cut across him in French. '*Emma's hardly been out of it.*'

Laurent shrugs. '*Luc must have thought to do it himself. He's a good boy, most of the time. He helps me more than some would.*'

'*How's Annette?*' I ask.

He puts his head on one side, his expression rueful. '*Ah, you know. Annette is Annette.*'

I glance at you but you're looking away, excluded again by the rapid French. I wasn't looking forward to you meeting Annette. You never knew what she would say next, what she might dredge up for her own entertainment. Her English was better than Laurent's.

'Who's Annette?' you ask, when we're out of earshot.

'Luc's mum.'

'Didn't you get on?'

I laugh and tug gently on a lock of your hair. 'How

did you work that one out?' I glance behind us but Laurent is no longer in view.

'The way you said her name.'

I sigh. 'Laurent was my childhood sweetheart and she never forgave me for it. She tried to kiss your father once, you know.'

It's cheap of me to tell you this, knowing you'll be seduced by the sort of adult details you're never usually party to.

'No way,' you say, as thrilled and scandalized as I thought you'd be. Adolescents are almost always conservative, all that nonchalance affected, a thin veneer. 'I reckon Laurent's still got a thing for you. I was watching him.'

I hide my smile at your precociously sage tone by turning to look at the sinking sun. It's beginning to burnish the vines to a deep copper. In the apricot sky over us, tiny bats ricochet back and forth, black sparks too swift to follow.

I'd bought a dozen cans of Panaché at the supermarket – your idea, the tiny amount of beer they contained making them cool – and you run ahead to fetch us one each from the fridge so we can drink them in the garden. Staying outside soothes the temptation to just pack up and go.

Every sense feels heightened since our return to La Rêverie, a little like they do in pregnancy. Wherever I turn, I'm accosted by beauty and sensation. I'd forgotten how the late sun turns the grey stone of the house golden, and the way the pale gravel of the path shifts underfoot.

The place feels like an old lover I shouldn't trust, trying to win me over again. You sense something of this attempt at seduction, too, I think, your eyes alert to the possibility that I might let us stay.

'I went into her room this afternoon,' you say, when we've finished our drinks.

I feel my shoulders rise an inch. 'Oh,' is all I can think to say.

It strikes me how much older you seem away from London, out of your school uniform. I notice the necklace then. You must have tucked it inside your T-shirt, but it's worked its way out to glint against your skin: a delicate silver chain strung with tiny turquoise stones I would recognize anywhere.

When you see my face, your fingers go to it, as though you're afraid I might rip it off. 'I mended the catch. But you don't want me to wear it, do you?'

I swallow. 'I don't mind, if you like it,' I say. 'But I thought we were going to sort through her room together.'

'You were busy with the books. Anyway, I only went through the drawers and there wasn't much. I found this down the back of them.'

I didn't need you to tell me that. I remember vividly how it got there; the skittering sound it had made as it hit wood and disappeared out of sight. It wasn't long after that we cleared much of her room. Greg and I had found it unbearable to leave it as it was: a shrine that seemed to leach misery throughout the rest of the house.

'Tell me a story about her,' you say, more gently, in the

tones of someone coaxing a nervous cat down from a fence. 'One I don't know.'

Reluctantly, I cast my mind back, trying to find something that I feel able to tell and will satisfy you.

'She loved the same music as me,' I say eventually, smiling at the connection that had meant such a lot. 'That's why I overreacted so much when you put that record on last night.' I reach out to stroke your cheek in apology. 'Anyway, it always annoyed your dad that she liked pop music. He tried his Frank Zappa albums out on her but it was always my music she preferred.'

She did, too, and despite herself, I think, because she always liked to please Greg. She always beamed when people remarked, as they so often did, that she was a proper daddy's girl. *Fille à papa*.

'As soon as the music started, she would begin to move, even when she was small and still unsteady on her feet. I don't think she could help herself.'

You smile into the gloom. 'Is that why your taste got stuck in the sixties?'

'I actually think I have very eclectic tastes.' I raise an eyebrow. 'I also listen to songs from the seventies.'

But it's true that my dog-eared LPs are rare survivals from that time. I couldn't bear to lose them as well — even the disillusioned ones that came later, flipping paradise over to reveal its underbelly, drive-thrus giving way to desperadoes. Some nights back then I would dream I was in California, losing myself in the lush canyons, wrapped in the soft orange haze of smog.

I don't tell you that part, or how elated I felt when I

saw her dancing and spinning to the music that lit up something deep inside me. Nor do I tell you how I once watched her move to a song I'd thought was hers and mine, her body pressed close to a man too old to be touching her. Thinking about all this makes me want to cry so I steer into safer waters.

'I was always wearing these cheesecloth dresses and skirts then. My hair was almost to my waist and I hardly brushed it. Maman didn't like it – she was always saying that it wasn't chic, that I looked like a grubby peasant.' I smile at the memory and do an impression of her to make you laugh, muttering, *'Mon Dieu!'* just as she had from the kitchen when the alien sounds and smells wafted down the stairs: joss-sticks and Joni Mitchell in full-throated wail.

But, even as I laugh along with you, I'm thinking of your sister again, moving instinctively to the music. She is suddenly there, as alive as us, breathing in the same violet air of almost-night, her feet, bare and dirt-soled, stamping out the beat. I know if I turn I will see her, crouching beneath the oleander, the expression in her eyes as hostile as it was when I last saw her.

1970

'*Ça va, chérie?*'

My mother has come to stay for a week. She's standing at the end of the bed having just opened the shutters. She thinks she's given me a lie-in but I've been awake since dawn. My father has been dead for a month, the new decade not meant for him. I'd assumed Maman would stay with us but she insisted on moving into my aunt Mathilde's cramped apartment in Toulouse. She said it was time Greg, Élodie and I had our own space.

'*But I'll miss you,*' I said, pride preventing me from saying what I really meant. *But I need you.*

'*Don't worry if you feel a bit overwhelmed sometimes,*' she says softly now, her hand cool on my forehead. '*C'est normal. I had it with you and Camille sometimes, you know. It gets easier.*'

I shield my eyes from the sunlight pouring in through the windows. '*I don't think it's that.*'

She perches on the side of the bed, and begins to smooth my tangled hair. '*Quoi, alors?*'

'*I don't know. It's nothing. I'm probably over-thinking things. Just . . . how did you feel when we were little?*'

She puts her head on one side, thinking back. '*Mainly

tired. Sometimes I couldn't think straight I was so tired. And I was always crying at nothing, like a tap.' She shakes her head and smiles. *'Your father was at his wits' end.'*

I open my mouth and shut it again. I want to believe that what I've begun to feel is what my mother felt; what so many new mothers feel. But this doesn't ring quite true to me. The unease that began as little more than a whisper is transforming into a black kernel of fear that has taken up residence inside me. I'd thought it would get easier as the months passed, not harder. I'd thought that it would begin to feel more natural, more normal between me and my child.

Perhaps it's all mixed up with grief for my father. One day last week, I forgot he was dead. I went to the field behind the house to scan for his slight figure bent over the vines, meaning to ask him if he wanted a cold drink, but there was no one. The truth winded me: the field sold to Laurent, and Papa lost for ever.

My brain slides away from that hurt. I go back to what I've been thinking about over and over since it first occurred to me: I can't remember Élodie ever laughing, though she's a year old now. And although she can already say a few words, she's mainly silent. The other day I had the strange notion that if she wasn't a baby – if she was a man, a lover – I would assume she had no feelings, that the reason I feel so foolish is because I'm simply not worth the effort.

I watch my mother deftly straighten the bottles and brushes on my dressing table. With just a little more pushing from her, I would admit it all. She turns back to me and I think she's going to say something but instead she leans over to kiss my forehead.

'*I'll see to Élodie,*' she says. '*You get dressed.*'

I nod, and the greater part of me is relieved. While I can hide my fears – and the guilt that is their shadow – there is still a chance I am wrong. That I do have some delayed version of the baby blues, rather than what it feels like, which is that there is something missing between us. Missing in *me*.

But a darker question keeps surfacing, however much I push it down. It whispers so the guilt doesn't hear: is something missing in *her*?

*

My mother returns to Toulouse and Greg is still away in London. It's just Élodie and me again.

These days, I'm finding it harder and harder to perform under my child's cool gaze. I lay her on the soft rug to change her nappy and begin to feel hot as I fumble to put the clean one on her. Its folds won't lie smoothly and in my frustration I accidentally prick the poreless flesh of her inside leg with the safety pin.

'*I'm sorry, I'm sorry,*' I cry, though she hasn't flinched, only the tiniest flaring of her nostrils to indicate she's noticed at all. I bend to kiss the pink mark I've made.

'*I'm stupid,*' I whisper. '*Stupid and clumsy.*'

I shake out a muslin square and hold it in front of my face. I haven't tried playing this game for a few months, but I make myself do it now: a peculiar punishment for the safety pin.

'*Coucou!*' I say, lowering it suddenly.

She doesn't move, let alone smile, but I do it again, and then a third time. She doesn't even blink and it occurs to me that those seconds when I'm holding up the muslin are a relief . . . the curtain coming down on a foolish act.

She stares expressionlessly at me and I wonder if tiny children are capable of contempt. This is such a horrible thought that I gather her up and hold her close, stroking the dandelion fuzz of hair at the back of her head, determinedly ignoring how limp she remains, how her little arms slide away from my neck to hang at her sides.

I love Élodie desperately, and perhaps there's a clue in that word. The closest I can come to it is not with words but an image: a pocket tucked away beside all the love I feel for her, invisible from the outside but there nonetheless. Every time she turns away from me, every time she screams, dry-eyed, for minutes on end, a new stone is dropped into it. The pocket bangs against my leg, heavier and heavier.

1993

The phone wakes me the next morning, after a broken sleep filled with dreams of leaving, the whirr of the old electric fan I'd left on transformed into the roar of jet engines at take-off. I blunder down the stairs and snatch up the receiver.

'*Sylvie? C'est Olivier Lagarde.*' His voice cuts through my morning haziness.

'*I have a couple of papers I need you to sign. Are you free this afternoon, if I come round with them? It's no trouble.*'

I hear the smile in his voice and find myself smiling too. 'Yes, of course. I'll be here. We'll be here.'

I pause at the phone when he's gone, then dial Camille's work number.

'*You're there now, are you?*' she says, when I explain. '*I didn't think you'd actually go. Is Emma with Greg?*'

'No, I had to bring her with me. He couldn't take her.'

'*What a surprise. So, I gather you've finally told her?*'

I don't say anything.

'*Zut, Sylvie. You haven't, have you?*'

'*I'll talk to her properly about everything when the time's right, but —*'

'*I think you're crazy,*' she says over me. '*Look, I've got to go into a meeting now. Tell her, will you? She's growing up.*'

'*Do you think you'll come and see us?*' I say, but she's already gone.

I put the phone down, wishing I hadn't rung her. It's an old habit, ringing Camille for reassurance, for her particularly breezy brand of advice, but she hasn't played the game this time.

I make myself a coffee and take it out to the garden where the heat and brilliance of the day are like a physical blow. A pair of unseen birds are scuffling in the thick of the oleander tree and there's splashing coming from the pool. I walk slowly, dismissing a ridiculous urge to check you're fine. My heart clutches when I see something red move behind the pines, a memory packed away for so long lighting like a flare, but it's only your beach towel, slipping off one of the loungers to the ground.

You're busy swimming laps and I watch you for a while, the path you're carving straight and clean. I go and lie down on a lounger and stretch out my limbs, eyes closed against the climbing sun, and feel the heat begin to unknit the tension in my muscles.

'Morning,' you call.

I sit up. Your elbows are propped on the lip of the pool, the water-darkened tails of your hair streaming over your shoulders.

'Hello, darling. Did you sleep well?'

You shrug one shoulder. 'Not really. It's so hot. I had a weird dream.'

I pause, draining my coffee while I decide whether to

ask what it was about, but then, as if you don't want to answer, you abruptly push yourself below the surface of the water, nothing left of you but your splayed fingers on the stone lip and a series of bubbles rising to the surface.

'I'll time you,' I say, when you rise up again. You used to do this in the bath when you were younger.

'Okay,' you say, humouring me, and take a deep breath in, one hand clamping your nose shut and the other grasping the side as you descend again. I make up how long you stay under, though you don't seem to notice. Perhaps you know I'm not feeling good this morning, that this is for me, not you: the comfort of an old ritual.

The squabbling birds have gone and the garden is quiet again. I try to focus on your submerged body, a distorted, wavering blur, but she's suddenly everywhere – thrumming in the air around me and flickering in the jade water around you. *Élodie. Élodie. Élodie.*

*

Olivier turns up later than I expect, just before six, when the shadows in the garden are stretched and turning blue. Because we're meeting for the second time, we kiss the customary three times on the doorstep, and though this *faire la bise* is simply what the French do, there's an undeniable frisson as our cheeks brush. His fingers touch the small of my back as we pull away, so lightly it might have been an accident, only I don't think it was. As I lead

65

him through the house and out onto the terrace, my hands go automatically to my face where we made contact. It's hot.

I pour the wine he's brought, pale and still frosted with cold. Above us, the swallows have begun their daily exhibition, skimming effortless loops between the house and the trees.

'*I was beginning to wonder if you'd show up,*' I say, smiling so he knows I'm not annoyed.

'*Yes, I'm sorry. It's been one of those days. I saved this for last – something to look forward to.*' He leans forward with a slow smile and we clink glasses. I catch his eyes flicking across my bare shoulders and shift in my seat.

'*I rang the police again today,*' he continues, '*to see if they'd talked to the Gattaz boys about the fire. Apparently, they were elsewhere that night. One of them was arrested for being over the limit on the A7 near Montélimar. Miles away.*'

'*So, if it wasn't them, do they have any other ideas who it was?*'

'*They did say there was a call that night. A lorry driver who had pulled up to rest on the main road between here and the village reported a gang of boys. They were racing up and down on their mopeds. They woke him up.*'

I swallow, remembering the night of the storm, and reach for my glass just as a hot needle of pain sears through my foot, the flaring agony of it making me cry out. I wrench off my sandal and a wasp crawls out from where it's stung the tender skin of the arch. It flies off, towards the side of the house where Élodie's slipped shutter has unfastened itself again. I'd been aware of it creaking when I was hacking at the lavender earlier.

Olivier kneels in front of me and lifts my foot to inspect it. Then he presses the curve of the cold wine bottle into the arch, his other hand firmly gripping my ankle. I can smell his cologne, lemon and something spicier, like cracked pepper. Slowly, the pain dulls to a throb.

He looks up, his face close to mine. '*Ça va mieux?*'

I nod, his proximity making me self-conscious now the pain is lessening. '*Let's go inside. We'll get eaten alive if we stay out here.*'

Limping, I show him into the salon through the double doors. As I close them to keep out the insects, in the split second before I turn back to Olivier, I see something pale move in the gloom beyond the glass. I peer harder but there's nothing.

For the last few weeks, Élodie has refused to eat anything I prepare for her. She is only two and a half but her willpower is astonishing, pushing away food even as her stomach grumbles with hunger.

'So she's a fussy eater,' says Camille. I can almost hear her shrug down the line. 'You were too, when you were little. God, the fuss about the grease at the top of Maman's cassoulet.'

I smile briefly at the memory. 'I know it's common. I know children dig their heels in at this age. It's just . . .'

'What?'

'She doesn't do it with Greg. Only me. And I worry about her because when he's away on one of his buying trips she doesn't really eat at all. I'd have to force her and I can't hurt her like that.'

'She'll get over it,' says Camille, and I can tell from the slight pause before speaking that her attention has wandered. I wonder what she's going to do with her afternoon, all of Paris waiting beyond her apartment door.

*

When Camille comes to visit – I've counted down the days to her arrival, though I would never admit it:

Camille hates neediness – Élodie has not got over it. In fact, I'm convinced she's lost weight. I'm terrified of what it says about my skills as a mother that I can't even manage the basic task of feeding my child.

Camille arrives just before noon, and by the time we sit down to lunch on the terrace, I'm ironically too anxious to eat myself. I silently will Camille to watch Élodie, but instead my sister is appraising Greg in her cool way.

'*Sounds like you've been away from home a lot lately,*' she begins, one eyebrow arched. '*The antiques business must be booming.*'

I pour myself more wine as he smiles thinly. '*It's not bad. I'd rather be here, of course,*' he reaches out to stroke Élodie's hair, '*but we need the money.*'

Camille pushes her half-eaten quiche to the side of her plate.

'*You on one of your diets?*' asks Greg.

Camille doesn't respond. She turns to Élodie instead. '*What about you, ma petite? You won't grow big and strong if you don't finish your lunch.*'

Élodie hasn't touched her food and I was hoping Camille would notice.

'*Actually, she's a very good little eater,*' says Greg, pulling Élodie into his lap. He spears a piece of quiche and pops it into her mouth, forgetting she won't eat anything with egg in it. She pauses and I wait – we all wait – and then she begins to chew. Another three mouthfuls follow and then Greg goes inside to fetch more wine.

Camille stands away from the table to light a cigarette

as Élodie opens her mouth and lets the food inside it fall out. It lands, wetly, on the front of her dress. She's eyeing me, head to one side, as she begins to smear the half-chewed mush of quiche into the cotton, not realizing Camille has turned back.

'*Arrête, Élodie! Arrête*' She pulls Élodie's hand away. '*What a thing to do.*' I meet Camille's eye and this acknowledgement briefly releases the pressure that's been building inside me lately, like the paint on the shutters that bubbles and cracks on the hottest days.

Greg is back on the terrace, clutching a bottle of red. '*What's going on?*'

Élodie begins to wail. '*She hurt me!*' she cries, holding up the hand Camille had pulled away. He sweeps her up into his arms and kisses her cheeks. He doesn't seem to notice that they're dry, but I don't care.

'*I certainly did not hurt her,*' Camille scoffs. '*All I did was tell her not to spoil her dress.*' She stubs out her cigarette and pours some wine. '*Children need to be told they can't behave like that, playing with their food and wasting it.*'

'*And you're the parenting expert, I suppose?*' says Greg.

I look from one to the other. I should intervene, like I normally do when the two of them start sparring, but this is not about politics for once.

'*I may not have children but I know they need boundaries,*' she says easily, lighting another cigarette. She offers Greg the packet but he ignores her. '*French children are brought up in the cadre —*'

'*Oh, yes, the cadre,*' he interrupts, rolling his eyes. '*That old authoritarian nonsense. It's nothing but a cage for children.*'

How can she be creative if she's being corrected and disciplined every five minutes? Children find their own way if they're left to their own devices.'

Camille laughs. *'You're such a hippie. Imagine what she'll be doing at fifteen. She's running rings around you now.'*

Greg's face darkens, but she's right. Though he would deny this vehemently, he treats Élodie as an extension of his politics: an experiment he hopes will prove him right about personal liberty and a life lived without constraints. He wants for her the kind of bohemian upbringing his arty friends in Hampstead are giving their children. He's desperate not to recreate for Élodie something as stifling and dull and *deeply uncool* as his own childhood in Surrey.

I can't help it. It's thrilling to hear Camille say what I never do, because I love him. Because I don't want us to fight over the daughter we've created together.

I look at Élodie now, in Greg's lap once more, staring back at me without expression, her face a beautiful blank. It's as if the storm never happened. She swivels round so she can lean against Greg's chest, and when she falls asleep, the instant slumber of the guiltless, long lashes casting delicate shadows on her almond milk skin, it's a relief. It's a relief to love her simply again. As her breathing deepens, the air loosens. My shoulders drop. Greg takes one of Camille's cigarettes.

When Camille goes inside for a nap – she and Greg have got through two bottles of wine between them – he turns to me.

'She's still going tomorrow, isn't she?' He smiles to

soften it. 'We'll drive each other insane otherwise. Lucky for me, I got the easy sister.' He reaches across the table and as I fold my hand into his larger one, Élodie wakes, her eyes instantly wide and alert, like those dolls whose eyelids snap open when you sit them up. She shows me her small white teeth, just for a second, then stretches out to sweep Camille's forgotten reading glasses to the ground.

I pick them up. One of the lenses has cracked. I show Greg and, to my surprise, he lifts Élodie out of his lap and stands her on her feet quite roughly.

'What did you do that for?'

She pulls in her breath and begins to shriek. He kneels in front of her, smoothing her hair because there are still no tears to dry.

'I'm sorry, I'm sorry,' he croons. 'She shouldn't have left them there, should she? Silly Camille.'

And because I want Greg on my side, because I want us all to be on the same side, because Camille will leave tomorrow, I say nothing. I let it go and it curls into nothing, burnt away by the heat of the afternoon.

The weather changes overnight. The clouds that tend to cling solicitously to the distant hills have rolled out across the whole plain, shrouding the gas-blue sky and turning it pearled and spectral. There's something comforting about it, something of England in its moderation. I open the shutters and remember that I've been dreaming of your sister. It's the old dream, the rare one that I always hoped would happen in real life: Élodie, sunshine behind her like a halo, hair sparking, her small hands reaching for mine.

Outside, the ferocious sun is wrapped in the same thick gauze, all the light and shade in the garden flattened. You lie dozing in the salon in your swimsuit and an oversized black Soundgarden T-shirt, a yellowed, translated paperback copy of *Bonjour Tristesse* splayed upside-down on your stomach. I resist the urge to replace it with something more innocent. At least when I lean over to kiss you good morning you smell like you again: not of chlorine or suntan lotion but simply my London girl.

I'm still fighting the urge to herd you into the car and drive north before the sun burns through, sending its shadows long and dark across the garden again, and this excess energy galvanizes me into action in the kitchen. I'm pulling ancient jars and tins out of one of the cupboards when there's a knock at the door.

I can see through the etched glass panels in the hall that it's a woman.

'*Camille!*' I can't keep the surprise out of my voice.

'*Thank God you haven't gone home yet. I left my damn key in Paris.*'

A dense cloud of perfume envelops me as she sweeps in. She's worn the same musky scent for so long that it's as much a part of her as her dark shining bob, and the tenacious way she enjoys arguing about everything.

She's already halfway to the kitchen when, as an afterthought, she turns back to kiss me, her dry, lipstick-bright lips not quite making contact with my cheeks.

'*You look great,*' I say, because it's impossible to break the old habit of trying to win over my imperious older sister. It's also true: she's a couple of pounds heavier than usual and it suits her. Her face has lost its pinched look and the lines around her mouth are softer.

She gives me a scornful glance that's so familiar it makes me yearn briefly for the years I saw that expression all the time, when our parents were still alive.

'*What I look is fat,*' she says emphatically. '*Work has been a nightmare.*'

She doesn't need to explain. I still know the way her brain makes connections without her having to fill in the blanks. She'd been too stressed and busy to keep up her usual starvation diet. Unless one of her admirers is taking her out for dinner, Camille generally subsists on undressed salad, plain omelettes and black coffee. But she was never meant to be skinny. As children, I was the slender one who ate what she liked, while my fleshier sister was put on a succession of diets by our mother. Camille has never quite forgiven me for it.

I smile gamely, dodging around the old rivalry. *'I didn't know you were coming. Emma will be so pleased. It's a lovely surprise.'*

She raises a sceptical eyebrow. *'I did ring, but no one picked up.'*

'We were probably outside. Emma practically lives in the pool.' I gesture at the fridge. *'Let me get you a drink. What would you like? Some wine?'*

She smiles slyly. *'Yes, I'll have a small glass. If it'll make you feel less guilty about having one so early.'*

Who drinks the most, who eats the least – this is old ground, too. I swallow the retort that rises to my lips and fetch two glasses, automatically checking them for smears against the muted light filtering in from the garden. Camille never knowingly misses an opportunity to find fault.

'Can you stay tonight?'

'Would you rather I didn't?'

I sigh. *'Of course not. I just wondered if you were going to. You never do and you didn't even mention you might come when we spoke on the phone. I'll make up a bed.'*

'I can always book a room in Laussac. I stayed there before.'

I turn to face her. *'Don't be ridiculous. It's your house too. It's been almost two years since you came to see us in London. I'd like you to stay.'*

As I say it, I realize it's true. 'Safety in numbers' is the phrase that absurdly comes to mind.

'*Well, all right, then,*' she says, with a tight little smile. '*It'll only be for a couple of nights, though. I haven't just come for you. I want to go through Maman's china, and I'll have to pay a call on Olivier Lagarde too.*'

'*You know, I think it's the dangerous thing,*' she muses, as I hand her a glass.

'*What is?*'

'*The difference between a handsome man and an attractive one. If there's no edge, good looks aren't enough. Olivier's got it.*'

I raise an eyebrow, a tiny gesture, but she still catches it, her answering smile full of mischief.

'*Oh, so you've seen him for yourself, then?*'

'*Come on,*' I say, picking up the wine. '*Let's go outside.*'

'*Anyway,*' she says, when we've sat down, '*how's it going? You're not getting much sleep, are you?*'

'*Look that bad, do I?*'

She tuts. '*Always so sensitive. You're a bit hollow around the eyes, that's all. No one in your position could be expected to sleep well here.*'

'It's just a house,' I say, though I know that's nonsense. The place reeks of the past: all the years with Élodie, and when I was a girl, too.

She leans in and I know what's coming.

'*No, before you ask,*' I say, as she goes to speak. '*I haven't told her yet. I need to do it in the right way.*'

'*God, Sylvie. Are we going to have to fall out over this again? She's a teenager now and you're still keeping her in the dark. What does she think happened, then?*'

78

I swallow. I can feel my temper rising but it's only because she's right. *'She thinks what she's thought since she was little. That Élodie died because she was ill. A girl in her class in London when we first moved there had a little brother with leukaemia. She thought it was something like that.'*

'She assumed, and you were only too happy to let her. That time I came to stay she kept asking questions about Heaven . . .' Camille shakes her head. *'I've never understood how she squared that with her memories of Élodie.'*

I fall silent but Camille knows me better than anyone alive. Not the mother, not the wife: me.

'You're hoping you'll get through this without saying anything, aren't you? That now you're here, her memory will come back and do the hard work for you.' She gives me the Camille look that has always driven me mad: triumph masquerading as disapproval.

'You know, if we'd just sold the house years ago, I wouldn't have been put in this position with no warning. But we've never been very good at coming to an agreement, have we?'

'Ah, I should have known. It's my fault you've been keeping secrets from your daughter all her life. No, I'm not taking the blame for this, Sylvie. You've had years.'

Of course she's right. I've had a decade. Countless days mounting up when it was just the two of us at home in London, you looking sidelong at her picture with that hungry expression in your eyes. I can't think now why I didn't just take your hands in mine. *There are some things I need to explain to you, darling,* I might have begun. *About what happened in France. Why we had to leave.*

The scrape of Camille's metal chair leg on the terrace

brings me back to the present. Very slowly, by tiny increments, the cloud is dispersing. As the sky brightens to white, areas of shade begin to darken, crosshatchings on stone and grass. Sitting up from where she's been rooting in her bag, Camille puts on a pair of oversized sunglasses and lights a cigarette.

'*Well, I suppose it's a blessing if she really doesn't remember anything.*' Her tone is gentler now. '*Christ, it's hot down here. You forget.*'

I put up a hand to shade my eyes. '*Unless she's not telling me. I don't think so, though, beyond finding the place a bit creepy at night. The only thing she's really recognized is the wallpaper in the blue room. She used to make up stories about it, do you remember?*'

Camille blows out a cloud of smoke. '*Memory is a peculiar thing. But maybe it's self-preservation. The brain is clever like that. And she was only four when you left, wasn't she? Has she gone anywhere near the barn yet?*'

She reaches forward to knock ash into a saucer as I shake my head.

Camille knew a lot of what was going on back then. There was a period when I regularly rang her late at night and she would let me offload what had happened that day. She didn't visit as much as I'd have liked but she was a support in her own way. I suppose it was the closest we ever were. Since London we'd grown apart, perhaps because I needed her less there.

'*Is it me?*' I would ask her, almost every time. '*Have I created this?*'

And she would always say no, in her wonderfully

emphatic way. *'That girl was born different. There was nothing you could have done.'*

For all our temperamental differences, she kept me sane during that time, her and the bag I had secretly — and guiltily — packed for you and me, stowing it behind a pile of spare blankets at the very back of the linen cupboard.

Now, I looked pleadingly at Camille. *'Remember how Emma used to wet the bed when we left France? Those terrible night terrors? Her asthma was awful.'*

'Yes, but moving away is one thing. I understood that. That's different from not telling her . . .'

I turn my palms up. *'I didn't know how best to help her back then. I hoped it would all miraculously sort itself out when we were in England, and some of it did. She loved her school, her asthma was suddenly under control. She still talked about Élodie but it was like she'd invented a completely different person, some composite girl based on her friends' older sisters. She wasn't pretending either. I know she wasn't. You saw it for yourself when you came. All the bad memories had just . . . gone.*

'But at night she was still wetting the bed, still screaming out in her sleep, having nightmares. When she asked if Élodie was the same as her friend's little brother who'd died of leukaemia, I thought it might close some door in her brain. And maybe it did, or maybe it was just time, I don't know. But over the next few months, things got slowly better, didn't they? God, I was so relieved. I played along with this made-up idea of Élodie during the day. I think I came to half believe in it myself eventually — and at night, Emma was okay. She stopped looking so tired, so constantly cowed and frightened. She put on weight. I would have told any lie for that.'

I stop because I'm about to cry, my throat aching with the effort of holding back the tears.

Camille drinks the last of her wine and pours us both another glass.

'*Élodie was always so much worse for me than for Greg, wasn't she?*' I say eventually, after I've lit one of her cigarettes, checking for sounds of splashing from the pool first.

She shoots me a wry look. '*Her beloved papa.*'

'*Come on, Sylvie,*' she says, taking off her sunglasses and rubbing between her eyebrows. '*You know why it was easier for Greg. He was hardly ever around. He could be in denial longer than you, even though he still had to face it in the end, didn't he? Élodie couldn't help but show you all sides of herself, not just the charm she turned on for other people. Most people want to be known, be understood, but Élodie . . .*' She shakes her head. '*I've never come across anyone as self-contained as that child, as single-minded. Sometimes she frightened me, too.*'

1972

I'm lying perfectly still in the heat of the garden. There's no breeze and above me the spears of the oleander leaves are unmoving, their shadows marking my bare legs with spike-fingered bruises. Like the air, I can't seem to make myself move. The day is already searing, the gossamer cloud of early morning long scorched away.

From the house behind me, a Charlie Parker track has been playing for a long time. Or maybe it's John Coltrane. I can't tell which, it's Greg's music, but every note of it finds me easily in the inert air. He hasn't spoken to me yet this morning. These days, we perform a strange dance around the house, both of us moving from one room to another, occupying the space the other has just left, mindful to avoid contact if possible.

On days like this, I wish I could sleep for ever. I've almost forgotten what it's like to feel refreshed and alert. The coffee I make in a daze doesn't do much good, making my heart skitter but unable to penetrate the featureless fog in my head.

Sometimes I think about the only London winter I experienced before Greg – freezing rain, dark by four, fingertips numb and reddened. I would be able to think clearly there, my thoughts as sharp as the wind. Here the sun is stupefying, a powerful *canicule* this year. *Canicule* for heatwave. The dog days. The news is full of Watergate, Nixon's shifty-eyed belligerence flickering on the black-and-white screen. Greg can't stop watching, swearing about fascists, but I can't seem to take in the particulars. I spend most of my days outside, waiting for the sun to begin its descent again, another day crossed off. My father's garden is turning brown and desiccated, though it's still early July.

A lizard brushes the hand I've let drop to the warm stone and I flinch, the first movement I've made in a while. Half an hour, an hour, I have no idea how long I've been lying here. I can feel the flesh of my legs beginning to cook. It must be close to midday.

It strikes me dimly, like the dull ting of a fork on cracked glass, that I don't know where Élodie is. Her hair grazes the tops of her shoulder blades now: sun-bleached at the ends, pale caramel at the roots. The gentlest of breezes ruffles the surface of the pool water, the movement reflecting on the dark underside of the oleander tree, ripples in every direction. I begin mentally to search the house and garden for my daughter, the worry of what she might be up to beginning to scratch at my insides.

At the edge of the parched lawn, I spot her at the top of the steps leading up to the terrace, crouching in the dark, dry earth of a flowerbed where nothing much ever seems to grow. Armed with a sharp stick, she's so intent on something behind a large stone that she doesn't notice my approach.

I open my mouth to ask what she's doing just as the stick comes down hard, once, twice and then a third time, like a spear, the movements precise and utterly focused.

'*Élodie?*' I say, as I run up the steps. '*What have you got there?*'

She turns at my voice, and there's something both wild and empty in her little face that stops me dead. Under the point of her stick is a small lizard, its belly ripped open, mushed innards spilling out. I step closer and see the clutch of pale eggs she has already smashed to pieces.

'Oh, *Élodie,*' I say, keeping my voice as steady as I can. '*Why have you done that? It's – it's not right to hurt things, to hurt creatu–*'

But she's already turned back to the skewered lizard. It twitches grotesquely, and I can't help snatching the stick and snapping it in half, throwing the pieces away.

She squawks with pure outrage, eyes blazing, and stands, tensed, I think, to run at me. But to my surprise, because she is never clumsy, she misjudges where she puts her feet and almost falls down the steps at her side. I see her sway, then right herself, but just as I'm reaching to pull her out of danger, she stills and, holding my gaze, very carefully steps sideways into nothing.

'What were you doing?' Greg shouts at me, as he scoops her up, her cries having brought him out of the house. 'For God's sake, you should be keeping an eye on her. It's not like you're doing anything else.'

He leaves the terrace without looking back, Élodie rigid in his arms, blood from her elbow seeping into his blue shirt and turning it purple. She is still holding my gaze as she continues to scream, her mouth a small round O, her eyes not screwed up or wet but unblinking. I try to remember the last time I saw her cry properly, with real tears, but I can't.

I would die for her, without hesitation; I am her mother. It's just that, sometimes, I wish I wasn't. There is no paradox in those statements for me. Both parts run in parallel through my head, twin convictions I find myself whispering, like a strange mantra.

1993

At Camille's insistence, we have dinner in the dining room, Maman's beloved chandelier – dull with dust, a couple of the bulbs blown – illuminating us in a flattering glow. The rest of the room, with its dark wood and marble fireplace, has faded into deep shadow. Moths bat softly against the windows.

'*I'll tell you another one who's going to be dangerous,*' my sister declares in French. She's had a few glasses of wine and is on good form, making a fuss of you and even eating a decent amount of the omelette I've made. '*Luc Martin.*'

You perk up at his name.

'*It was strange seeing him,*' I say. '*He turned round and looked so much like Laurent before I left for university in London.*'

Camille tuts. '*He's nothing like Laurent. Laurent was a puppy, following you around with his tongue out. I can't see Luc doing that for a girl. No, there's just enough of Annette in him to keep it interesting.*'

'What are you saying?' There's a slight whine in your voice.

'Boys, of course,' says Camille, giving you a wink. 'Did you like the look of Luc?'

Your eyes drop to your plate but you're smiling. 'Yeah, he's nice.'

Camille turns back to me. '*Sylvie, do you remember Julien Lefèvre? His father owned the Citroën garage out on the Alès road.*' She can't help herself, reverting back to quick-fire French. '*I saw him on the Métro looking ancient. He's lost all his hair. God, I adored him.*'

I laugh and something in my chest loosens. '*I haven't thought about him in years. He looked a bit like Alain Delon with those big blue eyes, but didn't he know it.*'

'*Ha, yes, I didn't stand a chance. I used to walk past his class-room with my skirt rolled up so high you could almost see my knickers. Papa would have had a fit.*'

I lean towards you. 'Camille's saying she had a crush on a boy called Julien. He was gorgeous, everyone liked him. He played guitar.'

'How old were you when you went out with Laurent?' You've never really asked me about when I was young, when I was your age. There's a strange pleasure in having elicited your curiosity – in having shown you that I'm more than your mother.

'Only a bit older than you, I suppose.'

'*He married that dreadful Francine, do you remember?*' Camille interrupts. '*Julien. The size of her backside. She only got him because she opened her le–*'

She stops as I glance pointedly in your direction, though you can't understand her. I regard her affectionately as she reaches for the wine. She looks younger in the soft light, and I think of all the meals we've eaten in this room together. Both of us had automatically taken the same seats we'd occupied as children.

Then her face sharpens. *'Didn't Élodie go around with the Lefèvre son's crowd for a while?'* Her red lipstick has bled slightly, and I realize she's quite drunk. *'They were older, weren't they? Pretty wild. Of course, there was that party, wasn't there? Just before . . .'*

I give her another look and, unable to stay sitting, hurry to collect up the plates. She gives me a tiny nod. I brace myself, waiting for you to ask why Élodie's name has come up, but you're smiling shyly at Camille.

'Has Luc got a girlfriend, do you think?'

You've missed it. I let out a long breath.

Camille turns to you with a smile, eyebrows raised. 'Why do you ask, *petite*? Have you got your eyes on him?'

You laugh and the shadows in the corners of the room still and settle.

We play cards after dinner, Camille, to my astonishment, letting you win. When we go up to bed I kiss her impulsively at the top of the stairs, though we've never been very physically demonstrative, not like some sisters. She touches her cheek in surprise.

'I'm glad you're here,' I say, and though she shrugs, I know she's pleased. It's not just that there's a third person absorbing the hum of La Rêverie's past, which seems to lessen the weight of the air. It's because of Camille herself. I've never told her, and never will tell her, but my sister has always been better than anyone at chasing the darkness away.

*

Camille sleeps late the next morning, and we creep around so as not to wake her. After breakfast, you don't go outside with your music and books as usual, though the weather has reverted to its previous brilliance and heat, the kitchen flagstones already warm underfoot where the sun strikes them.

'Are you okay?' I say, putting my hand to your forehead. It's cool but your face is pale.

'I got my period,' you mutter, a dull blush creeping into your cheeks because *les règles* are still quite new to you. And not just new, but discomfiting. You cried last winter, when the first one came, not with a few drops but a dramatic rush, just as mine had. It wasn't the blood or the cramps that had made you cry but the beginning of the slow farewell to childhood. You liked being a child. Élodie was quite different from you in that respect.

'Do you know what French mothers are supposed to do when their daughters get their first period?' I say, easing past your embarrassment.

You shake your head, not quite meeting my eye.

'They're supposed to slap them on the cheek.'

You look astonished.

'Not to hurt. It's a tradition. My mother did it to me and Camille, and her mother did it to her.'

You half smile. 'But why?'

'No one really knows what the slap is for. One theory is that the red mark it leaves represents the red of the blood.'

'That's just weird.'

I laugh. 'Yes, I suppose so. Look, go back to bed if

you feel rough. I'll bring you some painkillers.' You hesitate. 'Go on, it'll still be sunny later.'

I watch you go slowly up the stairs. Élodie never told me when she got her period. I only found out they'd started when someone from the village pharmacy rang. Another customer had seen her shoplifting a box of pads, as well as a bottle of nail varnish. *'Apparently she wasn't even trying to hide it,'* said the woman on the phone. *'She just dropped them into her bag and walked out.'*

'I'd have bought you a hundred packets if you'd asked,' I said to her later, after I'd paid the pharmacy five hundred francs not to call the police. *'Were you embarrassed to tell me you'd started?'*

'No,' she said, looking at a point somewhere over my shoulder. *'I just wanted to do it.'*

I wait until I hear the springs of your mattress creak as you lie down, then wander into the study. I've finished the books and my father's paperwork but there's still all of Greg's stuff to do. He was always a hoarder, and the desk and an ugly old filing cabinet are stuffed full of receipts, auction catalogues and bills. There's no system to any of it, and after a while I begin throwing things onto the rubbish pile without really checking. I wouldn't have noticed the small key caught up in a packet of ancient invoices if it hadn't clinked as it hit the floorboards. I recognize it immediately, slipping it into my shorts pocket. After an hour or so, my shoulders begin to twinge and I go outside for a break, resisting the temptation to pour myself some wine. It's fiercely hot and windless, the soil visible through the parched grass beginning to crack. I'm close to the pool when movement beyond the side boundary of the garden catches my eye.

There's an old path that leads that way from the pool, running down the edge of the property to emerge by the barn, quicker from here than up through the paint-peeling gate. I haven't been down it yet and it's clearer than I expect it to be, clearer than it should be, the weeds well trodden down.

I've never liked the barn, with its litter of discarded tools and air of neglect. As a child, I found its window-less bulk sinister and the events that followed years later only confirmed those early misgivings. Going closer, I see that one of the huge double doors stands ajar. I peer through the gap, but after the full glare of the sun it's too dark to see much, to make out the old scorch marks.

'*Sylvie.*'

I turn, heart galloping, to find Luc behind me. '*God, you scared me. What are you doing up here?*'

He lowers his gaze to his trainered feet, nonchalance replaced by furtiveness as he scuffs at the dry earth. '*I needed something for the pool.*'

'*Needed what? None of it is stored here.*'

'*Okay. Sorry. I'll try the shed.*'

He slouches away before I can ask him anything else and I wonder what I've missed. I nearly push the door open, drawn to see what might have interested him in there, but don't feel equal to it. I'd once wanted the place pulled down.

I pat my pocket for the key I found in the study, the

metal unbending as I press it against my leg. The barn has set off something in me, a masochistic kind of hunger that isn't dissimilar to the craving I feel for the wine waiting in the fridge. The push and pull Élodie always inspired in me.

Back in the house, I can hear Camille in the shower as I approach Élodie's room. I close the door softly behind me. I slip the key into the lock of the wardrobe door, trying not to catch my eye in the mirror. It's an old-fashioned oak piece Greg picked up somewhere, with the clothes rail positioned from front to back instead of horizontally. Élodie had always complained about it, saying it didn't give her enough room.

When the door swings open, the first thing to hit me is the dust and mothball smell of the faded shot-silk lining. Then a whisper of her own scent, which I'm not prepared for after so long. It makes a sob rise in my throat that hurts to swallow. As I press my face to the clothes, they sway gently, the hangers creaking dully against the iron rail. At the very front is the short white sundress she'd loved and I'd hated, so of course she'd worn it to death.

I can picture her in it during that last year as though it was yesterday – as though I'm standing at the window watching her cross the lawn wearing it. I close my eyes, seeing her luminous against the greens of the garden, the setting sun shining through the sheer fabric, outlining her shape, which is suddenly turning womanly, though her limbs are still slim and coltish. She is barefoot and slightly grubby and the combination, urchin and seductress, is deeply unsettling.

'*Qu'est-ce que tu fais, Sylvie?*'

I swing round. For an instant I'd thought it was her: she refused to call me Maman by the end. But, of course, it's Camille, wrapped in a towel.

She comes forward and fingers the dress, scarlet nails like blood against the white. '*I remember this. I always thought of it as her Lolita dress.*' She gives me a searching look. '*Why did you keep it all? Why were you always so intent on punishing yourself?*'

I don't answer, stretching instead towards the back of the wardrobe, the clothes heavy against my shoulder as I push them aside. My fingers close around a plastic Leclerc bag that crackles as I bring it out, brittle with the years it's been left untouched.

'*What's in there?*'

I put my hand in and pull them out, the tiny matinee jackets and bootees my mother had knitted her more than a quarter of a century earlier. The wool is still soft but the white looks grubby now. I remember dressing Élodie in them when we brought her back from the hospital; it was February and the house was freezing. I was so worried she'd be cold. I shake their creases out gently, as though they're in danger of falling into rags, and another sob hitches in my chest. I can't keep this one down.

'*Ah, merde,*' mutters Camille, as I press the jacket to my face. It still smells faintly of baby powder and Élodie's own brand-new scent.

She pries it gently away from me. '*This doesn't do any good, Sylvie. I've never understood why you're so hard on yourself*

94

when it comes to her.' She drops each small item into the bag and puts it carefully back.

Shutting the wardrobe door smartly, she turns the key and holds it up. I go to take it but she shakes her head. *'I'm keeping this. Now, go downstairs to Emma. It's her you need to think about now. Let the past rest.'*

1974

Greg is setting up a tripod by the pool. He's already taken a family portrait of the five of us: his parents, Margaret and Charles, are staying this week. I'm not convinced the visit is going well. Margaret is quiet, watchful, while Charles overcompensates, so hearty and appreciative of everything that it's beginning to ring false, though I know it isn't. The slightly strained dynamic is grating on Greg, who has already snapped like a petulant teenager a couple of times.

'*Papa, take photos of me now,*' Élodie said, after the group shots were done. '*Just me, not the others.*'

When he's ready, she perches on the very end of the low diving board above the deep end, the parasol pines a dark backdrop that makes her hair gleam palest gold, her toes just rippling the surface of the water. He wants to get her profile, first the left, then the right, and it takes longer than it should because she keeps turning to look straight down the lens of the camera, wanting to face it head-on.

Catching sight of me there next to Charles, hovering in the background as I often find myself, a silent extra or a servant standing by for instructions, she pouts.

This is a new face: I've seen her practising it in the mirror.

'*Arrête, Maman.*' She switches to English for her grandparents' benefit. 'Stop staring at me. You're always staring.'

Charles pushes out a laugh. 'Come on, Élodie, sweetheart. Your mother is only thinking how pretty you are.'

She flashes him a dazzling smile, her hair sparking as she shakes it back and poses again. I squeeze Charles's arm in a silent thank-you and find myself remembering all those times Greg came back from a buying trip, when a tiny Élodie would throw herself into his arms. '*Non, Maman, pas toi!*' she would say over his shoulder at me, little face set, hand batting me away. *Not you. Don't want you. Only Daddy.* And he would turn and give me a sympathetic smile. It still hurt.

I go back to the house. Margaret had said she was going in to find her hat but she's been gone for a while now. I find her in Élodie's room, holding up her white straw hat with an expression of disgust. It's frayed and crumpled, grubby with small footprints, but there's also something else on it I can't immediately identify. I see it then, discarded on the floor: the used menstrual pad she must have got out of the small bin in our en-suite bathroom. The hat is smeared with drying blood.

'Oh, God, I'm so sorry,' I say, the heat of acute embarrassment creeping up my neck. I can't meet Margaret's eye. 'I don't know what on earth made her think to do that.'

We stare at the soiled hat between us and then I reach

out to take it. There's a moment when I think Margaret isn't going to let go but she does. Her face is flushed too.

'I really am so sorry. I'll get you a new hat at the market tomorrow – there's a stall that sells ones just like it.'

She fixes me with her pale blue eyes. 'It's not just that,' she says softly, and I follow her gaze.

Élodie's room is always a mess. I used to tidy it daily but it just feels so futile – she only pulls everything out again. Although, if I'm honest, it's more that I have a deep aversion to the sight of her toys, not just unloved but often destroyed, everything seemingly smashed, kicked and pulled apart eventually. The violence unsettles me somewhere fundamental.

I think it has the same effect on Greg. I caught him in here once, holding the broken sections of a kaleidoscope he had once cherished. He seemed crushed. 'He always kept his things so beautifully when he was a boy,' Margaret told me, when I first met her. I know he worries about it too, the destructive streak she has inherited from neither of us.

So when I look to see what has stopped my mother-in-law in her tracks, I expect another destroyed toy. Instead it's a sketchbook I bought Élodie ages ago, and which she had never opened as far as I knew.

I push aside the wax crayons so I can see the pictures properly and they roll across her little desk and loudly drop to the floor, one by one. At first glance, they look like any childish drawings: stick people with round, bulbous heads. But then I look again and details begin to emerge: one figure lying along the bottom of the picture, black scribble where their stomach should be, a tongue lolling out. Another figure poking a disproportionately large knife into someone else. I turn the page, see a rudimentary cupboard with a bottle on its shelf. Drawn on the bottle, more carefully than anything else, is a skull and crossbones she must have copied from somewhere – a bottle of bleach on the highest shelf in the *souillarde*, perhaps. Pages and pages of fires follow: people, animals, trees, houses, all consumed by flames of vivid red and orange. In places she's pressed so hard the paper has torn. And then I realize that the same two figures crop up again and again: a man in a blue shirt and a woman in a long skirt, hair waving over her shoulders.

Later, I show the book to Greg. He's quiet for a long time.

'I used to draw guns and explosions all the time when I was a kid,' he says at last, voice straining to be light.

'When you were five?'

'Oh, God, I don't know. Probably.'

'Your mother seemed quite –'

'Quite what?' He cuts across me. 'Why are you bringing her into this?'

'I'm not. She found them. You saw what happened to her hat. She was worried. I'm worried. I think it's different from drawing explosions and monsters. I think these people might be us.'

He rubs his eyes. 'Let's just get through this visit and then we'll talk about it, okay?'

We don't, though. The next day, I pull the pages out

of the sketchbook and press them down to the bottom of the bin. I don't want to delve any deeper into it either.

When the film from that day is developed, I flip past the group shots to find the pictures of Élodie by the pool. I study them for hours. The girl with the amber eye looks to me like a different person from the one with the blue, in spite of the symmetry of her features, and the identical backdrop. It's the amber one I get framed. The blue I put into a drawer.

I have a secret theory. The girl with the amber eye is the daughter who got lost somewhere along the way, but who comes to me very occasionally in my dreams. '*Maman!*' she calls. And I turn to find her smiling, her hands reaching out for me.

You're still pale by evening, when we're due to leave for the circus. You've hardly eaten any dinner.

'Are you sure you want to go?' I stand behind your chair and smooth your hair back from your face. 'Why don't we just go another night? It'll be here for a week.'

'But Luc said . . .' You shake your hair so it half covers your face again. You're beginning to colour. 'Just that he might go tonight.' You get up, pushing back your chair. 'I'm going to get changed.'

Camille fixes me with a look when you've disappeared up the stairs. *'I told you she'd like him.'*

'Yes, it seems she's got a crush. I saw him today, you know, hanging round the barn. He said he was looking for something for the pool.'

'Well? Maybe he was just killing time before he had to go back to his mother. Wouldn't she keep you out of the house?'

I half-smile. *'Yes, I suppose so.'*

'Listen, I don't think I'll come with you tonight,' she continues. *'I want to carry on going through those things of Maman's in the attic. Besides, I don't like those provincial circuses. There's something creepy about them.'*

'I'm not too keen either, but Emma wants to go.'

We can hear the music from the circus as soon as we step out into the twilight to walk to the village. After the quiet of La Rêverie, evidence of so much life down the road is jarring. It gives me butterflies, the lurch of the innards just before walking out onto a stage.

The whole village seems to have turned out for the first night. Just as when I was a girl, the circus has been set up in an open space now used as a car park, to the north of the main square. The street leading to it is lined with market stalls manned by *dashiki*-wearing Senegalese men selling sunglasses, belts and knock-off designer handbags.

You're drawn like a magpie to one in particular, offering friendship bands woven from nylon in every colour imaginable. They're ten francs for three and you take ages to decide which combinations you like best, holding them against your wrist and rejecting the ones you say make you look pale.

While you deliberate, I glance furtively at the faces around us. A few seem familiar, a particular set of mouth or timbre of voice making me tense, but no one seems to notice me. I realize that your English chatter, your pinkened shoulders, have rendered us invisible. The villagers dismiss us as tourists and don't bother to look closer.

I relax a little, noticing for the first time how enchanting the scene must seem to you: lights strung through the plane trees, the air as soft and warm as breath, the noisy lure of the circus up ahead. Speakers pump out a dance track I've been hearing since before we left London, issuing from white vans and building sites, and now spread to

France too, its distinctive bass and insistent refrain lodged in my brain. 'What is love?' is the title. It seems apt.

There's no big top, as there would be in England: no one here is expecting any rain. Behind the ring, shadowy open-sided trailers house the animals and I feel an old fear prickle the back of my neck. As a little girl, I refused to go to the circus after Camille told me a story about an escaped tiger that had mauled an old woman before being shot dead.

I'd assumed they would have moved on from this kind of act, as British circuses have, but the flimsy cages are exactly the same as when I was a child, and exactly the same as when, years later, Greg insisted we take you and Élodie – with a row of gnawed wooden bars being all that separated us from the big cats. One year – the last time we went as a family – Élodie crept too close to an old male tiger in a cage on his own, first making faces and then hitting the bars with the flat of her hand.

She knew I was afraid: like a wild animal herself, Élodie could always smell fear on anyone, especially me.

'Attention, Élodie! Attention!' she mimicked, as she ran her hands along the bars, repeating my panicked entreaties for her to watch out and get back.

Greg was off buying drinks and, because I was carrying you, I was too slow to catch hold of her. Every time I tried, she danced away, laughing.

The tiger, who had been watching her intently from the shadows, suddenly launched himself at the bars, reaching right through them to swipe at her with a paw as big as her head, missing her face by inches and making me scream. As you burst into terrified sobs, Élodie whirled around, her face lit by the thrill of it. She had barely flinched.

'Do they have animals at this circus?' you say now, noticing the cages for the first time. 'Isn't that a bit cruel?'

'They still do that here,' I say shortly.

We move towards the stalls again, and I see Laurent from the back. Annette is with him, apparently haggling over a leather purse. She looks much the same as she always did, though possibly even thinner. 'It's all that disapproval of women like you,' Greg used to say. 'It burns off the calories.'

She looks up and notices me. Laurent, following her gaze, turns. His face lights up when he sees us, and I wish, as I always did, that he wouldn't be so obvious.

'Luc is here,' he says to you in careful English when he reaches us, his eyes twinkling. *'Annette, come and say hello to Sylvie and Emma.'*

We kiss the air near each other's cheeks. She smells of pine air-freshener and the plastic furniture protectors she always covered her sofas with.

'Do you think you'll be here much longer?' she says, after I've thanked her for Luc's help with the pool. Part of me has always admired her rudeness.

'I don't think so.' I keep my voice neutral. *'Camille is back and we're putting the house on the market.'*

Annette regards you, her head on one side. *'This one is nothing like her sister, is she?'* She turns to Laurent. *'You said there was a likeness but I can't see it. She looks so English.'*

I glance down at you, grateful again that you won't

understand. In fact, you've tuned out altogether, which means you haven't noticed Annette staring.

'*You must be thankful for that, at least,*' she continues, fingering the crucifix she's always worn round her neck. '*That lightning didn't strike twice.*'

'*Arrête, Annette,*' Laurent murmurs. '*Ça suffit.*'

'Mum, we need to go,' you say. You might not have understood the words, but you've picked up something uncomfortable in the air around us. I realize you're rescuing me. My lovely girl, I think, who already understands so much. I hate Annette even as I acknowledge that she's right. I am thankful you're different.

'I don't like her,' you say with feeling, once you've led me away. 'She seems like a bit of a bitch.'

'Emma!' I exclaim, but I'm smiling, most of it relief that the confrontation is over without much harm done.

You grin back. 'Is there time to get an ice-cream?'

*

Near the end of the first act, the ringmaster calls for volunteers from the audience. While the French children around us lift their arms, stretching towards the spotlight so they might be picked, I feel you shrink against me. You've always hated being the centre of attention.

The ringmaster asks for the lights to go up, his sharp eyes roving around until they light on you. A part of me knew they would: your white skin and shyness would be like a flare in the mass.

'*Mademoiselle,*' he shouts, gesturing towards you. '*Viens!*'

You shake your head. 'Mum, I don't want to,' you say urgently, but the big man on your other side is already passing you towards the end of the row. Everyone claps and cheers as you emerge, blinking, at the edge of the ring, the ringmaster's arm already around you, hustling you into the middle.

'*Comment tu t'appelles, mademoiselle?*' he says, leaning close, but you aren't looking at him, your eyes searching the crowd for mine. He grips you tighter. '*You are a very shy one, no? Don't you want to help me with my trick?*'

'*Je suis anglaise,*' you quaver into the microphone – the phrase I taught you in case you were faced with a round of rapid-fire French you didn't understand.

The crowd roars with laughter.

'*Voilà, la petite anglaise,*' the ringmaster announces with a flourish. '*She won't tell us her name.*'

Your task is thankfully easy. Another couple of children, a little younger, are brought into the ring and you're each given a set of balls. Clowns with buckets gesture for the balls to be thrown into them while they caper and trip. You do well, and I feel myself swell with an absurd pride watching you, your flushed face set with grim determination, hating every moment but too polite to walk off.

When you sit down next to me, I lean in close to your ear. 'I think you deserve some more of those friendship bands after enduring that, don't you?'

You give me a quick, tremulous smile and it's then, as I'm sitting upright, smiling back at you for your courage, that I think I see her. My heart stops and so does the world.

The easiest times between the two of us are at the sea. Élodie loves it there, like she loves dancing to my music. It forges a rare and fragile bond that I handle with the utmost care. It's why I have the urge to go there with her today.

Greg's parents left last night, Margaret unable to meet my eye as she waved goodbye. They were supposed to go at the end of the week but said they wanted to avoid the holiday traffic. I don't believe this. Margaret had the same expression I see on my own face sometimes, a preoccupied unease that makes her look drawn.

I sneak glances at Élodie in the mirror as I drive south, hair blowing because she likes the window wound right down, her eyes flicking back and forth as she watches the passing road. I turn on the radio and it's an Elton John song that seems to be played constantly. The uplift of the chorus makes my throat swell with tears I have to swallow hard. Her foot taps the back of my seat in time. I turn up the volume surreptitiously, because if she catches me doing it, she'll stop.

One of the stick figures from her drawings comes

into my head. It was wearing a long skirt like I often do – like I am now – and lying, eyes shut, in a swimming pool, the water scribbled right over her in lurid green. I chase away the image, and put my foot down on the accelerator.

Élodie likes the speed of the *autoroute*, especially when we overtake one of the huge transcontinental lorries, wheels spinning at eye level. On these journeys, it's possible to feel as though we are co-conspirators, even allies, no one watching us, no one knowing where we are.

It's late in the season, the holiday crowds thinned to nothing when we get there, the resort tired-looking, ready for its winter hibernation. As we walk to the beach from the half-empty car park, Élodie two steps ahead of me, the mistral whistles disconsolately through the metal shutters of deserted apartment blocks. There's something disquieting about it but I have grown so sensitized to atmospheres and tiny shifts of mood that I make myself dismiss it.

In the sea, we present a relatively normal picture of mother and daughter to anyone who might be looking on. Élodie insists on staying in for so long that we're both exhausted when we emerge. I roll out a couple of straw beach mats so we can lie down and dry off.

She seems to fall asleep almost immediately and I must nod off myself because the next thing I know I'm alone. There's nothing left of her but a pair of shucked-off armbands and the damp imprint of her body on the mat.

I jump to my feet and call her name. I scan the sand around me but she's nowhere. I run up and down the beach, screaming it over and over. Everything slows down, as moments of high drama do, and in the lulls between the fear and panic and horror, there is a speck of relief that shimmers, soft-lit and quiet. And I am so appalled by myself that I think I might be sick, right there in the sand.

It's another mother who finds her. She's holding Élodie's small hand when I race up to them, falling to my knees in the sand and checking her over in case she's been hurt. She watches me, dry-eyed and impassive, while I do this, our faces level. My hands are shaking but she doesn't appear remotely upset.

'*She said she didn't know where her maman had gone,*' the woman says from above. She can't keep the reproof out of her voice. Just behind her, three stolid little boys are digging in the sand.

I stand. '*She was right next to me. I closed my eyes for a second.*'

The woman nods, relenting, and pats Élodie's head. I wait for her to scowl and pull away because she hates to be touched like that. But she doesn't. She looks up and gives her rescuer a brave, tremulous smile.

'*You've got a little beauty there,*' the woman says, as I take Élodie's hand. '*Look after her, won't you?*'

'*Why did you go off? You frightened me so much. Anything could have happened to you,*' I say, as we make our way back along the beach, my voice strained with the tears I'm holding back. She's trying to wrench her hand out of mine but I'm holding on too tight. '*Why didn't you wake me?*'

But she won't answer. She refuses to speak a single word until we get home and Greg comes to the door, asking how our day at the beach went. She turns voluble enough then.

1993

In the concentrated heat of the circus audience, I close my eyes but when I open them again she's still there. She's standing at the back, looking towards the centre of the ring, where the entire troupe has begun to parade in a circle as the audience rises to its feet to applaud, slow-clapping in time to the music.

I crane to see past all the oblivious people now in my way, to try to spot the sharp little chin again, the familiar sway of long hair, the mesmerizing stillness she was always able to inhabit when she wanted.

'Come on, let's go,' I say, taking your hand. I pull you after me through our row, treading on people's feet in the rush. Your reluctance tugs at me, slowing us down like a puncture.

'Mum, what are you doing?'

You wrench your hand free but I blunder on anyway, running to the back of the raised benches, desperate to see her, terrified of seeing her. But people are starting to move now, wanting to get out ahead of the rush. I push through a large family, stupid and slow to part, and catch the reek of garlic sweat on the father as our bodies briefly make contact. He grumbles at me, '*Attention, Madame! Doucement,*' but I go on regardless.

Even in the sudden crush of people filing back towards the square, there's a curious hollow in the place where I thought I saw her, as though she's left a small force field in her wake. I look down at the straw as if, like something from a fairytale, I might spy some dropped token. One of the rings Greg brought her back from his trips, maybe – different shapes and styles but always set with a turquoise stone, like the necklace you've appropriated.

Of course there's nothing. Élodie was never there in the first place. I wouldn't find her, as I once had on a beach, nearly twenty years ago. It must have been someone with a look of her or the memory of the tiger or else I'm finally losing my mind.

I look around but I can't see you. Trying to slip inside the crowd, I find myself pushed back, unable to penetrate the wall of unyielding shoulders and hips. I hover helplessly in the small void Élodie's lookalike has left behind, an illogical panic spreading through my chest. I glance over my shoulder towards the cages. The tigers and bears will be back inside them now, locked in for the night. The old fear rears up again: the faulty bolt or the rotten bar, the tiger on the loose.

'Emma!' I shout, loud and desperate enough for a few people to turn. 'Emma!'

A hand on my arm makes me swing round. It's Olivier. He looks down into my face with concern. He seems taller.

'*Sylvie,*' he says. '*Qu'est-ce qu'il y a?*'

'*I saw her,*' I say breathlessly. '*She was here and now she's gone.*'

'*She's just over there. Look.*' He points.

I can't seem to catch my breath. '*Where?*' Everything has slowed down, the noise muffled. And then I see that it's you, not her, talking to Laurent about fifty feet away.

I close my eyes with relief, my body going limp.

Olivier touches my shoulder. '*See? She's fine. Let's just wait here a minute. There are too many people to get through.*'

I take in a lungful of too-hot air and force myself to let it out slowly, the panic ebbing with it. Olivier's hand on my bare shoulder is cool and dry. He's so close I can see every gold fleck in his brown eyes.

'*Doucement,*' he says, unwittingly echoing the man from before, but sounding completely different, the words slow and coaxing from him. '*Nothing's wrong. You need some air, that's all.*'

He reaches out and tucks a damp strand of hair behind my ear. I can feel a solid heat coming off the rest of him. He still seems bigger than I think of him in my mind, hard muscle and dense bone pressing into me. My heart is still fluttering in my chest, a different fear – or perhaps it's excitement now – sparking outwards to my every nerve-ending. We're standing too close to each other for almost-strangers, but I don't move away and neither does he. When he runs his hand down the sensitive inside of my arm, I feel a pulse deep inside me. He's gazing at me so intensely that it makes me flush and look away, unable to meet his eye any longer. I turn to beckon you over.

*

Olivier buys us ice-creams from the new *gelaterie* just off the square, open late to catch the circus custom. We walk slowly back towards the stalls because you want another look, and the cold ice-cream slipping down my throat is soothing. I'm acutely aware of Olivier next to me.

'*Okay now?*' he says, quietly so you won't hear.

'*Thanks for rescuing me back there,*' I murmur. '*I owe you.*'

'*Any time. Perhaps you can pay me back by coming to dinner with me.*'

'*I think I can manage that.*'

He smiles and guides me gently past a group of people, his hand warm at the small of my back, making my skin tingle.

I glance back to check on you and stop dead because you're no longer alone.

He's ten years older than when I last saw him and the sun damage has made it look like twenty but I still recognize him immediately. Marc Lesage. He'd run the *tabac* when I was growing up. He'd always been a bully people avoided crossing but I'd never drawn his attention until Élodie.

You catch my eye over his shoulder and I see how uncomfortable you are. His clawed old hand is on your arm, ice-cream dripping down your wrist because he won't let go.

'. . . *ta soeur*,' I hear him say, as I stride up. *Your sister.*

'*Bonsoir*,' I say, getting between the two of you so he has to let you go. '*Ça fait longtemps, Marc.*'

'*I was just saying that she doesn't look much like her sister.*' He slurs the words, his breath a hot aniseed fug of sour pastis. '*Probably a good thing, eh? You wouldn't want another like the first one.*' He laughs, baring yellow teeth, unknowingly echoing Annette's earlier barb.

He reaches for you again, staggering as his weight shifts, and I push you in the direction of Olivier, who is hesitating, wondering whether to intervene. Before he can, I lean as close to Marc as I can bear.

'*You're drunk, as ever. I told you ten years ago to mind your own business. Don't you ever come near me or my daughter again.*'

'*Why have you come back anyway?*' he calls as I walk away. '*We were glad to see the back of you. Vous nous avez apporté encore une brebis galeuse?*' Have you brought us another rotten apple?

And then he switches to English, raising his voice so you'll hear. 'Bad apple,' he shouts, his accent thick but understandable, as I hurry you away. 'She bad apple.'

People turn towards us, the background hum of the crowd abruptly switched off. A group of boys standing under the plane trees with their mopeds are laughing and whistling and I think we both notice in the same instant that Luc is among them, though he remains silent and unsmiling. I barely have time to absorb your stricken expression before you turn and run in the direction of the square.

Without a word to Olivier, I follow. People are dawdling and stopping, seemingly oblivious to anyone behind them. Ahead of me, you're pulling away, somehow able to weave much more deftly between the groups than I.

Just before reaching the square, where the clot of people is finally able to disperse, I lose sight of you, just like before. You've eluded me as easily as the mirage of Élodie by the benches, another ghost daughter vanished. I come to a stop, unable to think straight about what you might do next.

I make for the far side of the square where the road beyond the barriers erected for the circus will take me back to La Rêverie. I'm about halfway across when I see, at the very edge of my peripheral vision, the familiar swing of hair again. I wish it was yours, but it isn't. I cover my face with my hands, resisting the urge to scream. Somewhere in my mind, the thought registers that I badly need a drink.

When I take my hands away, she's gone, whoever she was. Almost everyone has gone from my end of the square, in fact.

'*Come on,*' I say aloud. '*Pull yourself together.*'

I set off again, determined that nothing will put me off this time. Beyond the village limits, plunged into sudden darkness, I run along the main road, ignoring as well as I can the flashing headlights of passing cars, the same dance song coming from one, a blaring horn from another, full of teenagers, high-pitched laughter Dopplering into something low and threatening as they fly past, so close my hair whips my cheek.

By the time I get back to La Rêverie, I'm breathing hard, my hair plastered to the back of my neck.

'*Mon dieu, Sylvie!*' Camille exclaims from the salon door. She's holding one of our grandmother's antique coffee cups in her hand. '*What melodrama. And you such an Englishwoman these days. Emma is upstairs. She wouldn't say a word to me, just ran straight up. What on earth has happened?*'

I take the stairs two at a time but you aren't in your room and, for a second, the panic returns and I'm ready to take to the streets again. As I turn to go back downstairs I notice the faint bar of light under the door at the other end of the hall. Of course. You're in Élodie's room.

As I reach for the handle, its brass plate gouged with half a dozen tiny Es if you know where to look for them, I feel the dread that always hits me on this threshold. Inside, you sit cross-legged on the dusty floor, surrounded by heaps of her clothes, torn from the rail in the wardrobe. Hanging from the open door is the key.

You've lifted your face, your eyes red. 'I found it next to Camille's cigarettes.'

I think you look more fearful than angry, which is something I never witnessed in your sister. Nothing ever frightened her, especially me.

I rush over and kneel to pull you to me, crushing the clothes under my knees. 'Oh, Emma, I was so worried.

You shouldn't have run off like that. That road is dangerous in the dark.'

You don't pull away, but you don't return the embrace either. When I lean back to look at you properly, a single tear runs down your cheek and falls to the faded blue shirt in your lap.

'Darling, what that horrible man said –'

'He said she was a bad apple.' You look down at the shirt in your lap and begin to pleat the fabric between your fingers, pinching each fold so hard that your thumbnails turn white. 'I know what it means but why did he say it?'

I look at the detritus around you and see the white sundress. The small splash of red wine staining the hem is still there, faded now to pink. I pick up an old flip-flop and trace a finger along the indentation her foot made long ago. There's something even more intimate about it than the clothes.

I take a breath. 'Em, you know I told you she was taken out of school when she was ten?'

You nod.

'Well, it wasn't because we decided to teach her at home, like I said. She was expelled.'

Your eyes widen. 'What did she do?'

'She was unkind to another girl in her class.'

'Is that all?'

You sound like Greg, never wanting to acknowledge that Élodie might have done anything wrong, and it makes me sharp. 'It was bad, Emma. The girl was seriously hurt. The point is that this is a small village.

Everyone knew what Élodie did and some people still remember it now. That's what that man meant. He should never have said it to you but I wanted to tell you why he did so you understood. Unfortunately, people have long memories in a place like this.'

You gesture to the clothes strewn around you. 'Can I have some of these?'

I shake my head. 'No, I don't think that would be –'

'Why?' You speak over me. 'She was my sister. You've never wanted me to have anything of hers.' Your hand goes to the turquoise necklace. 'You don't even like me having this.' It's then that I hear the wheeze in your chest.

I get to my feet. 'Choose a few things, then. And put the rest away, please. I'll get your inhaler.'

That she was expelled doesn't tarnish your image of her, I realize. Her hurting someone is just an abstract detail. It only makes her more fascinating.

'Mum?'

I'm almost at the door, thinking about your asthma and how, after years of absence, the symptoms are creeping back in. I'm also thinking about the wine in the fridge downstairs.

'What is it, Em?'

You pull in your breath and I wince at the sound. 'I found something else earlier. In the study.'

I wait. I've gone through that room, or at least I think I have.

'It's all in French but I worked out some of the words. I think it's her medical notes.'

1975

It's afternoon, Élodie is inside and, like a needle in a well-played record, Greg and I are slipping into the groove of what has become, in the last year or so, one of our most regular arguments. This one always comes out when another of his buying trips is announced, usually with little warning. It turns out he's leaving the next day and will be gone until the following weekend.

'It's easy when you can pick up and leave whenever you like,' I say, as I eat Élodie's abandoned lunch, already congealing in the sun. 'It's easy when you can drive to Paris or London with the radio on and the window down, alone with your own thoughts. When you can visit your interesting friends and talk about *art*. What do you think I do here when you're away, or locked in your study, when it's just me and Élodie and she won't sleep, or eat anything I give her, or even deign to look at me? You don't know anything about how it really is.'

There is relief in ranting like this. It distracts me from the fear that lurks underneath. It's all true, every word, but what it translates to, really, is *please don't leave me to do this on my own*. He would probably stay, if I asked like that, but my pride prevents it.

He reaches out to rub the back of my neck, a long-established gesture of affection between us that I would usually lean into, but not today. I remain stiff and his hand drops.

'Why don't you plan a day out? Take Élodie to the coast. You always have fun there.'

I'm about to reply when Laurent is suddenly in the garden. He ambles across the grass towards the terrace steps, little Luc wriggling in his arms, trying to get down.

'*Salut,*' he calls. '*Am I interrupting?*'

I shake my head and gesture for him to come up. He's always been a comforting presence, always brought out a version of myself I like more.

'*Bonjour, Laurent,*' Greg says tersely, getting to his feet. '*I'll leave you two to it. I've got some paperwork I need to get on with.*'

Laurent flashes him an apologetic smile. '*Of course, although actually it's you I was after. I wanted to get your expert opinion on something.*'

He often makes these flattering little overtures to Greg, as if he knows he's resented for our shared history. They seem painfully obvious to me, but usually have a softening effect on Greg.

'*Okay, sure, I'll help if I can,*' he says now, relenting slightly.

'*It's a brooch Annette wants me to have valued. It was her great-aunt's.*'

He shifts Luc to the other arm so he can reach into his pocket. The baby twists round, stretching towards the table and the remnants of our lunch.

'*I'll take him*,' I say, holding out my arms. I love Luc. He's a placid child, full of smiles and entirely uncomplicated. I like the dense weight of him in my lap. It makes me feel more solid. More grounded.

Élodie appears at the kitchen door. I see her eyes settle on Luc, who is now clutching my necklace in his chubby fist, fat amber beads the same colour as Élodie's left eye. She sidles over to Greg, one hand snaking around his neck to pull him down to her level.

'*What is it, darling?*'

She whispers in his ear, her eye on me. It's the right side, the blue side, the iris almost as dark as the pupil in the bright sunshine. Greg straightens up.

'Sylvie, she can't find her ladybird purse. Will you go and look while I talk to Laurent?'

I hand Luc carefully back to his father. '*I'll just be a minute.*' I look at Élodie. '*Can you remember where you last saw it?*'

She shrugs, her eyes sliding away from mine.

I swallow a sigh, and begin collecting plates to take in on my way upstairs. By the time I come down, having eventually found the purse stuffed inside her pillow case, she's gone. It takes me another second to realize there is no sign of the baby.

'*Where's Luc?*' I say sharply. Laurent and Greg are sitting at the table with a couple of beers, the brooch between them on the table in a velvet box.

'*Élodie's taken him for a little walk*,' Greg says, gesturing to the lawn below. Only I notice the slight challenge in his voice.

'*He's so restless since he started walking,*' says Laurent. '*He can't sit still for two minutes. She's doing me a favour.*'

I hurry down the steps but there's no sign of them on the lawn. There's a shady corner Élodie likes, just out of sight from the terrace, and I'm so sure she'll be there that when she isn't I stare at it dumbly for a long moment, unable to think what to do next. Then I hear a sound, so high and brief that it might have been a bird's cry. It had come from the direction of the swimming pool.

As I begin to run towards the parasol pines that screen the water from the rest of the garden, something bright flashes through the leaves, ruby-bright. Élodie is wearing a red dress today.

I arrive at the shallow end as Luc hits the deep water. It's not a small pool but I seem to be there instantly, as if I've leapt over time. I pull him out so quickly that his eyes are still round with shock from the impact. He doesn't even begin to wail until I start checking him for damage, his belated terror making both of us shake.

There's nothing wet or choked about his breathing and I feel my heart-rate go down a notch. As I cradle him tightly against my chest, letting him cry it out, I catch Élodie's eye. We stare at each other and it isn't like looking at a child.

She sees Greg and Laurent before I do and, as they stop in front of us, Laurent's face ashen under his tan, she points to Luc, whose cries are ebbing into exhausted whimpers.

'*Il est tombé,*' she says to her father, her voice more babyish than usual. '*Silly Luc fell in the pool.*'

No, I suppose I didn't see her push him. As Greg says later, I don't have any *proof*. But I saw how close she was standing to where he'd fallen in. And I saw the expression on her face, too.

'For God's sake, it was probably fear,' Greg says, when I try to describe it. 'She'd had a shock too, don't forget.'

He won't look at me, though, and there's not much conviction in his voice. I leave it then, but I know it wasn't fear. It was excitement, her face almost convulsing with it. It was in her eyes too – I'd never seen them brighter.

That night, neither Greg nor I sleep well, both of us awake, eyes open in the dark, until well after two. I put out my hand to rest on his smooth flank – an invitation for him to turn to me, to discuss it – but he only stills and deepens his breathing as though he's been asleep all along. It's the adult version of hiding from a monster by putting a blanket over your head. *If I can't see it, it's not happening.*

I draw my hand back.

1993

I can't remember the first time I asked myself the question. I suppose there must have been a first time but it's been a constant companion for so long, circling above me like a giant bird, shadow wings blotting out the sun, that pinning it down is impossible.

Was it me?

There were other questions too – *Was she born or was she made?* – but they were all variations on the first, the age-old question every mother of a child like Élodie has asked themselves: *Is this my fault?*

You'd found the medical notes in the old desk: a huge, dark-varnished monster of a thing with carved drawers running down both sides. The deep bottom one on the left had been locked when I tried it, with no sign of a key. I meant to look for it but then forgot. You admit you picked it with a straightened-out hair grip, demonstrating a rather disconcerting resourcefulness.

The folder, which you fetch now from your room, is bulky and lands on Élodie's bedroom floor with a thud.

There's a corner of yellow paper sticking out from the pile, a couple of words visible in cramped black ink, and I know it's Morel's writing. Docteur Hubert Morel.

He arrives in my head in his entirety: the way his pipe had worn a groove in his bottom teeth; cool, dry hands; gentle brown eyes that never judged.

Slowly, I pull the folder across the floor towards me, careful not to betray any alarm.

'Let's go out to the garden,' I say, and get up before you can object. I want to be in the fresh air. Camille appears at the doorway, unnoticed by you, her face enquiring, and I shake my head once.

Outside, the air is like a warm bath. You sit down next to me, both of us facing into the void of the now lightless garden. Camille walks over and presses a cool glass of wine into my hand, turning to go back inside wordlessly. The cicadas are quiet tonight, but somewhere in the near-distance, probably from the dried-up stream between the garden and the fields, a solitary bullfrog croaks.

I put my hand flat on the folder. 'We went to see a specialist about her. Just after you were born. I was ... *We* were so worried.'

'It must have been serious, then.' You reach out to pick at the frayed corner of the folder. '1975, 1977, 1979. Was she ill all that time?'

I pause. 'Well, yes. But not in the way you're thinking. The doctor we went to see was ... a different sort of specialist.'

'What do you mean?' You turn to look at me. In the light from the house behind your head, I can see a frantic mass of tiny insects thronging the air, darting in all directions, too many to count, and I get up to light a mosquito coil. You've been scratching at your bites all day.

'Mum, please,' you say more softly, when I've stopped fussing. 'It's not fair. I'm not a little kid any more.'

You are to me, I want to say, but resist. 'There were lots of phases,' I begin weakly.

'Phases?' You shake your head. 'What kind of –'

'Élodie wasn't easy,' I interrupt, and a bubble of hysteria threatens to explode out of me because it's such a ridiculous understatement. 'She had quite serious behavioural issues.'

You pause, taking this in. 'What – because she was ill?'

I swallow, reminded again how much easier it had been to let you assume Élodie was physically sick.

'Not exactly,' I say now.

I want to warn you then that knowing is not always a good thing – that once you do know, you can't unknow. That one revelation can upend everything else, flattening walls you thought were immovable, revealing rooms you wouldn't want to see into. But I'm so tired, and Élodie will be there again if I go and look under the oleander tree, long hair gleaming and rippling out of the dark like a moonlit stream. *Tell her*, she'll whisper. *Tell her, or I will.*

'Élodie wasn't ill in the way that you've always thought.' My voice is clear so it pierces the darkness. I don't think I'm speaking just for your benefit. 'She didn't have leukaemia or something like that. Her illness was in her mind. When I say she wasn't easy, I meant that it wasn't just . . . naughtiness. It was much more than that, much more complicated. It was something she was born with, how

131

she was made . . .' I falter. 'It couldn't really be cured, not with medicine.

'Your father didn't want to face that, not for a long time. I suppose I didn't either. But then, when I finally took her to see Dr Morel,' I gesture at the folder, 'and he explained there was . . . a condition, that it wasn't anyone's fault but there wasn't much we could do about it either, your dad and I had to come to terms with that.' I pause, because sometimes I don't think Greg ever did fully come to terms with the truth. In fact, the loss of her for a decade has enabled him to move further away from it than ever.

'I'm sorry, darling, that we didn't tell you this before, but you were too young to understand. I didn't want to remind you of how hard it was when we all lived together here. It was such a difficult time.'

I've been speaking fast and it's left me breathless. I want a cigarette. I wish I'd asked Camille to join us.

'But I can hardly remember anything about when we were here, Mum, you know that.' Your voice is high with emotion. 'I can't remember Élodie at all. Only from photos.'

I gesture for you to come and, to my surprise, you do. I pull you into a hug and you squeeze in next to me on the chair. You feel warm and solid, utterly alive.

'Why did you never say anything about this? Why didn't Dad? He's always told me more about her than you.'

'We both agreed it was best if we waited. We thought it would be easier for you this way.' It sounds awful out loud. I'm lightheaded with guilt.

'Everything seems weird now,' you say, after a while. 'It's like everything I've always thought about our family was wrong. Like it's been made up.'

'I'm sorry, darling,' I say into your hair.

'What was it that she had?' Your voice isn't much more than a whisper.

'It's hard to explain. Her brain didn't work like other people's. She couldn't . . .'

'Couldn't what?'

'I don't think she could feel what other people felt. I suppose that doesn't sound like much but it caused real problems, for all of us. It wasn't her fault but . . . it was hard, Emma. It was unbearably hard at times.' *Frightening, too*, I could say, but don't.

You still. I watch your profile as the moon comes out and spills its cool light over the garden. I can't quite make out your expression as you turn everything over in your mind, but I cling to the fact that you haven't gone back to your own seat, that your head is resting on my shoulder.

'But I always . . .'

'You always thought she was perfect. Clever, beautiful, the first-born. She was all of those things, but she was also very di– difficult.' I almost said *disturbed*, but I don't want to scare you. Truth and protectiveness are so hard to reconcile. 'When she was young she had these . . . rages. But then, as she grew older and learnt to control herself better, she became very . . . well, she became very cold.' I reach round for your hand, stroke it. You pull away, though you do it gently.

'Keep going,' you say, looking straight at me and, just

133

for a split second, I see a glimpse of Élodie in your face. I think it's the hardening expression: you're determined not to allow me to stop as you have in the past. You turn to look impassively into the garden, waiting, like a skilled interrogator, for me to fill the silence.

'Élodie was very good at manipulating people,' I say eventually. 'It was part of her condition. She knew that your father let her do what she liked if she was charming and well-behaved with him. So she was, most of the time. But I was with her all day every day. I knew her better than anyone. I saw other sides to her, too, when she wasn't . . . acting.'

You're quiet, taking that in, and I watch you, nerves wringing out my insides in case I've said too much. I can always read your face but it's too dark. I wonder if any memories are flickering on in your head and silently pray there aren't.

'So that's why she was expelled from school?'

'Yes. She stayed at home with me after that. With you and me.'

You hang your head. 'I can't remember. I can hardly remember her at all.'

'Well, you were only three. I don't remember much from when I was that young either.'

You now know the truth, though not the whole of it, not by a long way. And as we go inside to find Camille, I feel overwhelmingly relieved. With everything you've just discovered, you haven't thought to ask what your physically healthy sister died from. And being glad about that fills me with shame all over again.

I book the appointment with Hubert Morel the day after the incident with Luc in the swimming pool. I don't care any more what Greg will say when he finds out, or old Dr Bisset, the village doctor who's fobbed me off for a couple of years now. I know he thinks I'm an hysteric. When I tried to show him the drawings, he waved them away without even looking at them. *'My dear,'* he said, hands folded around his stomach as if he was already thinking about what to have for lunch, *'so she's a handful. She'll grow out of it.'*

Morel is a child psychologist, and his practice on a quiet street in Avignon is the closest I could find. This is not London or Paris: there aren't huge numbers of psychologists of any stripe to be found around here, let alone those specializing in children.

I am nervous on the journey there, not so much because I don't know anyone who's ever seen what Greg calls a 'head shrinker', but because I'm afraid he, like Bisset, will think it's nothing. That it's all in my mind.

Morel is tall and impossibly thin standing there in the waiting room when it's our turn.

'Madame Winters, why don't we speak alone first? Jeanne will

keep an eye on your daughter.' He gestures to the owl-eyed receptionist.

In one corner of the waiting room there are books and toys, drawing materials, a small wooden table and a chair. I watch as Élodie chooses a book and sits down quietly with it. As I follow Morel along the corridor to his office, I can't help glancing back because I can never get Élodie to read. She's staring after me, little jaw set, and I realize the book in her hands is upside down.

In his office, high-ceilinged and airy, Morel pushes a box of tissues towards me, though I'm not crying. Not quite.

'*May I ask how long you've had concerns about Élodie?*'

I let out a humourless laugh, which turns into a sob. '*About six years?*' I reach for a tissue.

He waits, one long-fingered hand folded over the other.

'*My husband doesn't know I'm here. She's completely different with him anyway.*'

I pick at a torn cuticle. I'm so worried that I'm not going to be able to make him understand either.

'*Different how?*' he says.

'*I feel as though she pretends with him and is honest with me,*' I say, then sigh shakily, because the words are so vague and inadequate. '*I see her every day, we're together all the time. I see her face fill with hate, or – and sometimes this is worse – this total blankness.*'

I am trembling now, and tears are spilling over. I dig my fingernails into the soft pads of my palms to make myself stop.

'*Can you give me an example of when you've seen her like this?*'

I tell him about the lizard and its eggs, how she'd destroyed them.

'*And she didn't do it to frighten me either. She thought she was alone.*' I swallow loudly. '*She did it for her own entertainment. For pleasure.*'

He nods, taking that in. Then he looks at me. '*Madame Winters, would you say that you are frightened of your daughter?*'

I jolt in my seat. No one has ever asked me that. I reach for another tissue but the box is empty. He hands me a perfectly laundered handkerchief, a blue H embroidered in the corner.

'*My mother does them for me,*' he says, with a rueful smile, and I think how much I would love to stay in that office for ever, with nothing to do but listen to the gentle timbre of Hubert Morel's voice.

'*I am the first child psychologist you've seen?*' he says, when I'm closer to composing myself. He sits down again.

'*Yes.*'

'*Was there a particular event that prompted you to come now? You said the incident with the lizard was a while ago.*'

I take a deep breath. '*Things have started to happen more frequently. I feel as though it's getting more serious. There was a dead pigeon. Élodie said she'd found it like that in the garden. Greg — my husband — said another animal had done it, a bigger bird perhaps, or a fox, but I —*'

'*You think Élodie killed it?*'

The word makes me stammer. '*I don't — I don't know. But there was no blood on it, no wound. Its wings were broken, as*

137

though they'd been pulled apart. I found a feather in her room.' I look up at him. *'I think it was strangled. Or maybe died of fright.'*

He makes a note, then puts down his pen. *'What else?'* He steeples his hands. *'Tell me.'*

And so I tell him about Luc.

Afterwards, he wants to speak to Élodie on her own. I sit in the waiting room, leafing through old magazines I don't absorb a word of.

'So, what's the verdict?' I ask, when I'm called back in, with an attempt at lightheartedness I don't even slightly pull off. I'm shaking again.

'Have you heard of the Rorschach method?' he says. *'Some people know it as the inkblot test.'*

A bell rings somewhere in my brain: a dim memory of listening to one of Greg's London friends who was training at the Tavistock Clinic. Red wine and an orange Habitat sofa, Greg and I still happy.

'It was developed in the twenties to test for schizophrenia but it's come to be used more generally, as an indicator of other . . . conditions. People assume there's a correct answer for each of the inkblots. That if you see a bat or a butterfly, you're normal. But it's much more complex than that. I take into account how long the subject might take to answer, for instance, and where in the picture they see what they see. I also look at how closely what they see resembles what is actually there, and many more factors.'

'And what did you find? What did Élodie see?'

He flexes his hands, turns the palms upwards. *'These are preliminary thoughts more than anything. I need to spend more time with her, perhaps in a month or so. There are further assessments I would like to undertake.'*

I lean forward. '*But you must have formed some sort of impression. She was with you for over an hour.*' I've crushed his lovely handkerchief into a damp ball.

He breathes out slowly through his nose. '*There were some . . . unusual responses. There are particular cards – I mentioned the bat – where most people see the same thing. When a subject doesn't, it can be significant.*'

'*What did she see?*' I whisper, full of dread and conviction that she will have described monsters and infernos where anyone else would see flowers.

'*It's more what she didn't see. She's obviously a bright child, but she struggled to see faces or animals in the shapes. Do you know what function the amygdala serves in the brain?*'

I shake my head.

'*The amygdala is shaped like an almond. It's buried deep within the temporal lobes. Put simply, it's where our emotional responses come from. It's there that emotions are acknowledged and processed. But occasionally, in some people, this part of the brain doesn't light up when it should. It stays quiet and dark.*'

'*And you think Élodie is one of those people?*'

He spreads his hands again. '*I think she may be. When the amygdala doesn't work in the same way it does in most people, there is a tendency to take risks more than is normal. You said to me earlier that Élodie never seems to show fear. That's different from bravery, where someone who is fearful of heights jumps off the diving board anyway. It might be that Élodie doesn't feel the fear in the first place.*'

'*But what about the other things we talked about? Is that all part of the same thing?*'

'*Madame, it's important to remember that Élodie's brain is*' *still growing. She is not yet fully developed. As such, I would be reluctant — any psychologist would be reluctant — to make a diagnosis of psychopathy. She —'*

'Psychopathy?' The room empties of air. 'You think Élodie could be a psychopath?'

'*I didn't say that. As I was explaining, we don't like to label a child with a condition that has such negative connotations while he or she is still very young.*'

'But if she was eighteen? Doctor, is — is this my fault? Is it how we've brought her up?' It's the question I've asked myself so many times and here is someone who might be about to say *Yes. It's your fault.* I feel like I might be sick.

But Morel only gives me a sad smile. '*There are two types of children who display unemotional or callous traits, such as you've described to me. The first have been exposed to abuse and violence all their lives. Their extreme coldness develops as a kind of defence mechanism, in order to survive the terrible situation in which they find themselves.*'

'But we —'

Morel holds up his hand. '*I said there was another type. It is clear to me that Élodie does not fall into the first group. The parents of those poor children do not seek help from someone like me. I am not talking about marital arguments or a smack on the back of the legs. These are children who are sexually and physically abused, neglected, left to fend for themselves from an early age.*

'*The other group are very different. They are rarer, too. These are children who appear to be wired differently. It's genetic with them, not learnt.*'

I put my hand to my stomach. '*It's inherited?*'

'*It's not really clear. Possibly. I would like to see Élodie again, preferably next month. As I said, there are further tests I'd like to perform.*' He stands.

'But what can I do? Is there anything I can do to help her? What if she tries to hurt someone again? I'm so frightened that she —'

'*Not all children with these traits are actively violent. Some are just manipulative and bent on getting their way. Often they do things just to see what happens. They are not stimulated by the same things we are. Adults with this personality type typically have a very low heart-rate, even in dangerous or what should be highly emotive situations. There is a theory that their urges to do things they know are wrong and will hurt people come from a desire to feel more, to be excited. This is naturally difficult to deal with but, with careful handling, it doesn't have to be dangerous.*'

'But it can be?'

He inclines his head. '*If she is aggressive, try to make sure she doesn't gain from it in some way. Try not to overreact and create a fuss that she might enjoy or find interesting. Punishment doesn't work with children like this. It's not an effective deterrent. They don't worry about people being angry with them. They don't feel shame when they upset someone. What is shown to work better is the very opposite: you reward the good behaviour instead of punishing the bad.*'

I think of Greg: the gifts he buys her, the treats I have always seen as naked bribery. And yet his relationship with her is so much less fraught.

'But what if she does something dangerous? Are we supposed to ignore it?'

'*Effectively, yes. A child like Élodie will not respond as another child would. It is hard to hear but she doesn't really care. At most, she will be fascinated by the effect she has on you: your tears,*' *perhaps, or loss of temper. I showed her some photographs, too. One of them was of a woman looking distressed and fearful, on the verge of tears. When I asked Élodie what she thought this lady was feeling, she had difficulty coming up with the sort of answer a child younger than her would know straight away. Do you know what she said in the end?'*

I shake my head, part of me not wanting to know, the other part morbidly needing to know everything.

'She said, "She looks like Maman."'

I briefly close my eyes. *'But you're saying I didn't make her like this, and that she can't help it?'* My voice is muffled by more tears.

He nods.

I don't feel any less frightened – perhaps I'm more so – but it still feels like an enormous stone has rolled off my chest.

'So, you'll do more tests,' I say, hope a faint glow in the core of me. *'And then you'll know what you can do to help her? Is there any kind of medication? Or talking therapy, perhaps?'*

For the first time, Morel doesn't meet my eye. I watch the Adam's apple in his narrow throat bob as he swallows. *'I'm afraid it's not as simple as that. She is what she is. There is no cure. But I can perhaps help you to understand her more, to manage her behaviour better.'*

He sees my face crumple and rushes on: *'There is hope, Madame Winters. I said before that children's brains are not fully formed yet. They are still malleable. That means they can grow out of it. It's thought that some four out of five children like this do.'*

I take that in. Four out of five is good. Eighty per

cent. I ignore the inner tremor when I think of the other fifth. I push away an image of her wild blue eye.

'But there must be something we can do in the meantime? Something that improves her chances of being in the four out of five.'

'There is a study I read about recently. The results appear to point towards parental affection making some difference, though it's early days. But if you can show her plenty of warmth and love, it may make a difference. I certainly don't think it can hurt.'

'But she doesn't like affection, not from me. She never has. She doesn't like it much from Greg these days either. Even when she was tiny, she didn't seem to need it.'

'So try again. What have you got to lose?'

He's right, and I ignore the little voice in my head that says it won't work.

*

Driving home in the car, Élodie silent in the back, I barely see the road passing underneath the wheels. I'm so afraid of everything ahead – from telling Greg to trying to deal with a child who has possible *psychopathic traits*, those words still clanging in my head.

And yet, underneath it all, I feel weak with a horrible kind of relief. It isn't my imagination, which Greg has implied for years. Something really could be wrong with her, a biological flaw hidden behind all that beauty.

I'm not mad. It's not me.

It's not my fault.

When I glance at her in the rear-view mirror, quiet and apparently peaceful as she watches the city thin out into fields again, I'm swept up in a welling of emotion so strong that it hurts my throat to cry silently. As tears spread in the lap of my skirt, I realize what this unfamiliar feeling is.

It's sorrow, deep and true. Not for me, but for her.

Though I haven't made a sound, she must sense something seismic taking place inside me. Perhaps sadness has a scent. She meets my eye in the mirror and I know she sees the tears and the smudged mascara, the blotches on my cheeks from the strain of stopping myself sobbing aloud. She takes all this in, then looks away again, her gaze returned to the road.

1993

The morning after you brought me Élodie's medical notes, the air curling in through my window smells strange, a note of something sour and herbal in it that's too faint for me to place.

I find Camille in the salon, a bowl of black coffee by her side, various boxes half packed around her.

'*You're awake early,*' she remarks, without looking up.

'*It's so hot. I feel like I've been trying to get cool all night.*'

'*Look, Sylvie, I think I'm going to head home this afternoon. Leave after lunch.*' The sunlight streaming in through the open doors cuts her in two. '*I've done what I need to do and can pop back if need be. I can't stand this heat and, anyway, I did say I'd only be staying a couple of days.*' She smiles wryly when she sees my face. '*Mon dieu, I thought you'd be relieved.*'

'*No.*' I cast around for the right words. '*I like having you here. So does Emma.*'

'*I've liked it too.*'

Suddenly I can't bear the thought of Camille leaving you and me alone in the house. There is something immensely reassuring about her implacable, uncompromising nature. It feels like a bulwark against all the uncertainty.

She sighs. '*Look, don't be angry but I've been thinking a lot about it and I don't feel completely comfortable here, with Emma not knowing the full story. I understand why you've done it, and I would probably have done the same myself, but I can't quite look her in the eye.*'

'*Camille.*' Something in my tone makes her put down her cup. '*I'm afraid.*'

'*Come on, Sylvie, there's not much more to sort out here. You can go back to England soon. If you want, let's just pay for house clearance. I'll go halves with you.*'

I let out a shaky breath and she regards me thoughtfully, her head on one side.

'*I think part of you doesn't want to let go. Even I've felt reluctant. It's our family home. But you've got so much more history here than me. Now you're back, it's got you in its grip again.*'

'*It's where it all went wrong.*'

Camille sighed. '*And maybe it's the only place where it can be put right. Tell her properly, Sylvie. Okay?*'

I nod, unable to speak because I'm suddenly in tears.

'*So I'm allowed to go, then?*' She smiles and hands me a tissue.

'*Yes, of course. I'm sorry.*'

'*It's fine. You've always been a weeper. You get it from Maman. It's not your fault.*'

'*I'm afraid Emma will never forgive me.*'

Camille shrugs. '*She might not, but she's much more likely not to forgive you if she finds out in some other way.*'

After that, I feel a little lighter, and in the sun-steeped garden, where the pigeons are squabbling companionably again, the weight of the past seems to lift a little. I'm suddenly full of conviction that I'll be able to explain everything. Tonight, after dinner, I will finally find the right words.

*

After Camille leaves, I set to work clearing up the garden. I get the old lawnmower out and drag it up and down in the intensifying heat, the sweat pouring off me freely, my hair plastered to my skin. It seems to take for ever, the grass too long to be cut cleanly and the lawnmower blades rusted and blunt.

About halfway through, I crouch to put a finger in one of the cracks opening in the dried-out earth. I think of Camille complaining about the heat and wish she'd stayed another night.

When the last section is done, I abandon the damn lawnmower where it is and jump into the pool without changing out of my shorts and T-shirt. The water is gloriously cool and I stay in for a long time, not really swimming, just floating, watching the water scatter like emeralds when I lift my arms towards the sky.

You've stayed in your room most of the day, only coming down to wave off Camille, and I tell myself the sun has finally beaten your desire for a tan because it's even hotter this afternoon. But I think it's more than that, and when I knock on your door and try to coax you down for some food about six, you refuse, turning towards the wall and saying your stomach hurts again.

I wash some deep red tomatoes, and they're so juicy

that when I cut into the flesh the seeds burst out of them. I arrange the slices on a plate, then scatter them with basil leaves and wizened black olives so salty they make my mouth water. I wash it all down with half a bottle of wine, which is a bad idea on an almost empty stomach, but the heat has taken my appetite. As I pass the phone, I consider ringing up the ferry company to enquire about return crossings but then I think about what Camille would say. *You just want to avoid telling her the whole story.* Instead I go upstairs to lie down, drifting on the woozy detachment the wine has infected me with.

The light behind the shutters is muted when I wake. I can hear music coming from downstairs, some jazz record I can't imagine you playing. I know I could sleep on and on, but that reminds me of the muffled days when Élodie was young, and the thought makes me get up immediately. I open the shutters and see that the searing afternoon has tipped into the gentle relief of evening, the light purpling the lawn below. Beyond the parasol pines, the last sunrays are glancing off the pool. I can just make out the glitter of them. As a tendril of girlish laughter silvers the air, I can see movement.

When I get there, the temperature in the garden is soft and perfect. I can only just smell the cut grass, the scent of the oleander flowers almost overpowering it. Hearing the laughter again, high-pitched and fluting, I go cold, despite the balmy air. It is as though the act of stepping into the garden has ripped open a hole in time. It must be you, but it doesn't sound like your laugh.

It's easy to creep up silently, shoeless as I am. Through the dense, bluish foliage of the pines, I can see a bare leg stretched out. The toes are painted a shell pink that makes the smooth skin of her foot look golden. *Her.* I move closer, blood roaring in my ears.

She's wearing white, which glows eerily in the spreading twilight. I don't notice anyone else because I can't take my eyes off her.

'Élodie,' I say, as I blunder into the open, the word coming out low and strangled.

But then she turns and everything distorts for a second, as it does under moving water. Because it isn't her. It's you. Of course it's you – as if moved by some unerring instinct to disturb me – wearing that sundress of your sister's. Her Lolita dress.

You're perched on the end of a lounger, your legs angled towards the boy stretched out along the side of the pool, his long body flat against the still-warm stone. Luc.

You look up at me quizzically and I'm glad you didn't hear what I said. There are some empty cans of lager under your lounger and they rattle as you knock them with your heel.

'What are you doing down here, drinking?' I say sharply. *'Luc? Why are you here so late?'*

He props himself up on one elbow. *'Salut, Sylvie.'* He laughs and you giggle in response. *What are you laughing at?* I want to cry. I can feel the nervous energy coming off you, like a scent, just as it did at the circus. That feels like years ago.

'Em, why don't you go up to the house?' I say.

You don't move.

'You're too young for . . . all this. Please, go inside and put something else on.'

'What's your problem?' you say, and there's a slight slur in your voice. I know you're only showing off in front of Luc but your transformation into someone like your sister in this moment, in that provocative, semi-sheer dress – which, in Élodie's case at least, was always too short and tight across her chest – makes me furious. I go over and pull you to your feet.

'Ow, Mum, you're hurting!' you say, though I've only taken your hand. You wrench out of my grip and sit down again, face determined and furious.

I turn to Luc instead. *'I think you should go home. Take the rest of those cans with you.'*

Though part of me wants to slap him, he looks quite beautiful in the failing light, every limb perfectly turned and browned; his soft, vulnerable mouth and gold-tipped hair. What he doesn't look like is a boy, not any more. I can't see Laurent in him now.

He begins to walk away but something falls out of his pocket. He turns to pick it up but I get there first. It's a Polaroid photograph and, though I've never seen it before, I know every millimetre of its subject. I take in the secret it exposes. Luc's face is in deep shadow when I look back at him.

'Where did you get this?'

He holds out his hand for it but I draw mine back.

He shrugs. *'Found it.'*

'*It's not yours.*' I put it into my pocket. '*You should go now.*'

He starts to walk away, but then looks over his shoulder. '*À bientôt*, Emma. Remember, I have a surprise for your birthday. *Un petit cadeau.*'

'*Va-t'en, Luc.*' It comes out almost as a snarl and he backs away, hands raised, though there's a mocking tilt to his mouth. I only breathe out when he's finally absorbed by the dark.

'That was so embarrassing!' you exclaim, when I turn back to you. You're livid, the words pushed out of you in staccato huffs. You go to the edge of the pool and kick at the water, sending an arc of it over the stones.

'Let me see what he found.' You hold out your hand.

I cover my pocket protectively. 'It's nothing. Just an old photo.'

'Mum, give it to me. If it's just an old photo, why can't I see it?'

'Because I said so,' I snap, at a loss for what else to say.

You sit down in a heap, landing heavily and slightly unsteadily. I think you're probably halfway to being drunk for the first time in your life. I lower myself next to you and lean out to dip my hand in the darkening water. It's so close to body temperature that I can barely feel it. I reach for your bare foot, which is the nearest part of you, but you tuck it under yourself and wrap your arms protectively around your body.

I look at you, unable to believe now that I mistook you for your sister. You look nothing like her, the white dress innocent on your still-childish frame, your poor face strained from the effort of not crying. Your burst of defiance has been short-lived.

I think about my earlier optimism, the promise I made to Camille to confess everything. The photograph crackles in my pocket as I shift towards you, my arms out. *Now*, I tell myself. *Now is the time to tell her the rest.* The photo should make it easier – a visual aid dropped into my lap by the gods – but now the moment has arrived I can't convince myself to jump. I don't know where we might land.

You resist me at first but then I feel you give way, like a sigh, your head coming down on my shoulder, your hair soft under my lips as I kiss the top of your head. Your warm breath smells slightly sour as you shift round until you're lying in my lap. I'm just thinking, gratefully, that your wooziness has saved me for now when you make a grab for my pocket. I twist away.

You get unsteadily to your feet. 'You're being such a bitch tonight,' you say, and I'm too shocked to reply – you've never said anything like that to me before. I reach out my hand for you, but you've already turned. I watch you flounce away, and for once I let you go.

I pull out the photo. It's hard to make out much. Night has almost overtaken day. That it's a Polaroid doesn't help, the image slightly blurred and the contrast too high, but even a conventional print would have come out strangely, her skin waxy and her eyes hooded and dark because she's lit from beneath by a blaze of birthday candles. Whoever took it has caught her in the second before blowing them out: she's bent over, one hand holding her long hair back from eighteen tiny flames.

Even in the low light, I can see the challenge in her eyes. Not the kind of challenge she had regularly aimed at me, which was something shuttered and flint-hard; this was playful, a studied kind of teasing. Whoever had been behind the camera was a man, I know that for certain.

If Élodie has become a ghost over the years, events now seem to be conspiring to make her real again: the medical notes, the Polaroid, even the spectre I saw at the circus. It feels as though my first daughter's outline is growing stronger, the vivid colours of her filling in again. It sounds absurd, like something from a dark fairytale, but I feel as though these revelations are giving her power one by one. That, somewhere, she's gathering strength.

Anxiety clutches at me. I can't seem to take deep enough breaths. Today we are hosting a children's birthday party. Not for Élodie but for a little girl who also goes to the village school. Her father is a civil servant Greg got talking to one day while buying cigarettes at the *tabac*. Yesterday Greg heard that their pool filter had broken, with little Marie-Laure inconsolable because she'd so wanted a swimming party, and he offered ours.

'But Élodie wasn't even invited,' I said in astonishment when he informed me. 'Will she be allowed to attend this party now it's taking place in her own garden?' My fraying nerves made me sound petulant, though this had happened many times before: Élodie the only child excluded.

'They probably don't know each other,' Greg said blithely.

'There are eleven children in the class.'

I caught the roll of his eyes.

'You won't have to do anything. Monique has all the food ready to go, apparently. I just thought we'd help them out, that's all. She and Yves will take care of it – we're just providing the garden and the pool. You know we're the only other house in the village with a decent-sized one.'

'Well, if you've offered there's nothing I can say, is there?'

A muscle ticked in his jaw and I wished he could still read me as he used to.

I don't mix with the women in the village much. I didn't intend it to work out that way: when I returned home from Paris I expected to slot back into old friendships from childhood. It was difficult with Élodie, though. She wasn't like the other children and, in the end, it wasn't worth the disapproval. Occasionally, I exchange a few words with one of them at the market but it never seems to go further with these women, some of whom I've known my whole life. Greg and I don't get invited to much either, unless Laurent surreptitiously intervenes. Since Élodie started school, it's got worse. Coolness has curdled into judgement: I know they whisper in the street when they see us. They disapprove of Élodie but they disapprove of Greg and me more – for the assumed parental failures that have made her the way she is.

I once overheard a conversation between two mothers at the school gates, who hadn't realized I'd come back for Élodie's coat. '*Sylvie Durand's girl has a terrible mean streak,*' one said.

'*Oh, but it's more than that, don't you think?*' the other replied. '*She might be pretty but I don't think there's anything behind the eyes. Nothing good, anyway.*' And then she shuddered. She actually shuddered, and I was filled with a fury that was oddly liberating. It wasn't often that I found myself jumping to my daughter's defence – such a normal maternal instinct a novelty for me. I didn't say anything, though, to my later shame. They had articulated my own fears and I was too frightened they would see that in my face if I dared tackle them.

It's been a month since Luc ended up in our pool, a month since I took Élodie to see Morel. The follow-up appointment is next Wednesday. Annette hasn't spoken a word to me since it happened. She came round that evening, when I was upstairs putting Élodie to bed. She wanted to talk to me but Greg, to his credit, said I was in bed and couldn't be disturbed. She shouted at him instead and, though I closed the windows, I could still hear every word she said and knew Élodie must be able to as well.

I had stolen a look at her, sitting up in bed in clean pyjamas, her cheeks scrubbed and glowing from the bath, but there was nothing in her expression to betray any stress or emotion.

'Annette's very upset because of what happened to Luc by the swimming pool,' I said tentatively.

She fixed me with those incredible eyes, long lashes made longer by the nightlight above her head. *'He's stupid. A stupid cry-baby.'*

'Is that why you pushed him?' I hid my hands in the covers because they were shaking. *'You can tell me the truth now. I won't tell anyone else, not even Papa.'*

She smiled quickly, no more than a pearly flash of teeth, and then it was gone. *'He fell,'* she said, in a flat monotone, and turned away to face the wall, her nose just a couple of inches from it. As I reached up to turn out the nightlight – which she'd never needed: Élodie was impervious to nocturnal fears – I glanced down to see that her eyes were open and unblinking. The smile was back.

When Annette had finally gone, I went down to find Greg at the kitchen table nursing a large cognac, his face flushed a dark, ominous red.

'That fucking woman,' he said.

I began to knead the tension out of his shoulders. He reached back to take my hand and we stayed like that for a long time. I had the feeling he wanted to be outraged when really he felt defeated. Strangely, an outsider explicitly accusing Élodie of not being like other little girls had brought us together. For that night, at least. He was getting some of the treatment I got, and it made us allies again.

Now I am hiding in our bedroom, though the party for Marie-Laure has already begun. The swell of voices rises from the garden, like the buzz of hornets. Greg has already been up twice to see what's taking me so long. I will him to understand that I'm not being rude or sulking because this was his idea, that what I am is scared – scared of the collective judgement of the mothers if something happens.

The thought of Élodie running unchecked finally gets me down the stairs and out into the blinding day. The first couple of hours pass without incident. I drink a couple of glasses of the Crémant de Bourgogne Yves has brought over for the parents, which froths palely out of the bottle, still chilled enough from the box of ice to cloud the glass. My muscles slowly loosen and the beauty of the day comes into focus for the first time: the brilliance of the sun-struck pool, the dark gloss of the oleander leaves, the unfamiliar sounds of a large group of people enjoying themselves. I haven't experienced this since I was a child, handing round trays of hors d'oeuvres at my parents' parties.

At first, the cry that goes up is not immediately discernible from the rest. Children jumping in and running around a pool are noisy. It takes a second, maybe two, for the wail to lift the fine hairs at the back of my neck. Silence settles around it fast, like blanketing fog. And then, as though released from a spell, everyone is suddenly moving. A little boy – Jean-Claude – is pulled from the water, his father grasping him under his arms and lifting him free.

As I run towards them, I see the long graze that stretches the length of his thigh. As it reacts to the air it darkens into a purple welt, though in fact the skin is only broken in one place, where pinheads of bright crimson rise. It will scab and bruise, though. It might even scar.

I look towards the pool for an explanation, expecting a broken tile, but there's nothing. The boy is sobbing by now.

'*Qu'est-ce qui s'est passé, chéri?*' his mother Claire cries, her dress wet from kneeling in the pool of water her son has made, the water running off his small body.

I look for Élodie and spot her at the far end of the pool. She's not looking at me. She's watching Jean-Claude. Her head is cocked to one side and she's studying him closely. Her hands move under the water, pale and distorted, and I can see there's something in one of them, pencil-thin but shorter. I move slowly round the pool towards her. She did this, I think, the thought as clear as any I've ever had. I try to push it away, like I always do, for her sake and for Greg's, for mine too, as her mother. I want to look away, in case anyone catches me watching her and reads my mind, but I have to know. I'm a metre or two away when she heaves herself out of the pool, lithe shoulder muscles flexing.

I glance back towards the other end but the adults have closed in on Jean-Claude, all eyes elsewhere. I grab Élodie and pull her into the shadow of the oleander, reaching round for the hand she's put behind her back. Before I can get whatever it is, she throws it at my feet and wrenches away. I hear the dull ting of metal on stone as I let her go.

It's a dart. There's a craze for them among the boys, who swap them for their brightly coloured flights. One of them must have brought it with him because I would never let Élodie have them. This one, sky-blue and silver, has only just missed my bare foot before bouncing into the dead leaves at the tree's base. Without thinking, I push it deeper into the soil and turn back to the pool. Élodie is nowhere to be seen.

Jean-Claude stops crying eventually, though his chest still heaves. Claire is a sensible woman who grew up with three brothers. She's wiped the blood away with a tissue.

'*You're fine now,*' she says, with a last kiss on his fore-head. '*No more tears.*'

His lip wobbles but he's given a chocolate biscuit and soon it's almost as if nothing had happened. I drink another glass of the Crémant, but I'm keeping a closer eye on the pool now, and I notice Greg is too.

And then, right at the end of the afternoon, it happens again. Some of the families have gone by now and most of the pool is in shade. Cake crumbs are scattered across the stones around it. There are only four children left in the water and Élodie is one of them. Jean-Claude is another. I've gone inside to fetch cotton wool and disinfectant for a child who has slipped and grazed her knee. Greg is seeing someone off at the front door.

There is no cry from Jean-Claude this time. One of the other children raises the alarm, shouting, '*Papa! Papa! Viens ici!*'

I rush down the steps and across the lawn, clutching the disinfectant, the last to arrive. I am just in time to see a strange re-enactment of earlier, except it's a different father lifting Jean-Claude from the pool.

The little boy is silent this time, his eyes closed, his lips indigo. Claire's face is a mask of horror as she lunges for his hand. The father lays him gently on the stones and is just about to start mouth-to-mouth when Jean-Claude coughs wetly, pool water running from the side of his mouth. I sink to my knees, boneless with relief, the glass bottle I'm still holding chinking against the stone as I lose my grip on it. I look automatically for Élodie, and she is back at the very opposite end of the pool, in the corner where the shade is thickest. Her mouth is moving in a strange way, as though she's talking to herself or – my heart skipping at the thought – trying not to laugh.

I'm so intent on her that I don't see the girl who summoned her father lift her arm to point.

'*It was her*,' she says, her voice high and clear. '*It was Élodie. She pushed him down under the water and wouldn't let him come up, even though he was kicking. She thought it was funny. She was laughing.*' The raw shock and outrage in someone so young cuts through every parent present.

The other mothers – and it is the mothers, who have flocked together as if by instinct – don't look at Élodie. Instead they turn as one to me, still kneeling like a penitent. Claire, of course, and Pascale, who had been next to me in the school register, Adèle, with whom I'd swapped pencil cases when we were seven, Jeanne Dubois, who was best friends with Camille for a time. They stare me down, these women, and I know I am no longer Sylvie Durand to them. I am no longer a fellow mother. There's nothing left for me and my family but distaste and horror, even fear.

1993

Olivier rings the next morning and suggests we meet at the café again. My heart lifts at the thought of seeing him, and leaving the house, too, which we haven't done since the circus. You flatly refuse to leave the poolside at first and, though you're ostentatiously cross with me about the previous night with the Polaroid, I suspect you're also hoping Luc might appear if you stay put.

'But I think the filter's getting blocked,' you say, once I've persuaded you into the car, the whine in your voice grating. You're inspecting the lightening ends of your hair. 'Luc will definitely have to come and sort it out. It's full of twigs.' You steal a glance at me but I don't react.

'Mum, are you even listening to me? We could call in for him on the way back.'

'Maybe.'

The road to the village unfurls ahead, the oncoming cars shimmering in the heat haze. The air that blows in through the window is tinder-dry and hot, like a hairdryer, even when I put my foot down. A figure walking along the hard shoulder makes my insides plummet, but as we draw closer it becomes obvious it's just an old man in a flat cap, shuffling along with a basket over his arm. I slow to a stop.

'*Bonjour, Monsieur,*' I shout across you through the open window. '*Vous allez au village?*'

He peers in at me, unsmiling, then nods.

'Go on,' I say, chivvying you to get out and let him sit in the front, which you do with bad grace. I don't know exactly why I've stopped for him, but I think it's probably another attack of superstition. Paying my respects to the gods.

You don't like being relegated to the back seat, insult heaped on injury, and your expression is sullen in the rear-view mirror as I try to engage the old man in conversation. Neither of you deigns to respond to my bilingual wittering, and by the time we reach the outskirts of the village, I've given up, a loaded silence descending.

The road to the square when we get there is closed off and I remember it's Saturday: market day. I pray we don't bump into Marc Lesage again.

It takes ages to park, and I can feel my blood pressure going up as the dashboard clock ticks on, afraid we'll miss Olivier. Finally, I find a space just vacated by an orange camper van with German plates.

Olivier is a still point among the bustle of the square, his appearance as crisp and casually elegant as before. He stands to kiss me and bright speckles of sunlight filtering down through the plane trees dance across his face. His skin smells of limes and I feel the same sensation I had at the circus, a warm dissolving inside.

'*Désolée d'être en retard,*' I say. '*I forgot about the market.*'

He smiles and pulls out a chair for you. *'It doesn't matter. I've been enjoying myself here, watching everyone come and go.'*

When the waiter appears, I order a Perrier for me and a lemonade for you. You're still quiet but Olivier's relaxed air is contagious and you no longer look so mutinous. I feel myself unwind a little, and take in the market properly for the first time.

A stall selling a vast array of salami and cheeses is closest to where we're sitting and I can smell a little of all of it, strong and savoury. Further on, another stall is selling soap, chunky squares of Savon de Marseille in pastel shades: rose, lavender, rosemary and olive oil, like my mother once used. I see your magpie eye drawn to the chequerboard of colours.

'I'm going to go and look.'

'Go on then. But don't wander off. Stay this side of the square.'

You tut, and I'm no longer sure you'll do as I ask. I've always taken that for granted, until now.

I watch you wander over to the stall.

'It's a good sign, don't you think?'

I look at Olivier questioningly.

'The soaps. All those pretty colours are for the tourists. The market's been changing the last couple of years. It's getting more like the ones you'd find in the touristy villages further south. This will be good for selling La Rêverie.'

My gaze is still trained on you when I become aware of Olivier's warm hand on mine. *'Look, Sylvie, about the other night . . .'*

'Oh, God,' I say, shaken out of my distraction. *'I'm so sorry I ran off like that without a word.'*

165

He puts up his hands. *'Please, don't apologize. I'm just sorry Emma was upset. Lesage has never been a nice man and he's getting worse with age. Anyway, I have some news.'*

My heart clutches. 'News?'

'It's nothing to worry about, just that someone wants to have a look at the house.'

I pause, then arrange my face into a grateful smile. 'Oh, a viewing. I thought . . . Yes, that's good, thank you for finding them. Who are they? Are they local?'

'No. A couple from Amiens with two little girls. They want a place in the south for holidays. Somewhere with more sun.'

Amiens. The nearest city to where Élodie had to go. I remember skirting the place on the way to see her that last time: the sky lowering almost to the road; the spitting rain that wasn't enough to stop the wipers shrieking; and then, as the clutter of Amiens fell behind and the land flattened out, nothing to see but battlefield signs and pylons marching on the horizon.

'Martine can't make it so I said you wouldn't mind showing them round yourself. Was that all right?'

I nod, watching the bubbles speeding to the top of my glass. I glance towards the soap stall. You're still there, sniffing each in turn, smiling shyly at the woman running the stall.

'Sylvie.'

I look back at Olivier and he takes off his sunglasses. His eyes look more tired than the rest of him and it makes him less intimidatingly handsome but somehow more attractive.

'I was really enjoying myself with you and Emma before . . .

166

what happened,' he says, so low that I automatically lean towards him. He holds my gaze a beat too long and I'm aware of every inch of my body.

I smile and look down at the table. '*Yes, so was I. It was a shame it had to end so . . . abruptly.*'

'*So, that dinner I mentioned, at the Routier place with the lights?*' He's still looking at me and it's hard not to touch my hair, adjust the thin straps of my dress.

'*Yes, perhaps we could.*'

He smiles. '*Good.*' He reaches out and I think he's going to stroke my face but there's a tiny insect caught in my hair. It's a long time since anyone has made me so aware of myself physically. I'd forgotten how heady it can be.

'*Do you really think the house will sell?*' I say in a rush.

'*La Rêverie is a magical place. Those people are stupid if they don't buy it.*'

'*Thank you. It is special. People see things differently, though, don't they? For everyone who sees something magical, there's someone who will see a roof that needs replacing in a few years.*'

'*Let's hope they're romantic souls, then, like me. Though are you absolutely sure you don't want to hang on to it? I don't think I could part with a place like that. It would . . . well, it would be nice to know you were coming back here each summer.*' For the first time since I met him, he looks a little unsure of himself. '*I don't have much in common with the people I work with.*'

'*Why are you here anyway? It's a bit of a backwater.*'

'*Not like London.*'

I start to apologize for being condescending but then I see he's teasing. '*I didn't mean to be rude. It's just that it's unusual.*

167

You were in Avignon for school, you said. Not many people come back to the village from the city, not till they're ready to retire anyway.'

He pauses. *'It was the usual reason people do foolish things.'* He looks away across the square. *'A woman. My ex-wife. She's still in Avignon. I washed up here.'*

I feel absurdly jealous and something of it must show in my face.

'It was a long time ago. I can't think now what we saw in each other. All we did was make ourselves unhappy. I look back and it's like watching someone else's relationship — like watching a film. A depressing film.'

I laugh. *'Yes, I know what you mean.'*

He looks at me intently. *'Do you? Was it the same for you? I always think it must be so much harder when you share chil— a child. I could move on and not look back.'*

I glance away, feeling the mood shift. He turns his coffee cup in its saucer. I suddenly want to be back in the present. His discomfort makes me feel braver. I lay my hand on his arm and he looks up at me.

'Look,' I say, *'now that Camille has gone back to Paris, and it's just me and Emma, it might be easier if you came round to the house like before. Maybe on Monday, after the viewing. I could . . . I could let you know how it went.'*

He smiles and I know he wants to, that the mood has shifted back.

'Come on Monday,' I repeat. *'I'd really like you to.'* He reaches out and smoothes the twisted strap of my dress. The gesture, swift but intimate, makes my blood swarm.

'Then I will.'

*

For most of Sunday, I barely think about Élodie. The seductive promise of Olivier's visit has done the seemingly impossible and edged her out of my thoughts. I go outside to escape the guitars howling from the salon, where you've been playing the same Nirvana tape over and over, and become aware that it's even quieter than usual outside. The only sounds are from insects and the church bells that echo across the fields between us and the village, out of time with your music, sonorous and slightly discordant.

The state Olivier has put me into – warm and liquid, brimming with promise – has also made me think of your father. You'll understand when you're older, Emma, that just because things don't work out in the end it doesn't mean they were wrong to begin with. Perhaps it was like that for Olivier, but it wasn't for me and Greg.

Oh, London in those early days. The luck of arriving in 1967, when Twiggy was in *Vogue* and the Beatles had just opened their Apple boutique, the sober old Baker Street bricks painted in psychedelic swirls of colour.

I was a bystander to all that, really: a strait-laced little French girl, my *maman* voicing her disapproval in my head every time I went out without stockings on. A bystander until I met Greg, anyway. In those winter months before he persuaded me to give up my degree and return to France I was the most alive I'd ever felt.

I remember everything about our first proper date. It was like we were in a film: the two of us walking together through a series of lovingly lit shots. My senses were so heightened that I knew I would remember everything, not just what we would earnestly discuss or which pub we would end up drinking in, but the texture of the lint under my fingernails at the bottom of my coat pockets, the precise sensation of my breath-dampened scarf as it brushed my lips.

The city around us, rendered in many shades of grey, was so perfectly the winter-struck London I had imagined from France, the freezing air like crowds of ghosts, the pigeon-coloured sky lowering with rain that would soon fall. He bent towards me as we talked and I could smell the wool of his duffel coat and the salt-soap blend of his skin. His eyes glittered above wind-reddened cheeks as I turned to look at him.

Greg Winters. Even his name was perfect. I wanted to know everything about him, and everything about him was fascinating to me. I wanted to take a train back to where he'd grown up and see all the places he had known as a boy.

I'm going to love this person, I thought, though we hadn't kissed yet.

Even after we had, even after we were sleeping together, I liked to frighten myself in the hours before dawn, too jittery with love to sleep, by imagining scenarios where we had missed each other by inches: him approaching another girl in the Union that day, her in my place next to him in the dark, their breath mingling to fug the cold air, his warm arm flung across her stomach instead of mine.

You surprise me out of these memories just before the sun sets.

'What are you thinking about?' you ask, but I don't tell you. Maybe one day.

I rouse myself to clean up the ancient brick barbecue at the far end of the terrace and tip in half a bag of charcoal. When it begins to turn orange and grey, I make a salad and take a packet of thin, paprika-stained merguez sausages out of the fridge.

Because of the barbecue smoke, it isn't until we've finished, plates wiped clean with bread that I catch another scent in the air. It has a different quality from our little fire, catching the back of the throat, nothing comforting about it. This is astringent, almost caustic.

We become aware of it at the same moment, you frowning and leaning back in your chair to check the barbecue hasn't set light to something. I don't need to look: I know that smell of old and, like the tigers at the circus, it awakes a fear so vivid and primal that, for the first time all day, my heart briefly loses its rhythm.

'Is that . . . ?'

'Come on,' I say, holding out my hand. You take it, yesterday's mood finally forgotten.

Our bare feet thud loudly on the dusty wooden treads as we run up the stairs. I wrench back the shutters in my room, which I'd left closed to keep the heat at bay. There's still a little light left in the western sky, but what I'm looking for is to the east: towards the hills that undulate greenly even when the fields and gardens of the valley have been scorched brown by the sun. What we smelt on the terrace is burning pine trees. Somewhere out there, a forest fire is blazing.

You lean right out, my hand automatically going to your arm to hold you steady.

'How close are they?'

'Not close at all.' I gently move you a few inches back from the window. 'Don't worry. They don't get this far.'

'Why is your voice all shaky, then?'

I do my best to smile. 'They used to frighten me as a little girl, that's all. There were fires almost every summer – you must have seen the road signs, *"Attention au Feu"* with the tree and the match? The worst that happens is that some of the forest roads get closed off.'

'What about the animals?'

I stroke your hair. Your tenderness always surprises and touches me. It relieves me as well: proof that I must have done something right as a mother.

'They'll move to another part of the forest before it takes hold,' I say. 'It's huge up there, miles and miles of trees. They'll be fine.' I don't know if this is true.

'If it did come this far, what would we do?' You scrabble under the bed and bring out your inhaler.

'It won't, darling,' I say, as you take a couple of puffs. When your breathing is back to normal, I take your hand and lead you out to the hallway. It's got darker while we were looking out of the window and I have to feel around for the light switch.

'But what if it did?' you persist. 'We could get in the pool until the firemen came, couldn't we?'

I smile over my shoulder as you follow me downstairs.

'That's a clever idea, but we won't need it. Don't worry about the smoke – it'll have gone by the morning.'

*

But the smoke hasn't gone. If anything, it's grown more intense overnight. By lunchtime, the pall of it is suspended above the garden, like dingy gauze, the usual painterly, pin-sharp light dimmed and vaguely nicotined. In the mirror that afternoon, as I smarten myself up for the viewing, my eyes look hollow. I haven't slept well again.

The Bernard family arrive precisely at midday. The two little girls are plainer than their parents and dressed in matching outfits. They say barely a word. Their father, on the other hand, asks a stream of the sort of practical questions I've been dreading: when was the heating installed, how much does the pool cost to maintain, does traffic noise from the main road carry into the garden during August?

La Rêverie is threadbare and dated, but the kind of buyer I need won't care about any of that. They will reach a hand through it, and grasp at what Olivier recognized as its inherent magic. Some houses are almost alive, hearts beating just under our hearing range, and however mixed my feelings for my childhood home are, La Rêverie is one of them.

'*And what about the fires you get down here?*' Monsieur Bernard says in the garden, fixing me with a look through his rimless glasses. '*The smoke's stronger than it was at the other houses we've seen. I suppose you're quite low here, and the air doesn't circulate much.'*

'Actually, this is unusual. It'll have blown away by tomorrow.'

'Hmm.' He looks sceptical. *'Peut-être.'*

They follow me back towards the house, none of us speaking because he's run out of questions and I out of energy. You're swimming your daily lengths as we pass the pool and I see the first kindling of interest in the Bernard girls' stolid faces as they take you in, your body sleek and efficient as it cleaves the green water.

'Is that your daughter?' Madame Bernard asks. It's the first time she's spoken beyond her initial murmured *bonjour.*

'Yes, that's Emma. She loves it here.'

'Perhaps you shouldn't sell it, then.' She smiles twitchily, embarrassed at how rude the words sound aloud. *'Perhaps you should keep it for her, I mean. For when she has her own children.'*

'Don't let her catch you saying that. I'll never hear the end of it,' I say, suddenly jovial, because in just a few minutes they will climb back into their city car and we'll be alone again. I'll be able to join you in the silken water.

When they've gone, I do just that, glad that the awkward episode is over and Olivier is still to come. I wonder if part of my relief lies in the confidence I feel that the Bernards won't be making an offer. La Rêverie is still ours for the time being. I want to leave as soon as possible. I do. But I also find that I want to stay, a hankering that has crept up on me stealthily. The coexistence of these absolutes reminds me of how I always felt about Élodie, love and fear so tightly entwined as to be indivisible.

1977

It's high summer, a cloying August day when the heat seeps into the house like tar, turning milk and dazing flies, which gather in listless piles under the windows. I'm looking for Élodie, who has disappeared again. My T-shirt is stuck to me with sweat.

'*Élodie, s'il te plaît!*'

I have been calling her for a while but she doesn't answer, though I know she can hear me, that she's in the house somewhere. I always know if she's nearby, as though we're still attached, womb to navel, by a cord that can't be cut.

I find her in Greg's and my room, where she is scratching a large E into my antique jewellery box with a metal nail file.

'*Oh, no, no!*' I rush forward and wrench the file out of her hand, throwing it hard at the floor where it hits the skirting board with a clatter.

The jewellery box is made of rosewood and inlaid with delicate mother-of-pearl leaves. Papa bought it for me when I was seventeen – the only present he'd ever chosen himself because my mother usually took care of that sort of thing. It wasn't even my birthday. '*I just saw it and thought of my Sylvie,'* he said, shrugging and embarrassed, after I unwrapped it.

Grief and fury burning through my insides, I feel as though she's taken that nail file to my own flesh. I pull her to her feet. She's eight now and we've been back to Morel twice more, making four visits altogether. In fact, there's little point in going. Morel's opinion, however gently put, remains the same: *You'll just have to wait and see.* She'll grow out of it or she won't.

There's no sign of her growing out of it yet and, while she's often destructive, this particular incident feels deeply personal. She's watched me carefully polish and rearrange the contents of that box so many times. Clenching my jaw against tears, I lift the lid. She's slashed at the velvet lining, which is old and has frayed easily into ragged ribbons. My amber beads are missing, too. A present from Greg I've always loved, each one as big as a marble. He'd given them to me when I got home from hospital after giving birth to Élodie.

'What have you done with them?' I'm kneeling, my face close to hers, voice shaking with the effort not to shout the words. *'Where are my beads?'* I point to the box. *'Do you really hate me so much?'*

She won't look at me, but it's not as though she's looking at her feet with contrition. Her odd eyes, warm and cold, follow a fly as it buzzes in slow circles around the overhead light.

'Look at me,' I hiss. *'Look at me when I'm talking to you. Where are they?'*

Her lips curl into a smirk. *'Gone.'*

176

'*Gone where?*' I look desperately around the room, but she's been upstairs a while. She could have taken them first, coming back to destroy the box afterwards.

I wish she'd chosen anything but those beads, which I treasure not only because they're from happier times, but for their colour: the darkest ones so closely match her left eye. It's nonsensical but I feel as if she's thrown away all hope of that other Élodie, as if she's telling me she'll never grow out of this. That the blue eye is the only Élodie after all.

Something inside me snaps. I pick her up under her arms, holding her away from me because I don't want to feel her hot, unyielding body against mine. She's heavy, especially when she goes completely limp, but I make it down the stairs, half dragging her dead weight the last few feet, the muscles in my back screaming.

It's deliciously cool in the *souillarde* and I wish I could shut myself in there instead. My mother had used it as a place of punishment when Camille and I were girls, though it was hardly that during the stifling summers. It's funny how we repeat our parents' ways, even their stock phrases, with our own children. Perhaps it's nothing more than a reflex but it feels like a comfort to me to pretend occasionally that I am my *maman* and Élodie is me. I always understood that relationship.

'*I don't want to look at you so you'll stay in there for ten minutes while you think about what you've done,*' I say through the door, cringing at the cliché and the quaver in my voice.

I know it's a futile punishment. It was enough for me as a child to think I had fallen out of my mother's favour, that, however briefly, she disliked or disapproved of me. Élodie won't care, perhaps can't care. I am well aware that this is going against Dr Morel's advice, but it's almost impossible to follow that when she's at her most extreme. It goes against the human need for justice. I suppose the punishment is for my sake.

Feeling weak, I rest on my haunches for a minute, forehead against the door, and I wonder if she's just the other side, my mirror image, faces close enough to kiss if it wasn't for the inch of wood between us.

Back upstairs, I inspect the jewellery box properly. She's scraped the varnish down to the bare wood, splintering the surface, which must have taken some force. I get into bed with it and pull the covers up over my head, though it's much too hot for that. Curling into a ball with the box pulled into me, I let myself cry, the sobs loud in the dark little nest I've made. I am so frightened, I think, and my heart skips and stumbles as if to prove it; as though Greg is here giving me the look that says, *You're exaggerating.*

After the ten minutes have passed, I go to the door. I can't face going down to her.

'*Élodie, you can come out now,*' I call.

She doesn't answer, but I hear the creak of the *souillarde* door as it opens. After a moment the television is switched on in the salon. I go back to bed and burrow under the covers again.

The next thing I know Greg is shaking me roughly awake. My eyes feel swollen and crusted as I open them.

'Get up,' he says from above, voice cold. 'Get the

fuck up and explain to me why you locked our daughter in the *souillarde* for so long that she wet herself.'

Disorientated, I twist round to look at the clock on the bedside table. Only about forty minutes have passed since I called down to her.

'She was only in there for ten minutes, Greg, and you know there's no lock on that door. She went to watch television, I heard her come out and turn it on.'

'She says she tried to turn the handle but couldn't get it to work.'

'I heard her! I heard her come out and go and switch the television on.'

'You didn't go down to let her out yourself?'

'I heard her come out, Greg.'

'Do you really think she would have wet herself if she didn't have to?'

'Actually, yes, I do.' My heart races as I let the words fall.

He pauses, his gaze going to the damaged jewellery box on the bed, and I think for a moment he's going to consider the possibility that I may be right, but then the shutters come down. It's so much easier to be angrier with me. He shakes his head, face stiff with disgust, and slams out of the room.

Later, when I look in on the two of them, they are watching television together – some old Monsieur Hulot film. He doesn't see me but she does, another smirk lifting the corner of her mouth, that pretty little dimple. A muscular anomaly masquerading as beauty.

We both know what Morel has said. Greg saw the aftermath of her nearly drowning that little boy. But he won't agree, not out loud anyway. Morel was 'stigmatizing a tiny child'. Jean-Claude 'got a little fright'. 'She's wilful, I accept that,' he said the other day. 'But I actually think the main problem is that she's so bright. She gets frustrated and it comes out in the wrong way.' I didn't reply, and where once he would have picked a fight about that, he fell silent instead. Oh, yes, he knows.

After I've searched the house and garden for the beads, I go back upstairs and stuff some clothes and toiletries into a bag, along with the thousand or so francs I keep at the back of my sock drawer. Perhaps it's unforgivably selfish even to contemplate leaving a child, but it doesn't feel it, not in that moment. It feels like survival.

I walk to the village because I don't want the sound of the car starting to alert Greg. Along with the clothes and money, I've packed a couple of photographs of myself, taken by Laurent the summer before I went to study in London. Sitting in the village square waiting for a bus to take me away, I clutch them like talismans: proof that I once faced the world with equanimity. I don't think about where I'm going. I'm not really thinking at all. The only place I want to go is back to my old self.

After a long time, I don't know how many hours, ancient Madame Perrot opens a window just across from the bench. Her curls bob in the warm breeze.

'*Sylvie Durand, is that you over there?*' she calls. '*There are no more buses today, petite. You'll be waiting till Monday.*'

I walk slowly back to La Rêverie, my feet scuffing the dry earth at the side of the road because I can't summon the energy to lift them. She had called me Durand, instead of Winters, as though I'd fallen backwards through time to before I was a married mother, when everything was ahead and nothing frightened me.

I let myself in and stand in the hall but no one comes. I'm like the runaway child who briefly leaves home after some unbearable injustice: neither Greg nor Élodie has even noticed my absence.

1993

Olivier arrives, only a little late this time, clutching two glass bottles: wine of palest salmon pink and Pschitt lemonade for you. You snort with laughter when you see the label and he grins back.

I'm relieved. Earlier, as I'd got ready, your face in the mirror as I brushed my hair had been almost scathing.

'God, Mum, you're making such an effort. What's even the point if we've got to go home soon?'

Now, as I take the wine from Olivier, I see you witness the brief contact our hands make and roll your eyes. For once, I hope you'll go upstairs, taking your adolescent contempt with you. I need this evening.

'*So, how did the viewing go?*' he says.

'*I don't think we'll be expecting an offer any time soon, but I'm still opening this. It looks expensive. Thank you.*'

He shrugs. '*It's their loss if they don't buy. What did they say?*'

'*Not much. He asked about the smoke, of course. Are the fires getting bad this time?*'

'*Oui, ils sont très graves.*'

You stop pouring lemonade. 'How serious? You're talking about the fires, aren't you?'

I send Olivier a pointed look.

'There's no problem, Emma,' he says haltingly. 'They will send planes tomorrow. You know, with water? They take it from the sea. If the wind –'

'Darling,' I interrupt him. 'I promise you that we are not in any danger. Do you honestly think I'd let us stay here a minute longer if we were?'

'I'm not scared,' you say, with a shrug like Olivier's. But for all your nonchalance, your eyes are too bright. You're a little frightened, and you're also excited. You duck your head so I can't see your face. 'I'm going upstairs now.' I resist the urge to ask if you've got your inhaler. It'll only make you cross, so I let it go.

When you've gone, taking the lemonade bottle with you, Olivier and I wander through the garden, ending up at the pool. The smoke is slightly stronger here, as though the pines are hemming it in, though the proximity of the water makes it seem less intrusive.

Olivier lies back on one of the loungers and lets out a long breath. *'Ah, that's nice.'*

I smile and hand him a glass. *'I think I could have been friendlier to them, you know.'*

'Who?'

'The people who came to see the house.'

'Maybe you don't want to sell after all. Maybe you should just stay for ever.'

I laugh and sit down on the lounger next to his, kicking off my sandals, sensing him watching as I do.

'What was it like?' he says, when I'm leaning back like him. He angles his body round to face me. *'Growing up round here, I mean? Everyone knowing everyone else.'*

'It was exactly as you'd expect. Horribly incestuous because it was impossible to keep any secrets, but strangely comforting for the same reason. In London, you don't feel like you make any impression on the place. It's like you move so lightly over it that it wouldn't miss you if you went away and never came back. Here, for good or bad, you mean something. You're someone.' I hadn't meant to say so much and I look down at my hands, embarrassed.

'Maybe that's why I've stayed on here for so long,' he says. 'To be someone.' He tops up my glass. 'Now, tell me about these teenage secrets you were trying to keep.'

I smile and sip the wine. His eyes are on my mouth. I can feel the alcohol in my bloodstream now.

'Come on, Sylvie. Didn't you break Laurent Martin's heart when you went off to England?'

'How do you know that?' I wonder if he's asked about me and the thought makes my heart speed up.

'His is the next property over, isn't it? Did you smuggle him in here after dark?'

I raise a disapproving eyebrow but I'm laughing. 'That's none of your business. There are lots of shadowy corners in this garden, though.'

He smiles. 'For the first time, I think I'm regretting being sent away to school. I could have been here instead, doing my best to woo the beautiful Sylvie Durand.'

There's a long beat when we look at each other without speaking.

'I've been thinking,' he says eventually. 'I've only got one meeting tomorrow, early. Why don't I come and pick you both up afterwards and we'll go out for the day. The three of us could go to the gorge in the Ardèche.'

'*That sounds lovely. But tomorrow is Emma's birthday.*'

'*Oh. Well, of course you'll want to do something with her.*'

'*No, I . . . Look, let me talk to her. I think both of us could do with a change of scene.*'

We sit quietly, not needing to say anything, and I think how natural it feels to be close to him. Natural but charged at the same time, like it was with Greg in the early days.

'*They think it might have been started deliberately, you know,*' says Olivier, jolting me out of my thoughts. For a moment time warps and kinks, as it sometimes does here, and I half expect to see Greg in the lounger across from me. I can almost hear the splash of Élodie in the pool as she turns somersaults in the water. *Regarde, Papa! Regarde-moi!*

'*Sorry, what?*' I try to soften my abruptness by smiling.

'*The forest fires. They think it might have been arson.*'

'*Arson?*' My voice sharpens again.

Quite suddenly, the idea of staying on in the house seems absurd. More than that: foolhardy. The old familiar urge to run washes over me, cold and clammy.

'*What is it?*' says Olivier. '*You've gone pale. Look, don't be nervous. They'll get it under control soon. We haven't had a bad one for years now. Even with the drought in 'eighty-nine we didn't have one. It'll just be a couple of stupid kids. Like it was here.*'

'*I know. It's not that.*'

But I'm lying. It's exactly that.

'*Sylvie, are you okay?*'

'*It's just been a strange day. And I don't like the fires. They've always unsettled me.*'

'*All the more reason to get away from here tomorrow, then.*'

186

He reaches out and brushes my hair back, letting his hand rest at the nape of my neck. He begins to massage it gently and the warmth of his fingers spreads down my body, my muscles unclenching again. A different kind of nervousness begins to creep through me, a bright, fluttering hum after the dark beat of anxiety. He moves even closer, so that I can feel his breath on my shoulder.

'*You know, I've been worrying about you,*' he murmurs, his mouth brushing my ear now. '*I've been thinking about you.*'

He tips my face up to his and runs his forefinger slowly along the groove of my collarbone and up to my lips.

'*Olivier,*' I begin, but he's already kissing me, and no part of me wants to pull away. I twist towards him until we're pressed against each other, and his hands are on my waist, pulling me into his lap. He smells of summer – hot skin and something like coconut. He twists me round so he's on top of me and I think about saying we should stop but I can't think of a good reason why. I like the weight of him on me, his ragged breathing in my ear. I'd almost forgotten what this was like. I let myself go.

'Mum!' you shout from the house, I don't know how much later.

Olivier and I have been kissing and kissing. '*Like teenagers,*' he'd whispered, smiling into my hair.

Now I scramble up, Olivier moving aside reluctantly, a hand reaching out to stroke my thigh as I hunt beneath the lounger for my sandals.

The last of the daylight has seeped away, the moon blotted out by the smoke drifting across the sky like black chiffon.

'Mum, come up here a minute!'

'Hang on, Em,' I call towards the house.

'Have another glass of wine,' I say to Olivier. *'I won't be long. She might have lost her inhaler.'*

When I get to your room, you're stationed at the flung-open window. Thankfully you can't see the lounger from there, the pines obscuring the view. You turn when you hear me and I see again that slightly manic look in your eyes, fear melding with exhilaration.

'Look.' You point and your hand has the chemical tremble that's becoming too familiar. 'Look out there.'

Beyond the dark smudge of the garden, the unrolled satin of the pool, way off in the distance, but not so far that it doesn't make my stomach lurch, the hills are ablaze, orange tongues leaping and dancing in the black. I think about what Olivier said before, about kids setting fires for fun, and shudder.

We went on a family camping trip when Élodie was nine. It comes back to me sometimes, often at unexpected moments, and the memory still has the ability to chill my blood. I remembered it when I walked into the *souillarde* that first day and saw the scorch marks on the wall.

In English, a memory is *sparked*, a dark and overgrown neural pathway, almost lost for good, lighting up again. Fitting, then, that the spark for this one should be the fires out there in the hills.

1978

The trip is Greg's idea. I've never enjoyed camping so I'm reluctant but end up capitulating, mainly, if I'm honest, to deprive Greg of the point against me if I spoil his plan.

We don't go far – we don't need to: the forests are only half an hour by car. We're soon winding up into the green-swathed hills, leaving behind the stifling heat of the open plain below. The pines flank the road, impossibly tall and straight, the canopy a hundred feet up, throwing us into shade for the first time in the journey. I feel myself relax a little – the air streaming in through the windows is not only cool but wonderfully clean. Perhaps, I think, relenting, this wasn't such a bad notion after all.

I reach forward to turn up the music. It's the scratchy compilation tape that Greg put together for me – all my favourites squeezed into ninety minutes. It took him hours, not just the recording but the track names written in such neat, tiny capitals, a peace-offering he couldn't make in any other way. I've insisted on playing it all summer, my own olive branch.

'California Dreamin'' comes on with its plaintive

refrain, the half-kaput speakers of the old Citroën favouring the backing harmonies over the lead vocals, turning them echoey and ethereal as we drive through the cathedral of silent trees.

The campsite is only small, little more than a clearing with a basic shower block and room for about fifty pitches, most of which haven't been taken. It isn't high season yet. The afternoon passes uneventfully, with Greg and Élodie heading into the thick of the forest on bikes, while I stay behind to read at the picnic table outside the tent. Dinner, too, is peaceful. The clean air of the hills is so soporific that we are zipped into our sleeping bags by half past nine.

The first I know of it is the high note of a baby's cry. It's not a normal cry, but a bright thread of alarm that pierces the dark. Moving lights answer it as people begin to turn on torches. Greg crawls to the end of the tent to open the flap and the smell of smoke seems to roll inside like a choking wave. He scrabbles for our torch.

'Shit, where is it?'

'Here. It's here,' I say, turning it on and throwing it to him before grabbing a cotton top to cover my nose and mouth. I fumble for my jeans, which are damp and hard to pull on lying down, my heels slipping on the nylon of the sleeping bag.

'Sylvie,' Greg says, voice hoarse with sudden fear. 'Where's Élodie?'

He points the torch to where her sleeping bag is thrown open, unzipped to the bottom. Her clothes and shoes are gone. *She* is gone.

'Oh, God,' he says, hand raking through his hair. He

ducks outside the mouth of the tent. 'I'll find her. You get everything into the car.'

From the back of the little campsite, where the trees grow thickly again, I can hear the fire itself now, a noise apart from the spit and crack of burning wood, a monster beginning to roar. I think I can feel the heat of it on my face, but perhaps it's just panic and imagination. The smoke, blacker than the night, is starting to billow in earnest.

The car is parked close by and I say a little prayer as I go towards it. *Please don't be lost in the jumble of the tent. Please.* And they aren't: the keys are in the ignition, the metal glinting dully in the glow that's now turning the sky an apocalyptic orange. *Who up here is going to nick a car?* I remember Greg saying. It seems like years ago.

I go back to the tent for as much as I can carry, trying not to dwell on where she is, where Greg is. I am desperate to go and look, too, but I know it's sensible not to change the plan. I can't possibly sit in the car just waiting, though. A strange combination of fear and fury is already beginning to boil over inside me – at Greg, for thinking we could play happy families for a weekend, and at Élodie, for doing exactly as she likes, for putting herself and her father in serious danger. The anger is easier to reckon with than the fear.

A couple of minutes later, Greg runs into view, Élodie on his back. Relief floods through me, cool and clear. I check them over and they are dirty but unhurt. He tumbles her onto the back seat, throws himself into the front and starts the car.

'All right?' he says to me, as he rams the gear-stick into reverse. His face, sickly in the weird light, is lined with real fear, his eyes wild and unfocused. I nod because I don't trust myself to speak yet, unsure what will come out if I open my mouth: frightened sobs or a terrible accusation.

I was watching Élodie as Greg ran up with her, and again as he bent to open the back door, the perfect heart of her face clearly visible over his shoulder as she clung to him like a monkey. Her hair was grubby and tangled and one of her cheeks was streaked with soot, but her mouth was curled into a small smile. I know all her smiles and this was one of triumph. I think I'd known in my bones that it was arson, that she had started the fire.

Olivier comes for us just after ten the next morning. You've already unwrapped your present, which I'd brought from London: a silver locket in the shape of a heart. Inside, I'd put a tiny picture of you on one side and me on the other, taken when I was about your age. You'd put it on straight away, though without taking off Élodie's.

'Won't the chains get tangled together?' I said, but you shook your head.

When I asked you last night if you wanted to go to the gorge with Olivier, I thought you looked relieved. Perhaps I wasn't the only one relishing the idea of putting some distance between us and the house, between each other, even: Olivier's presence was bound to keep things light. I also felt I needed to widen the gap between past and present. The two tended to overlap at La Rêverie, the boundaries too permeable for comfort.

The roof of Olivier's sleek car is down and my heart lifts at the thought of the day ahead.

'*Did you see the news?*' he says, after he's wished Emma a happy birthday, and we've turned on to the main road. '*They say the fires will be out by tomorrow or the next day at the latest.*' He switches to English. 'Emma, did you understand? There will be no more fires.'

You look at him, surprised out of your thoughts, and lift a shoulder. 'I wasn't that bothered.' You don't mean it rudely. In fact, you look miles away, fingers worrying at the neon bands circling your wrists.

Olivier glances at me and I shake my head minutely. You're sitting behind me and I can see your face in the wing mirror, small and very young today, not like you've just turned fourteen at all. You love birthdays but you don't seem yourself, a sharp line marking the smooth skin between your brows and your thumb at your mouth now, teeth nibbling at the cuticle. I haven't seen you do that in years. My stomach twists when I remember the Polaroid. I'd hidden it in the inside pocket of my suitcase, but could you have found it? You can't have, surely. If you had, and you'd looked closely enough, there's no chance you wouldn't have said something. *How can you have this photo, Mum? It doesn't make any sense.*

'It'll be lovely to be somewhere new today, fires or not,' I say brightly, so Olivier doesn't think we're ungrateful. 'The gorge is in the opposite direction, Em, and it's very beautiful. It's the most dramatic in France.'

You nod absently.

'How's your chest?'

'Fine, Mum,' you say wearily. You'd woken up wheezy. *I had a bad dream*, was all you would say. When I reach back for your hand, between the seat and the door, you squeeze mine only briefly.

194

The gorge's dusty car park is almost full when we get there.

'Ah, the crowds have already descended,' says Olivier. 'I thought it would be quieter in the week.'

It occurs to me that I haven't been to the gorge since my teenage years. Somehow, Greg and I never got round to taking you and Élodie there.

The long absence makes it untainted, which is just what I need today, and what I suspect you do too. The wide river snakes between towering walls of stone, so tall they block out the sun and turn the water a dark turquoise. Picnics are already being spread out where the stone flattens, and a platoon of life-jacketed kids in canoes is paddling towards the arch the gorge is famous for: a curved slab of rock that seems to blot out half the sky. The scents of damp stone and the *gaufres au chocolat* for sale at a stand, sweet and heady, mingle strangely.

Still, I find myself combing through the crowds for long wavy hair and a certain way of standing. I remind myself this is habit, not intuition, and make myself stop.

Olivier has brought a picnic too, lugging it down from the car park in a red cool-box. When he got it out of the boot, seeming suddenly sheepish that he'd made such an obvious effort, I reached out and squeezed his arm, touched by his thoughtfulness.

He has forgotten to pack any plates or cutlery so lunch is a messy affair. You get the giggles watching him try to spread cold butter with a bendy plastic knife from the *gaufre* stand, baguette crumbs scattering all over his nicely pressed chinos. He's remembered a bottle opener, though, and there's more Pschitt for you and bottles of chilled Pelforth beer for us.

'*Thank you,*' I say, when you go off to find a toilet.

'*What – for this gastronomic splendour?*' he says, gesturing to the debris of crumbs and empty packets around us.

I laugh and lean closer towards him. '*Not just for lunch. For being something good. You've made today feel like a holiday.*'

A strand of hair blows across my face and he tucks it behind my ear.

'*It's just a shame this visit has to come to an end. If there's any way I can persuade you to reconsider selling . . .*' He runs a finger around the neckline of my top and my skin immediately responds, goosebumps rising despite the heat. There's a beat when neither of us says anything, and I think he's going to kiss me.

'*I can't,*' I say softly, before he can. '*But I haven't booked our ferry back yet. We won't be leaving for a little while.*' I meet his eyes and I can see the desire in them, which makes something twist inside me. I trail off as he looks away, eyes narrowed at the bright water.

'*I see. I must have misunderstood the other evening.*'

Before I lose my nerve, I lean in and kiss him. There's a suspended moment when he hesitates and I think he's going to pull away, but then he kisses me back, his mouth hot and urgent. His hand goes to my waist, then begins to move up, fingers easing under my top to make contact with bare skin.

We pull apart at the same moment, smiling and then looking furtively around for you. I spot you in the near-distance, intent on a board with prices for boat hire on it.

'*We've turned my poor Emma into a chaperone.*'

'*She's a good girl. She doesn't really mind.*'

'*You've bought her off with lemonade.*'

'*I think you're worth it,*' he says, smiling. '*And now I'm going to bribe her some more, by hiring a pedalo for us all.*'

I watch him go, heart beating hard from his touch, the rest of me molten. My mind is already moving towards evening, you upstairs in bed, he and I alone.

At the end of the afternoon, ours is one of the last cars left, the gorge shadowed and silent now, and much more magnificent for it. It's almost seven by the time Olivier turns off the road and on to La Rêverie's drive. All three of us are tired and peaceful. I'm not quite ready for the soothing rhythm of the journey to end, my legs heavy with relaxation, Olivier's hand on one knee. The light is the colour of goldenrod, soft-focused and saturated, like a seventies postcard. Slanting through the scrub oaks on the drive, the lowering sun is the perfect temperature. Behind me on the back seat, you're asleep, your head lolling gently with the movement of the car, your lips parted. Watching again in the wing mirror, I witness the very instant you wake, your face reanimating, your hand coming up to rub your cheek. Your eyes open slowly, drowsily, but something ahead on the drive makes them snap into sudden focus.

I look round and see a figure at the gate. It turns at our approach.

As the world begins to shudder on its axis, thoughts flicker like lightning through my brain.

There's someone there.

Can it be?

It's her.

She's here.

Élodie.

Élodie.

PART TWO

People say that if you tell yourself something for long enough you start to believe it, that it becomes an almost perfect forgery of the truth. But while the rational part of me always knew Élodie wasn't dead, it's also true to say that, after a while, she didn't quite seem alive either. She became someone who was neither here nor there, caught between the layers of existence. She was the hairs standing up on the back of my neck, the movement in the mirror of a dark room, the unease and creeping guilt that for no earthly reason steals over an ordinary day. She haunted me. And when I didn't want to be tormented by the thought of her any more, I made her into the girl with the amber eye, who didn't have a bad bone in her body.

It was easier than you might suppose to perpetuate such a huge lie, particularly in the village. Both my parents were gone by then, and of course Greg's were in England. Your dad was in Paris and you and I had gone to London. And Élodie? She had been spirited away to the other end of France, where the land was flat and the skies leaden.

Not a dead girl after all, then. A girl who grew up,

who had just become an adult in the overexposed Polaroid Luc had dropped. A girl who, just a few days after that photograph was taken, would leave the Institut Médico-Éducatif, where she'd spent the previous three and a half years, and disappear without trace.

The knowledge she was out there became a chronic pain I learnt to live with. It grew more acute when the letter about the fire arrived, and cut deeper still when we rolled off the ferry at Calais and began the journey south.

They rang Greg when she vanished six years ago – his phone number in Paris was listed as the emergency contact once I had left La Rêverie with you and settled in London. Paris was so much nearer the Institut.

'They're going to stop looking for her,' I remember him saying on the phone, a couple of months later, his voice ragged with emotion. 'They said there's no trace, and because she's now legally an adult she's no longer the Institut's responsibility anyway. I contacted adult services but they weren't interested, I could tell. She's had a completely clean record for the last three years.'

For months, I expected her to show up at his place because she'd had that address. But she never did. That shook Greg, I think, part of him believing she would have forgiven him for her necessary removal because it was more my doing, even if we'd both signed the papers. But she never did appear and the weeks piled into years. And whatever Greg might claim, and however complicated it was by other feelings, I was as shattered by it as he was.

I made a wish once. For a daughter who would be

special. I didn't think to wish for more modest traits, such as being ordinary, or gentle. And she was special, just as I'd hoped. She was extraordinary. There was no denying that.

See how I talk about her in the past tense. It became habitual long ago. She *is* special, just as she is beautiful and clever. But part of me still can't get my head around her continued existence, even as she stands there in front of me on the drive, La Rêverie rising up behind her, her eyes refracting light and her lungs pulling in air. She's just like any other person.

No, not like any other person. Never that.

My beautiful daughter. My beautiful adversary.

It felt different the second time. I could sense it, even before they cut the cord. There you were, my precious girl: pearl-skinned and limpid-eyed, a glossy conker whose world had just cracked open, fresh air whistling through it, and you so delighted by everything, from sunlight flickering on a wall to the soft nap of your blanket, your limbs pumping, priming for life. If Élodie's birth had been a *coup de foudre* – a bolt of lightning, a love at first sight that felt almost violent – something in me quietened and calmed when you came along, Emma. It was like stepping from the tumult of a storm into still darkness, a place as safe as my own mother's womb.

But it doesn't last, this sense of security. It isn't long before I'm shaken out of this gentle, cushiony night. Like a diver wrenched to the surface too quickly, I come up gasping.

One day, when I go upstairs to wake you, see if you need changing, I find your older sister framed in the doorway to your room. I ask her why she's there but she slinks away without answering. The bruise I find later, on the inside of your tiny thigh, is shaped like spread butterfly wings, dark blue in the centre. I stare at it while you lie quietly on the changing mat, legs frog-kicking. Part of me wonders what could have caused it while another, older part of my brain, more reliant on instinct, knows it's a pinch-mark made by fingers smaller than my own.

In some deep cellar of my consciousness, I've been dreading this moment since the day I brought you home from the hospital two months ago – no, since the day I found out I was pregnant again.

Élodie is ten now, and at school during the week. For those hours at least, I have some respite. After they leave in the mornings – she always wants Greg to walk her if he's home – I feel my body let go slightly, and it seems to me that La Rêverie does, too, the overstretched atmosphere deflating like a lung.

'Greg,' I call. 'Come and look at this.'

He peers down at you. 'What? That?'

'Yes, that.' To me, it's as obvious as a sailor's tattoo on your new-hatched skin. 'Don't tell me you can't see it.'

I peel up your Babygro, hands unsteady as I search you for other marks. There's nothing on your torso but there are what look like fingerprints on your left arm, just above the elbow. Four little smudges that can't be wiped away.

'What about these, then? I suppose they're nothing too.'

'They're just bruises. She must have knocked against something.'

I turn to him, trying to keep my voice steady. 'She can barely move on her own. How does knocking against something do that? How can she have bruised the inside of her thigh when she can't even crawl yet?'

He gives me his best forbearing look. 'I'm sorry, Sylvie, but I don't know what you want me to say. A bruise won't do her any harm.'

'Are you being deliberately obtuse? Those are fingermarks.'

A blend of complex emotions crosses his face. Then he hardens. 'You don't know it was her. I actually think she's been pretty good since the baby arrived. The new camera has been a real success – she's been going round taking photos of everything, especially Emma. But you can't bear to give her the benefit of the doubt.' He shakes his head.

Tears roll off my chin and land on Emma's leg, just below the bruise.

'And now you're crying again,' he says. 'I don't know what to say to you, Sylvie, I really don't.'

His face changes again, turning implacable, perhaps even bored, and for the first time I can see Élodie in his features.

1993

Everything has slowed right down, just like in the seconds before the impact of a crash. Walking towards her seems to take long minutes, my thought processes strangely ordered and calm. She had turned at the sound of the car, but doesn't now make any move to approach. I force myself to keep going forward.

As I get closer, I see that her face is thinner, the cheekbones more pronounced, which makes her odd-coloured eyes seem larger and even more arresting. Her skin is browner than I remember it, as though she spends most of her time outside. She's lost some of that ripe and dangerous lushness she possessed when I last saw her but her features, set harder in the intervening years, are more eerily perfect than I've recalled in my dreams. My heart lifts and swoops: a huge kick of maternal love to the chest, which also wakes the old fear. I feel it surging in.

And then she smiles and I'm thrown because it isn't one of the Élodie smiles I know. This one is tentative, even nervous, and for a fleeting moment, I wonder if she's an imposter.

A hand on my arm makes me jump. You've come up

behind me, your fingers digging into my skin, but you aren't looking at me, not even for an explanation. You're staring at your sister, wide-eyed, drinking her in, like you could never get enough.

'Mum,' you wheeze. 'I don't . . . Is it . . . ?' I upend my bag and watch loose change and tissues and lipsticks fall to the dirt. You scoop up the inhaler just as I bend down to get it. No one says anything as you suck in the medicine, Élodie's face unreadable as she watches you.

'It's your sister,' I say, when you've handed it back to me, though I'm not sure I'll be able to speak until the words come out. 'I know I need to explain. But . . . this is your sister. It's Élodie.'

At her name, she turns her gaze from you to me, and as our eyes lock I think she flinches minutely, as though it's hurt her to do it. I watch the nervous bob of her throat as she swallows, and I can't help marvelling at it, even in my shock, because I have never seen Élodie show nerves about anything, not even the day Greg drove her away.

I am so transfixed, so fundamentally shaken, that it takes me a while to register that your pupils looked huge as you used the inhaler, black pooling over blue. You're much more shocked than I am, of course you are. Here, standing before you, is a ghost made flesh. Your almost-mythical sister, miraculously resurrected. I look at her again, half expecting her to have dispersed into the golden light, and it's then that I see Luc in the background, moving out of sight on the path that leads to the barn. Then my eye returns to her, and he drops out of my mind – just like Olivier, until he taps me gently on the arm.

'*Sylvie, I'm going now. You need time alone with . . . with your family . . .*' He tails off. '*I'll ring soon, okay?*'

I nod absently, the words meaning nothing. As he drives away, it strikes me that I haven't touched her yet. I haven't even managed to say anything. I cannot think straight.

And then she steps towards us and I automatically mirror her. As she embraces me I realize we are exactly the same size. Her arms around me are strong. She is utterly alive.

'*Maman, you're shaking. Your heart is beating so fast,*' she says, into my ear. So close, I feel overwhelmed by her, like I don't know whether to weep or faint. *My child*, I think, the words sliding cleanly, simply into my mind. She smells different and the same – of fresh air, the sea, patchouli. Her hair, when I clutch at a lock of it, has lost some of its girlish silkiness, replaced with the same tensile strength I can feel in her body. While I tremble, I notice that she is completely calm.

'*Let's go in,*' I find myself saying.

I turn after I've ushered you into the house and catch her momentary hesitation on the threshold. But then she steps inside and, like all old lives revisited, it's as profoundly familiar as it is dizzyingly strange.

We go through to the salon. I make coffee with sugar for all of us, though you don't drink it and I have no idea if Élodie does.

I glance over at you, clutching your cup of coffee,

like it's the only thing stopping you spinning away. You still have that dazed expression; you look like I feel. Across from us, sitting with perfect upright posture on my mother's armchair, Élodie is looking around the room.

'*It's just the same,*' she says, in apparent wonder. '*It's been here all this time, unchanged.*'

'*I've been packing up,*' someone says. Me. '*Trying to clear the place out.*' I reel at the absurdity of our conversation, this chit-chat that signifies nothing after ten years.

'*Pourquoi?*' Her eyes are soft, vulnerable.

'*It's for sale. La Rêverie is for sale.*'

'*Oh. You don't want it any more?*'

I shift in my seat, check you again. 'Emma, sweetheart, you still look pale. Why don't you go upstairs for a while, until you feel better? I'll come up and talk to you soon, I promise. I'll explain everything. I just need some time with your sister.'

You're outraged. 'No way. I want to be here. I want to know . . .' Your eyes fill with tears, and a terrible guilt sluices through me. 'You told me she was dead!' Your voice strangles as I look at Élodie, who flinches, more obviously this time. Guilt that she should hear that makes me sway in my chair. I put my hand to my face and realize it's wet.

Élodie gets up and goes to kneel in front of you. Gently she pulls your hands away from your streaming eyes as I wipe my own.

'I am so sorry, Emma,' she says gently, musically, in slightly stilted English. Her accent is stronger than it used to be, as though she hasn't spoken anything but French for a long time. 'This is my fault.'

You exhale shakily. 'Your fault? How is it your fault?'

'I told them not to see me. I say to them, "I am dead now, to you." And then, later, I disappear, so they would think I really was. *Tu comprends?* I make everyone think it.'

I sit frozen as you look at me, then back at her. 'But why?'

'I was angry. I was a bad person then. I thought only of myself.' She places her hand on her heart.

I stare at it because I don't know what I'll see if I look at her face. She's taking the blame and it makes my head spin.

'Emma, go upstairs. Just for a while.' It's not fair of me but I can't cope with this right now. I need to sort things out. I raise my hand when you open your mouth to object. 'Please, just go. I'll come and get you when Élodie and I have spoken.'

You do as I say, thank God, stamping up the stairs and slamming your bedroom door, which seems fair. Besides, I'd rather your temper than the blank shock.

When I turn back to Élodie, a hundred other moments with her in this room flash through my mind, like a magic lantern being spun. Out of the evening light, she looks younger, blurrier, closer to the age she was when she left.

We need a proper drink. In the kitchen, hands still shaking, I open the fridge and take out a new bottle of wine. Élodie reaches up to the cupboard where the glasses are kept and it's that casual gesture – her unthinking familiarity with the kitchen – that finally brings it home to me that she's back. It makes me sway again. I feel like I'm already drunk.

'*Ça va?*' Her hand on my bare shoulder is cool. I jump and then flush, with shame or embarrassment, I'm not sure.

'*I'm sorry,*' I say, after I've drunk the first glass straight down. '*I just – it's such a shock, that's all. There's so much to say, to ask you, that I don't know where to start.*'

'*It's a shock to me, too.*' Another wavering smile. '*I didn't think anyone would be here, but then I saw the British number plate on the car, and the shutters were open. I was about to leave when the other car drove up.*'

The possibility of that makes me dizzy again. Would I ever have known she'd been here if we'd missed her? I think I would. The air would have had a different weight, a different colour.

'*Come outside,*' I say, wishing my voice sounded steadier. '*Come and talk to me.*'

On the terrace, she sits in the chair opposite. She curls her legs under her in exactly the same way I do. I'd forgotten that. She holds her wine glass like I do, too. Learnt or innate? I never did know the answer to that one.

'*Élodie –*' I begin, but she talks over me.

'*It's so strange. Apart from Emma, everything looks the same as I remember, even you.*' Her finger traces the dimple in her cheek and I find myself copying her again, finger to my own face.

'*How are you, Élodie?*' I begin, unsure how to convey that I need to know everything suddenly: where she's been, how she's coped all this time without her family, perhaps without anyone. This thought makes me crumple inside. But all I have are the same words I'd put to a casual acquaintance in the street. *How are you?*

'*Are you well?*' I try again. '*You look well. You're still so beautiful, maybe even more than you were.*' I put out my hand but draw it back when she doesn't move. '*Élodie, where have you been all this time? Where did you go when you left the Institut?*'

Her fingers flutter to her hair and begin to twist a lock of it round and round. A couple of her nails are broken off at the quick and there's an angry-looking graze from her little finger to her wrist bone. It strikes me then like a body blow: this is my own daughter and I have no idea how she came to hurt herself. She's been out in the world on her own for so long, fending for herself. Shame eddies through me again.

'*I've wanted to come back,*' she says, looking away across the garden. '*Lots of times. I often thought about it. But I never actually did it until now. I must have known, in here.*' She lays her hand flat against her chest again. '*Something told me I had to come back now.*'

'*But then you were just going to leave again? Without seeing us?*'

'*I got afraid. When no one answered I lost my nerve. I thought that maybe it wasn't the right time after all.*'

'*You were afraid? But I have never known a child as unafraid as you.*'

She shrugs. '*Like you say, I was a child. I guess I didn't know fear until I . . . went away.*'

'Oh, God, Élodie.' I hang my head. '*You know we would never have done that unless . . .*'

'I know. I didn't say it to make you feel guilty. You and Papa did what you had to.' I watch her scratch carefully around the edges of the graze. 'What did you tell Emma about me? Apart from the fact that I'd died, I mean.' Her eyes flick towards me and then away as I wince.

'I – She was told that you had to go away. That you were – ill.'

'And that I died of it, this illness?'

I sigh shakily. 'We thought it was best, that it would be easiest on Emma – she was still such a little girl – if we let her think you were physically sick. I'm – I'm so sorry for that, and I'm grateful for what you said in there. I really am.'

'But did you actually say I was dead? Did you say those words: "Élodie died"?' Her voice trembles.

I hang my head again. 'No. Someone in her class gave her the idea that you must have gone to heaven, and when she asked me I let her believe that. Look, I know how awful it sounds but I never . . . I never said the words –'

'I understand.' She cuts across me. 'It was easier for her to believe that then. She was only little, like you said.'

'Your father was against it at first. I should say that. He was angry with me about it. Still is, I think.'

'Will you tell him I'm here?'

'Of course. I'll ring him later.'

'Later. Does that mean I can stay here tonight?'

Blood pounds in my head. 'You must.'

I still don't know where she's been all this time, or why she's chosen to come back now, beyond a nebulous feeling that it was the right time. As I watch, two tears roll simultaneously down her cheeks and I move to comfort her instinctively, even as it strikes me that she never cried, not really. It had never looked like this. This looks like proper crying, an overspill of emotion that can't be contained. I had always felt Élodie was too much in control for that.

I hurry inside and rip off a piece of kitchen roll. Kneeling next to her chair as she wipes her eyes, my hand comes to rest on her back.

'*Perhaps I shouldn't stay after all,*' she says, after she's gathered herself. '*Perhaps it would be better if I went somewhere else.*'

'*No, no. You can't go. You've only just come back. You'll sleep in your own room. It's just as it was. I mean, some things have gone, of course, but your clothes, your bed . . .*' I run out of breath. Three words circle in my head. *She's my daughter. She's my daughter.*

She nods. '*Thank you.*'

We lapse into silence again. I watch her surreptitiously as she wipes her nose. A sudden breeze lifts her hair, a golden pennant rippling out behind her.

In the pit of me, my old friend Anxiety strikes up a new beat, faster than before. It'll be dark in a couple of hours. And for the first time in ten years, Élodie won't be out there in the vastness of the world, but under the same roof as you and me.

1980

She stands motionless, luminous in white, another finger of the moonlight that falls across your cot. The cotton of her nightdress is so fine that it floats around the silhouette of her body. It makes me think of a jellyfish propelling itself across a dark sea. A loose floorboard creaks under me and she spins round, long hair flying after her. With the window behind, her face is a dark blank.

Truly it's one of the most frightening moments of my life. As I move towards your cot, taking in the fact that the side has been lowered, that you haven't yet made a single sound, my heart falters and skips. I lift you out, already certain you're dead. But then you open your eyes wide and begin to wriggle and I have to choke back the screams that are almost out of me.

She hadn't made any noise getting from her bedroom to yours. As I take her back to her own bed, my fingers tight round her wrist, I notice how cool her skin is. She's been in there for a while. I wonder if some ancient instinct alerted me to the danger, waking me with a silent alarm only a mother's blood would hear.

The next morning I ring around until I find a man

who will fit a lock to your door today. Not a bolt or a latch, but a proper turning lock that requires a new handle and drilling into the frame. A lock with a key that I can have with me, that will keep you in and safe, and out of her reach.

When Greg gets home that night, his eyes are red. John Lennon has been shot, and they've been playing 'Imagine' on the radio all day. He's so upset and disenchanted with the world that I don't tell him what happened with Élodie, but of course he sees the new handle that doesn't match the rest when he goes up to bed. I brace myself for a fight but he doesn't say anything. He rests his hand on it for a moment, the brass garishly shiny in the gloom of the hall, then walks slowly towards our bedroom. He looks so beaten-down, I don't have the heart to repeat what Élodie said after I'd led her back to bed. *'Je n'aime pas ça,'* she had whispered, a sharp little hiss in the dark. *I don't like it. I don't want it here.*

1993

Élodie turns in just after nine, saying she's exhausted. I make up her bed with fresh linen, so tired myself that the strangeness of carrying out this mundane task in Élodie's room, for Élodie, feels thankfully remote. We embrace awkwardly when I've finished and I close the door softly behind me. I stand there for a while, marvelling at the small sounds on the other side of it: the floorboards creaking under her feet, the sigh of the mattress as it takes her weight for the first time in a decade. *She is here.*

When I tear myself away, I find you waiting for me in the salon.

'Explain, then,' you say flatly, mouth a hard line that makes me think of your father in the last years of our marriage. 'You said you would.'

I rub my scalp, which is tight and sore. 'Yes, I did.'

'So Élodie's not dead.' The words are blunt. You're angry, and not sure who to direct it at. Not yet.

I try to organize my thoughts. 'What you have to remember is that everything your dad and I ever did was to protect you,' I begin. 'Perhaps we got it wrong, but . . .'

'Because you lied about what she died of, you mean? When, actually, you didn't even know for sure that she was dead at all.'

'Yes.'

'Why didn't you look harder for her? She said she *made* you think she was dead, but what does that even mean? And why did she want you to think she was dead in the first place?'

You're much quicker than I am tonight.

'I suppose we didn't know, not for sure. But when you assumed, we let you because we thought it would be easier for you than knowing she might be out there somewhere.'

What I don't – what I *can't* – add is that I hadn't known how much you remembered of what she'd done to you. I didn't want you to think she could come back and get you.

'So basically she lied to you and Dad, and you lied to me?'

I sighed. 'Yes, I suppose so. I'm sorry, Emma love, I really am. I know that's totally inadequate.'

You don't soften. 'So what about why she lied?'

'I think she must have been angry with us, with everyone, because of the help she had to have. You know from the notes that she had to go to a special clinic where they treated children like Élodie. We didn't see her much while she was there because that was what the doctors advised. I'm not sure they would do the same now.' I shake my head. 'I know it's a mess but perhaps you'll understand better when –'

You get to your feet. 'Don't say I'll understand when I'm older. That's all you ever say. Anyway, it looks like being older just makes you into a better liar, if you're anything to go by.' And then you're gone, thundering up the stairs. Your bedroom door slams, making me flinch.

*

I tiptoe into your room just before midnight and, as La Rêverie drifts along the dark seabed of night, I watch you sleep. Between the quiet sighs of your breathing, I listen for the tiniest sounds beyond the closed door. I wish I'd left it ajar like I found it, but I don't want to risk waking you by opening it now. I don't want to frighten you, a Gothic spectre in a white nightdress standing over your bed. I wish this room had a key so I could lock you in, just like the old days.

My head pounds from too much sun at the gorge and too much wine on an empty stomach. The disorientation of standing in the near-blackness makes me unsteady on my feet. I creep to the far wall, halfway between you and the door, and lower myself carefully to the floor, back up against the cold wall. Outside, through the half-open shutters, I can see the dull glow of the forest fires in the distance.

Sometime after one, an insistent tapping noise, like a fingernail on a door, makes my head jerk up. It stops and then starts again, my heart beating almost as loudly in each of the lulls. Then my thoughts clear, and I realize I know this sound. It's a death-watch beetle in the wall somewhere close by, eating away at the old wood of La Rêverie's fabric. Bad news for the house, and for whoever buys the place, but nothing that can harm you. Still, it chills me. They're named for those who would sit up through the night, watching over a loved one who might not see morning. In the old days, people believed the sound heralded tragedy. Rationally, I know that's just silly superstition. And yet.

Before I got pregnant with you, Greg and I had relinquished the idea of having another child. Prior to Élodie, I think he had fondly envisaged a whole brood and I liked the idea too, in a naive sort of way. After, though. After I knew what it could be like, I told him Élodie was the only child we would have.

'I just can't risk it,' I said, when Élodie was a few years old. My voice shook. 'I couldn't possibly cope. I can't.'

He wouldn't talk about it but I knew what he was thinking – we were still close enough for that then. I knew that at some low frequency pulsing beneath his hearing he was already troubled by her, too, even before I took her to Morel. In the years since, I was sure he'd gone over the doctor's words almost as much as I had, some of them sticking fast, impossible to budge. Callous. Unemotional. Cold. And, of course, *psychopathic*. That word like a siren echoing across the fields of my dreams.

As it was, the issue of having another child was taken out of our hands and, oh, Emma, I'm so glad it was. It still makes me smile at the ridiculous irony of it, but it was Annette Martin who gave you to me. Annette and her badly prepared Coquille St Jacques.

We hadn't been invited to the Martin house since Luc had ended up in the pool, but Laurent must have over-ruled Annette so that Greg and I were among the numbers for his birthday party. Half of us went down with food poisoning the next day and I was one of the unlucky ones. I felt so awful I didn't care about any-thing, even what Élodie might be doing, as I lay in bed with the shutters closed and a bowl at my side. It cer-tainly didn't occur to me that I might have thrown up my pill. And I'd almost forgotten that Greg and I had slept together when we got home the night before, when the scallops had yet to poison my system: a quick release that might not have happened if we hadn't drunk so much. When I finally realized – late because I was too busy getting through each day to notice something as mundane as my menstrual cycle – I was almost four months pregnant.

Another irony is that, after feeling so ill with the food poisoning, you never gave me a single day of morning sickness. And how typical of you was that? You were always so easy on me, even when you were still strug-gling into existence.

But I didn't know you would be you then, and I was terrified. Before I told Greg, I went around in a daze of dread and disbelief, checking my knickers for blood a dozen times a day. In five months' time, I told myself, there will be another one, another one like her.

My head whirling with *Then*, I must have dozed off. The next thing I know the room has lightened to grey, the faintest blush in the eastern sky signalling that the sun

225

is finally creeping up the horizon. The beetle has stopped. I jolt when I remember why I'm here and not in my own room.

I know I should leave now, before you wake. I get to my feet, body stiff from the hard floor, hips clicking as I move towards the door. I used to hanker after the past all the time when I first became a mother but I haven't felt such a visceral craving to reverse time for years. Now, as I tiptoe along the hall towards Élodie's room, the force of this desire almost undoes me. Not that I know when in time I would go back to. To my own childhood? Perhaps. It would be nice not to be in charge: as I learnt when Élodie was small, it's hard to assume responsibility when you don't feel in control. But, then, if I went back to being a little girl, I wouldn't have you. And I could never wish you away, Emma. I couldn't wish your sister away either. Perhaps it's a biological impossibility. The thought of either constricts my throat.

Élodie's door is shut and there is silence behind it. My logical brain knows she is sleeping just like you are – the heavy slumber of dawn – but I have an unnerving vision of her sitting bolt upright in bed, eyes fixed on my shadow under the door as I hover there. There was no answer when I rang Greg last night. My hands had still been shaking so hard that I'd had to dial twice.

'You were never there, Greg,' I'd muttered aloud, as I slammed the receiver back into its cradle. 'And you're still not.'

From downstairs, the ormolu clock chimes five, and

I'm hurtling back to our first night here, eight or was it nine days ago? Resisting the urge to go back and resume my vigil over you, I make coffee for something to do, taking it out on the terrace to drink. The sun is growing stronger all the time, the lemon-rind sky turning blue by imperceptible degrees. I've made the coffee strong and I drink it fast, aware that I'm creeping around, already on eggshells.

I'm clenching my jaw so tightly that my teeth hurt. I make myself breathe out slowly, counting up to five before I allow a breath in. But then I hear the creak of a shutter and tense again, gooseflesh rising despite the sun. I look up at your window but I know that it came from the other side of the house. I brace for more noise but everything goes quiet again.

'*Maman.*'

I nearly drop my cup because she is suddenly there beside me. I probably never told you how light she was on her feet. *Is.* I almost never heard her approach when she was growing up.

'*Do you mind if I go for a swim?*' She is already dressed in a turquoise bikini that brings out the coppery lights in her left eye, the rich gold of her hair.

I let out a startled laugh, at a loss to know how else to respond to such a normal request in such abnormal circumstances.

She turns to go and I call after her. '*I tried to phone your father again but he's obviously away.*'

'*He was always away, wasn't he?*'

I look at her in surprise. I can't remember her ever

criticizing Greg. She's looking thoughtfully up at the house and I wonder what she's remembering. My eyes flick over her half-naked body. The skin of her midriff is only a shade lighter than her legs and arms. On the right, just above the line of her bikini briefs, is a neat scar, silver scoring the gold.

'*Did you have your appendix out?*'

She regards me from above, head on one side. She's a different Élodie today, this one far more self-contained than she was last night. '*My appendix?*' Her finger trails back and forth across the scar. '*Yes. I'll swim now, I think.*'

I watch her go. She is still utterly without self-consciousness, though she must know I'm watching her. The sight makes old memories fire painfully in my brain so I get up and go inside to the phone again.

The line connects after only a couple of rings. '*Camille?*'

'*Who else were you expecting on this number?*' she says with her usual bite but then, when I don't say anything: '*Sylvie? Ça va?*'

'*She's back,*' I manage to get out.

'*Who's back?*'

'*Élodie.*'

'*Oh, my God. Are you all right?*'

'*No. I don't know what I am.*'

'*Did she . . . How was she with you? And, oh, God, what about Emma? I hope you told her before . . . ?*'

'*She had an asthma attack from the shock. I stayed in her room most of the night.*'

'*Where is Élodie now?*'

'*In the pool. It's as though all this is completely normal.*'

'*Merde.*'

In the background, I can hear the rumble and spit of her coffee machine and wish I was in her light-filled Paris apartment with her.

'*You haven't said what you told Emma.*'

I peep into the hall to check for you but it's still quiet upstairs. Softly, I close the salon door, taking the phone with me.

'*Élodie took the blame. She said she made everyone think she was dead.*'

'*She did? Why would she do that?*'

Something loosens inside me. Tears well up from nowhere. '*Christ, Camille. I don't think I can cope with this.*'

'*You were probably always going to have to at some point and, actually, I think you're as ready as you're ever going to be. I think that's precisely why you're there after avoiding it for a decade. Why did you go back now? Because you heard about that damage in the souillarde and you thought it might be her.*'

There's truth in this. Camille had always been completely clear-eyed.

'*Look, maybe she's changed, grown up,*' says Camille. '*Grown out of it. That's what the psychologist in Avignon said, didn't he? Things were going in the right direction, weren't they, at that place, before she took off?*'

'*You honestly think we can be a normal family?*' It comes out facetiously but I want her to convince me of it, too. '*I can't help it, Camille. I'll always be afraid of what she might do. I didn't sleep last night. I sat on the floor in Emma's room, keeping watch.*'

'*And what happened? Nothing. She's swimming in the pool. She's probably got her own life now to get back to, once she's made up for lost time with you and Emma. Did you think of that?*'

I contemplate her leaving and I don't know how it makes me feel. Relieved, of course; I can't deny that. But also empty, hollowed out in some crucial way.

'*You're still going to have to tell Emma the truth, though,*' Camille says, softly for her.

'*Which part? It's so complicated.*'

'*All of it. Tell her why you don't trust Élodie. That she had to go away for good reason.*'

I shake my head. '*I can't do it to her. I can't tell her that her sister hated her so much she tried to hurt her. I've spent ten years protecting her from that.*'

She sighs. '*Look, Sylvie, I would come, but I really can't take any time off work this week and –*'

'*It's fine,*' I say dully. '*I understand.*' And I did. There was a limit with Camille; there always had been. It was enough that she hadn't said *I told you so.*

'*Greg should be there. This is on him too. Ring me back if you need me to go and knock on his damn door.*'

'*I will. Wish me luck.*' I can feel tears starting again.

'*Bon courage, Sylvie. You know you can ring again.*'

I take the phone back into the hall. The air is cooler than it is in the sun-steeped salon, and among the familiar smells something potent and heady is suspended in its particles, like the smoke that stains the breeze. Patchouli and sea salt.

I have to say it aloud. *She's really back.* And though an old version of myself screams at me to get us both in the car and drive away, I am just about able to ignore it. Partly because I want to believe she may have changed; and partly because I don't think that's possible, and that something will happen soon to force my hand. I don't want to think about what this might be. I know I'm backing myself into a corner but feel helpless to stop it. And there's another reason I'm trapped. Just as I have something on Élodie that could spoil her for you for ever, so she has something on me. And I can't ever let you find that out. You would never look at me in the same way again. I wonder if we're already in an accident unfolding in slow motion. I wonder if I'll recognize the last moment we have to jump clear.

1980

Élodie has always been something of a loner at school. It's one of the things her teachers brought up, right from her earliest days at the village crèche. '*Élodie doesn't seem to have many friends*,' they said, though I knew they really meant 'any'. Only one teacher, young and earnest, in her first year of the job, made a slightly different observation, but for me it was a crucial one. '*Élodie doesn't seem to need friends*,' she said, and that was much more like it. I could never imagine her as the girl sitting alone, wistfully looking on as the others played. She simply wasn't interested.

And then she was.

I don't know what changed, possibly just boredom, or else a growing awareness that there is pleasure or at least interest to be had in playing with others. I don't mean playing only in the straightforward sense, of course. In French there's only *jouer* but in English there's *toying*. That's more apt.

There are two girls in her class, Thérèse and Sophie. Their mothers have been friends since childhood so, inevitably, their daughters are close too. They are more than that, though: these two are inseparable. They sit together, they eat together, they hold hands in line, they plan how they will both wear their hair the next day.

Three is always a crowd with little girls. As far as anyone can tell from what Thérèse, Sophie and the other children are willing to say afterwards, Élodie worked on Sophie first. She was the shyer of the two friends; if one was to be brutally honest, she was a paler version of Thérèse in all ways. I don't know why Élodie mounted her charm offensive on Sophie first; perhaps because Thérèse was a more formidable opponent to go up against.

Élodie started wheedling Greg to buy her sweets behind my back. The school frowns on anything like this. She sneaked them into school and began to ply Sophie with them. I don't suppose any of her classmates had ever experienced the full beam of Élodie's charm before. It's a fact that even babies prefer beautiful faces and Élodie's looks, combined with her new-found smiles and contraband sweets, made her irresistible to little Sophie, who chose to pair up with Élodie, turning away whenever Thérèse tried to join in. Thérèse's mother noticed how angry and tearful her placid daughter had become but didn't know how to tackle it. She hoped it was just a phase that would pass.

This was the point at which Élodie switched. According to another girl in the class, she simply walked up to Thérèse one morning when the bell to line up had been rung, and took her hand instead of Sophie's. From then on, Thérèse and Élodie were as thick as thieves. Or so we were told afterwards. Élodie never mentioned Thérèse at home. There was no change in her whatsoever, despite her apparent discovery of intimate friendship for the first time.

Unfortunately, Sophie didn't have Thérèse's pride. While the other girl vented her frustration and sadness at home, Sophie became desperate. She followed the other two around, trailing in their wake, her little face pinched with misery. The teacher intervened and said the three of them must be friends, and this was when the real trouble started.

After some weeks of ignoring Sophie, or holding their noses and saying she stank of shit, Élodie told her that they could all be friends again if she did a dare. Sophie, who had never done so much as talk back to her parents, stole money from her teacher's purse, scratched bad words into her desk and broke her lunch plate.

All this was unpleasant but arguably not out of the ordinary for little girls flexing their muscles in the playground for the first time. Perhaps. But then the dares took a darker turn and Thérèse started backing off, taking days off school, telling her mother she had a stomach ache.

On one of the days Thérèse had absented herself, Élodie told Sophie she had to climb up onto the high, flat roof of the dinner block. When she'd done that, Élodie told her to jump off. Ground down by months of bullying, she barely hesitated. She broke both legs, one of them so badly that the jagged tibia pierced the skin.

That was last week. Today, Greg has insisted we take Élodie to the hospital where Sophie lies in traction, to 'let them sort this out'. When we get there, the girl takes one look at Élodie, who is approaching armed with chocolates, and begins to tremble violently, her small hands clutching at the bed sheet, her mouth opening and closing in silent terror. She tries to sit up – to back away – the metal traction equipment above her groaning as it resists, and her face blanches with pain.

'Take her out,' I say to Greg, my voice like steel, and for once he doesn't protest. Neither does Élodie.

'I'm sorry,' I whisper before I follow them out, deep shame and horror making me shake almost as hard as Sophie herself. *'I'm so sorry.'*

You emerge just after I've finished talking to Camille on the phone, hair tangled and eyes puffy. You've dressed hurriedly, your T-shirt on inside-out, but I notice you've taken off the locket I gave you, favouring Élodie's turquoise necklace. Hurt flares inside me.

'Where is she?' you demand, without any kind of greeting.

'In the pool.'

You drag a chair back with a screech of metal and throw yourself into it. You look a bit like I feel: stunned and slightly frantic. I brace myself for more questions that I won't be able to answer properly, infuriating you further, but you don't seem angry any more, just totally preoccupied. Teenagers live their lives so immediately. I'm not convinced death seems so final to the young. You hear of teenagers committing suicide for reasons that seem almost trivial to an adult, and I've always thought it's because the end of a life is still an abstract concept. I'm not sure they can process 'for ever', let alone in relation to their own death. And, of course, Élodie has never been entirely dead to you anyway. She has lived on in dreams and photographs and the cherry-picked stories your father tells you. She's halfway to being your religion.

You go back inside without warning, and when you reappear, the straps of your favourite swimsuit are visible beneath the T-shirt. You hover by the steps down to the garden, suddenly hesitant.

'Do you want me to come with you?'

You shrug, but I know you do. Is it shyness, I can't help wondering, or some old instinct lighting up in your brain?

I would have followed anyway.

At the pool, we watch Élodie gliding underwater, a lithe shadow moving through the green, hair streaming over her shoulders as she surfaces, the shining water running cleanly off her smooth limbs.

She props herself up on her elbows, her lower half still in the water, two shades paler.

'You know, *ma soeur*, when I last saw you, you still needed . . .' She gestures, making a ring around one slim upper arm.

'Armbands!' you cry triumphantly.

'Yes, armbands.' She winks. 'I am certain you are faster than me now.' You go over to a lounger and pull off your T-shirt, your cheeks pinking as you drop it. Then you turn and dive so abruptly into the deep end that you almost misjudge it. I watch you touch the bottom, then kick hard up to the surface. Your front crawl to the side is ragged.

'Mum . . .' you suck in a breath '. . . Mum, will you get my inhaler? It must be the chlorine.'

I kneel down at the edge and put my face close to yours. 'There's hardly any in the water. Breathe for me.'

It's not nearly as bad as yesterday but the wheeze is definitely there. 'Emma, you have to take it everywhere with you. I know it's boring but you have to remember.'

You roll your eyes. 'Sor-ry. It's by my bed.'

I hesitate, looking from Élodie to you. She's floating on her back in the middle of the water now, face serene, golden hair fanned out around her face. She makes me think of a Greek icon.

'No, you go and get it. You've got to learn.'

You glare at me but clamber out, something in my voice halting any objections.

'*She doesn't speak much French, does she?*' Élodie says, when you've gone. '*Even though it's half of her.*'

She lifts herself out of the pool so she's sitting on the edge, a fine gold chain around one ankle glinting in the bright light as she flexes her toes. Lifting her hair, she lets it fall with a wet slap. The movement reveals an inch more flesh at the base of her spine, and with it a small black tattoo. It's a symbol I'd never seen, three delicate swirls arranged in a triangle.

'*I thought it would be easier for her to adjust,*' I say, looking away. I still feel as if I'm dreaming, that I can't really be having a conversation with Élodie by the swimming pool at La Rêverie.

'*In London, you mean?*'

'*Yes, that's right. I told you we were moving there when I came to visit you that last time.*'

She moves her feet in circles, churning the water. A

butterfly hovering too close is soaked and begins to struggle on the surface. She goes still, watching it. I get up and reach in to scoop it up, placing it carefully on the warm stones to dry out.

'Emma can't remember being here, when it was the four of us?'
'Not really, no.'

She plucks a stray oleander flower out of the water and lays it next to the butterfly. *'Maybe she does remember somewhere. I think we all remember everything, like a videotape running inside our heads from the moment we're born. You just have to find where it's stored. I have a very good memory. I can find things quickly, up here.'* She points to her temple. *'I remember everything. Being here only makes it clearer. Maybe it'll be the same for Emma, once she's been here a little longer. Maybe it'll all start coming back.'*

'Élodie?' She looks round and I take a breath. *'Where have you been?'*

But suddenly you're back, three cans of cold Panaché clamped between your hands and the inhaler tucked into the top of your swimsuit.

'It's a bit early, isn't it?' I begin but, seeing you flush with embarrassment, I hold out my hand for one of the cans.

'She got angry when I drank at your age.' Élodie smiles conspiratorially at you. I marvel again at how I've come to be in such a situation.

After lunch we return to the pool. I sit stiffly on a lounger pretending to read, when I'm really observing Élodie surreptitiously through my sunglasses. I've decided the house can wait. I need to stay with you.

You've dug out an old photo album from somewhere and the two of you are sitting cross-legged on the ground to look through it. I've tried to ask Élodie about the intervening years a few times now, but each time she's batted away my questions.

'Come and look at these, Mum,' you call. 'You look weird in this one, and so thin.'

I know then that they must be some of the pictures Élodie took with her little pink camera. Apart from a particularly disturbing set of pin-sharp shots, which eventually made me confiscate the damn thing, her photographs always came out blurred or otherwise off-kilter. Lots were of me, though I often had no idea she'd taken them until they came back from the developer. Our little voyeur. I made the mistake of saying this to Greg as we looked through the photos, making my voice lighthearted, but he shook his head. 'A little voyeur?' he said. 'Christ, Sylvie.'

I don't want to look at them any more. I turn back to my lounger and it's then that I see Luc. The red of his T-shirt catches my eye, blazing among the dark foliage of the pines. It takes me straight back to that day when he fell into the pool as a baby, Élodie in a red dress.

'*Luc est là,*' I say. As Élodie turns to see the new arrival, I think I catch the cold flare in her eyes that means she's working something out. For that split second, I glimpse the Élodie I used to know and, though it chills me to the bone, it's also a strange relief.

'*Luc and I already met,*' she says, with an easy smile. She hasn't got up to greet him so he goes over to kiss her the usual three times, bending over her to do it. I see his eyes rake down her body as he straightens up. There's an ease between them that seems off. I suddenly remember him slipping away yesterday, when I was still stunned by her return.

I'm trying to piece it all together when I catch sight of you, your smile faltering as you absorb the effect Élodie is having on him, the fact he's forgotten to greet us at all.

'*So, what can we do for you, Luc?*' I say sharply.

He shoots me a quick smile that doesn't reach his eyes. '*Two things. First I came to invite you to my parents' anniversary party. It's next week. There'll be food and a band.*'

For a second I'm perplexed that Annette would want us there, but then it would be just like her to want to show her marriage off, especially in front of someone like me. *We're whole*, would be the message. *You made the wrong choice.*

'*Thank you for the invitation – thank your mother – but I'm not sure we'll be able to come.*'

'Mum, what's he saying?' You look suddenly miserable, picking up the animosity between me and Luc.

'I was inviting you to a party,' Luc says in smooth English. 'But your mother says no.'

You look at me, your eyes pleading. 'Why can't we go? Mum, please.'

I sigh. 'We'll see. I don't know if we'll still be here then.' I look back at Luc. 'What's the second thing?'

'*I just wanted to make sure Emma had got her birthday surprise.*' He glances over at Élodie. '*But I see she has.*'

She narrows her eyes at him, so fast that I only just catch it. Luc does too, and it makes him flush along his cheekbones.

'*Wait a minute,*' I say. My head is whirring. '*You said you had a surprise for Emma days ago. A little present, you said.*' I take a step towards him. '*How did you know Élodie would be coming back then? How do you know her at all?*'

I look from him to Élodie. She's staring at Luc, unsmiling and completely still. He shifts about, clearly uncomfortable, eyes cast down to his feet.

And then she stands and shakes her hair back. '*Oh, Luc, you have given away my secret,*' she says and laughs her silvery laugh – the one that was once capable of making me quake, the one she always used in front of men. '*I'm sorry, Maman. I came earlier than I said. I was . . . what is it in English?* "Getting my courage"?'

I don't correct her. I think of the clock that had wound itself; the swimming pool already filled; the presence I've felt in the house and garden since we arrived. Has she been here all along, watching and waiting, not just an electric hum in the air, but real?

Confusion clouds your face.

'Mum? I don't understand. What's everyone saying?'

'It's nothing, darling. Just a mix-up. Luc was asking if it was a surprise to see Élodie, that's all.'

You smile uncertainly and just as I reach out, hoping you'll have forgiven me enough to take my hand, Élodie swoops in and kisses you on the forehead.

'Isn't my little sister beautiful?' she says in English for you, and Luc nods, smiling tentatively again. You blush and laugh shyly, covering your mouth with your hand. 'Luc, you must go now,' she adds, with a toss of her hair. 'I am going to swim with Emma.'

'*Arrête*,' I say, and she swings round. '*Have you been here, at the house, before yesterday?*' I'm speaking in French again, too fast for you to begin to follow.

'*Non, Maman,*' she replies. '*I swear. I was in the village, staying with a friend of Luc's. That's how I know him. I didn't come back here until last night.*'

It surprises me more than anything that I want to believe her, even if I'm not sure I do.

1982

You are three, and have lately turned your teddies into school pupils. I have bought you a small chalkboard and an exercise book of squared paper, which I've made into a class register. I've written down the teddies' names in a column, but you're dexterous enough with a pencil to mark everyone in and out. Your current favourite pupil, though he's naughty, is Maurice, a plush monkey in dungarees and a flat cap. I've invented a funny voice for him.

Your sister was expelled nearly two years ago, and because Greg has resisted enrolling her anywhere further afield, I am supposedly conducting lessons at home for her. The reality is that she does what she wants, moving through the house and garden, and lately beyond its boundaries, like a semi-feral cat. If I'm brutally honest, I prefer it when she's out. When she's here we do nothing but circle each other, hackles up. It's exhausting.

It's mid-afternoon, and I'm in the kitchen, trying to work out why the fridge light is flickering, when it dawns on me that the house is too quiet, that it's been too long since I've heard you moving about upstairs. That I haven't seen Élodie for hours.

I crash through your bedroom door but you're not there and neither is she. Élodie has recently taken to hitching lifts from the main road to go and see friends she won't tell us about, disappearing for hours without explanation. She's probably been gone a while already, her thumb out to the cars heading south to the sea, hair and dress billowing in the hand-dryer-hot breeze. Probably.

I'm about to leave, my mind already frantically listing other places to search: the garden, the pool, the road. But then I hear a tiny whimper and freeze. For a second I think it's coming from one of your soft toys that are, as usual, stacked high on the bed. But then I hear it again and realize it's coming from the tall cupboard in the corner.

I fling back the door to find you cowering at the back behind a couple of bags of old clothes, your knees brought up to your chin and tears spilling over at the sight of me. Silent tears, though, because she's tied a silk scarf of mine around your mouth, tight enough to leave marks. I wrestle it off, wringing wet with tears and spit and snot, and resist the urge to tear it into strips. Your face is flushed with panic and from being in the airless cupboard, but you also have two bright pink circles drawn on your cheeks. A different pink, darker like peonies, stains your lips. Spidery lashes are drawn above and below your eyes, each one a black line two inches long. It's then that I notice the felt tips scattered across the floor.

You don't have any dolls. You don't like them. Camille sent an expensive one from Paris for your third birthday, which I quietly put away in the same cupboard because, standing only half a head shorter than you, it terrified you. It takes me a moment to comprehend what I'm seeing because I haven't thought about, let alone seen, that doll for months, but Élodie has stripped you of your usual T-shirt and shorts and dressed you in Claudette the doll's scratchy nylon dress. It's too small and the elasticated capped sleeves have made red rings on the delicate skin of your upper arms, to match the gag marks on your face. It's the same around your neck.

It's as I lift you out that I spy Claudette there, at the back, and of course she's in your clothes. She smiles fixedly at me and the thought of you being trapped in there with her, when she frightens you so much, makes fury sear through me like acid.

The felt-tip takes a long time to scrub off. As we sit together in the bathroom, you and I – Greg absent as usual and Élodie God knows where – your skin sore from all the rubbing and the salt in the tears that continue to course down your cheeks, you tell me again and again.

'Élodie said I was Claudette. Élodie said I was Claudette now and Claudette would be me. That I would have to stay in the dark.'

Back in your room, I pull out the doll and notice what I didn't before, in the gloom of the wardrobe. Her face is scribbled on with red felt-tip, and stuffed in your shorts pocket is Maurice, his small plush body ripped open to reveal the white stuffing inside, his head lolling where it's been half torn off. I only realize you've followed me in from the bathroom when you begin to wail.

A couple of weeks later I venture into Élodie's room to change the bed and find a roll of used film on her bedside table. She still uses the pink camera Greg bought her, the only gift that ever stuck.

When they're developed, about half of them turn out to be of Élodie. I have no idea who's taken them, though I guess it's a boy, from the way she's smiling and pouting. She's always preferred men, and the way men look at her makes me queasy – not only that they do it, but her precocious ease in wielding that power.

Élodie has been in a hippie phase for months now, not caring that she is years out of date with her embroidered smocks, her hair hanging to her waist, her dirty feet. The look fits her and she's stuck to it longer than any that preceded it; the chameleon that has found the perfect colours in which to hide. The soft lines and fabric make a clever disguise, just as her physical grace has always masked her iron determination. Sometimes she makes me think of those Manson girls that were all over the news the year she was born: flowers woven in their hair, drifting on the music, sloe eyes opening to reveal the void.

The other half of the photos are of you, dressed as Claudette the doll. In some you're posed on the bed with your beloved teddies, the felt tip already marring your little face. Others were taken after she pushed you into the cupboard, like an unwanted toy. Anyone looking at them would know instantly that you were afraid, your pupils dilated, your bottom lip drooping. You're holding fast to your monkey in all of them, and I wonder when she tore it out of your hand, and whether she destroyed it in front of you. I wonder when she tied the gag tight around your mouth.

The next day, when Greg returns from his trip, I go to my bedside cabinet where I've hidden the photos inside a book, only to find they're gone. She's taken them, probably burnt them. And though they might have been the proof I have been subconsciously looking for – the proof that will finally force Greg to admit what we both know – most of me is simply glad they no longer exist.

1993

We end up in the salon by mid-afternoon, you and Élodie trying to tune in the old television while I hover,
packing and repacking the same box and seemingly getting nowhere. I've tried to phone Greg again but there's
still no answer. Though Élodie seems unaffected by the
heat, the two of us – unused to such extremes – have
been driven inside by it. I want nothing more than to go
upstairs, run a cool bath and submerge myself, but I
won't leave you. I close my eyes against the light streaming in through the open doors, voices flickering and
receding as you turn the dial, anxiety roiling inside me.
It's a relief when the phone rings at about four.

'*Allô,*' says a breezy voice. '*It's Martine here, from Century
21. No offer from the Bernards yet, but we've had another request
for a viewing, from an English couple. I can do this one so it
doesn't matter if you're going out. Tomorrow at eleven okay?*'

'Oh. Yes, I think that's fine. Thank you. We'll probably be
here, though. Me and . . . my daughters, I mean.'

I glance towards Élodie to see if she caught the plural
that feels so rusty in my mouth but she's still facing the
television, where a half-tuned news bulletin stretches and
fragments. When it briefly settles, a reporter is talking in

front of a line of burnt-out cars. A pall of smoke has turned the sky to lead behind him. I squint to read the place name at the bottom of the screen and see, with a lurch, that it's less than an hour from here. Élodie's expression, reflected imperfectly in the television as the blizzard of static takes over again, is hard to make out.

Martine talks on for a few more minutes, her light chatter washing over me. I'm dimly relieved that she doesn't seem to know or care about Élodie's return. Perhaps people in the village aren't aware of it yet. As for the viewing, I wasn't expecting more interest so soon. It makes me feel agitated – there's too much going on. I'm not sure I trust myself to say the right thing to these English people who might want La Rêverie. For the first time in a long time, I'm thinking of the English as Other and myself as French. And that wrong-foots me again.

As evening approaches, the three of us still ensconced in the hot salon, I realize that, even as I'm trying to ensure you're never alone with her, I'm also avoiding being alone with you. It isn't very difficult for me to pull this off: you're like her little shadow already and, unlikely as it seems, given the past, Élodie appears to want to be wherever I am.

I try Greg yet again, letting it ring out for a good five minutes before giving up. He must be in Normandy and I don't have the number.

Élodie insists on cooking that night. I need to go shopping but she says there's enough for some approximation of a *salade niçoise*, waving me out of the kitchen when I try to protest. I join you at the table on the terrace. You've changed into something floaty but slightly grubby, which must have come out of Élodie's rucksack because I don't recognize it. I resist telling you to go and change.

'She lent it to me,' you say, catching me looking. 'She said if I wanted, I could keep it.'

'It's a bit big, isn't it?'

That's true – it keeps slipping off one shoulder – but what I really mean is that it's too old for you. Too provocative.

'Élodie says it suits me.'

What can I say to that? I'm beginning to feel as though I have to tread carefully or you'll choose her. That's how the dynamic already seems to be shaping up, and she's only been back twenty-four hours.

By ten, you can no longer keep your eyes open. Reluctantly you head upstairs, leaving your sister and me alone. Although I'm exhausted, my body thrums as though it's over-caffeinated. I'm too alert to sleep now. It's the first time Élodie and I have been alone together since the morning.

She isn't going anywhere; playing Patience with a soft old deck of cards on the glass coffee table she learnt to walk around. I can see her tiny fingerprints in the sunlight as though it were yesterday.

I watch as she goes over to the record player and checks what's on the turntable before turning it over to side two and dropping the needle. It's a James Taylor LP I'd put on a couple of nights earlier.

'*You didn't come to see me again,*' Élodie says softly, after

'Fire and Rain' has finished. *'In the centre. I waited for you, every week. But you never did, not after that last time.'*

'I – I'm sorry. But don't you remember? The doctors said it was a bad idea. They said that with . . . cases like yours, it was better if there was no family contact while they worked on treatment.'

She smiles ruefully. *'They told me that, too. I thought they'd made it up. I thought they were avoiding telling me that you didn't want to see me. Do you think you would have come, if it had been allowed?'*

The guilt rushes in again. *'Of course. I often rang to see how you were getting on. Didn't you know?'*

She shakes her head. *'Look, like I said before, I'm not bringing any of this up to make you feel bad. I understand now. I would understand if you said you hadn't wanted to see me.'*

She's sitting cross-legged on the floor, her back against the sofa, her loose hair half covering her face. I'm holding my breath because I think she's about to admit what she did. She had never done that before, not directly – not even during that last visit. But then she veers off again.

'It was when I got to the ashram that I truly began to understand,' she says. *'All the anger – and I had been angry for a long time – just melted away. I was taught about forgiveness, about letting things go. We meditated every morning, and each time that ball of grief and hate was smaller and then one day it had just . . . gone. I felt the last of it disperse through the pores of my skin. I felt as light as air. There's no anger in me now, no negative feelings. I'm clean, Maman. I was reborn that day.'*

'Ashram?' I say stupidly. *'What ashram? You went to India?'*

She laughs. *'To Spain. Up in the mountains in the north. We*

I draw my hand back. '*You forgive me?*'

She smiles again. '*I do. I forgive you.*'

'*Doesn't it have to work the other way, too? Don't I have to forgive you?*'

Something flashes across her face, too quick to interpret. Then she nods. '*You're right. I ask your forgiveness too. I'm sorry I wasn't the daughter you wanted.*'

'*No, hang on.*' My voice cracks with emotion. '*That's not asking forgiveness. If you don't mean it, you shouldn't say it.*'

She puts her head on one side. '*But it's true. It wasn't until Emma that you wanted to be a mother, that you felt you were a mother.*'

I shake my head. '*No, no, that's not how it was at all. You don't know. If you had seen me when they put you in my arms for the first time . . . I wanted so badly to meet you while I was pregnant, and when I did, the feeling was instant. It was a fierce kind of love, like nothing I'd ever got close to before. It* is *a fierce kind of love. Nothing changes that.*'

She rescues me then, returning to the subject of the ashram: the wildflowers that grew on the mountains even as snow lingered on the peaks; the guitar chords someone taught her to play; the profound peace the place helped her find. I want to believe in it. Part of me does.

Slowly, fatigue begins to overtake me. It's so warm in the salon. Her voice too, which has deepened and softened with the years, is having a soporific effect.

'*Aren't you tired?*' I say.

'*Not really.*' She smiles sadly. '*I don't need much sleep, not since the Institut.*'

'Oh, Élodie.'

She shakes her head. '*No, I didn't mean it that way. It's ancient history, really. It's just that there was always something happening there at night, something to wake you up. I feel as though I did nothing more than cat-nap during those years.*'

I hang my head. I don't know what to say. She comes over and takes my hands. The physical contact, like yesterday's, is a shock.

'*Maman, you must understand. I'm grateful to you and Papa for sending me there, not resentful. They helped me. If I hadn't gone there, and then to the ashram, I wouldn't be cured.*'

'*Cured*,' I repeat. '*I mean, I can see you're different, of course I can.*' I can hear Morel's words in my head. *She could grow out of it.* There was an eighty per cent chance of it. But then he also said there was no cure.

It occurs to me that the only way I can know is to find out more about her. I gather my last reserves of energy and lean forward. '*Élodie, what else has happened to you?*'

'*I told you, I was in Spain and* —'

'*Not just the ashram. I mean, who have you been with, where were you before Spain, how did you come to be there at all? What has it been like for you all this time, without us* — *without your family?*' My voice breaks on the last word.

She turns up her palms. '*I will tell you everything, Maman, if you really want to know.*'

'*I do*,' I breathe. '*I do.*'

So she tells me about her life without us. I listen from the sofa with my eyes closed. After she left the Institut, she went south, hitching rides to the coast.

'I was always so cold in the north. It didn't feel like France to me. It wasn't home.'

She spent almost two years on the Côte d'Azur, working her way east towards Italy and then west again, as far as the Spanish border and then beyond it, to Roses, where Dalí lived.

'Everything was white and blue there. White fishing cottages, white sand in the calas – the little coves. Blue skies every day.'

'You always loved it by the sea.'

I open my eyes and she's smiling in the lamplight. 'You remember.'

I want to cry. 'Of course I remember.'

She worked just enough to live, never staying anywhere long, mostly waitressing. 'I always got good tips,' she says, and I smile, the tears receding again.

'I'm not surprised. Élodie?'

I open my eyes and she's moved closer, so that we're in touching distance now. I didn't hear her move. 'Tell me where else you went,' I say. 'Who you met.'

She sits back. 'I went to California once. Someone got me a passport. I went for the whole summer.'

That makes me sit up. 'You did? I never got there. I wanted to, once upon a time. What did you see there?'

'Oh, so much. I met a man. He had a house on stilts, looking out over one of the canyons.'

Her smile is another I don't know, sphinx-like. 'Tell me.'

'I met him in the desert, at a festival. He had a Mexican name but he was from LA. I asked him to take me to the Troubadour club. They weren't playing your music any more. It was all rock bands by then, but I wanted to go. I thought of you.'

'*How did you know?*' My voice is thick with emotion.

She gestures at the records stacked underneath the old player. '*I told you, I remember everything.*'

'*What happened to the man?*'

She shrugs. '*I left LA, went back to Spain. I liked to keep moving. I was always looking for something and not quite finding it. I think, really, I was just trying to get back here.*'

I let that land and settle. The silence stretches out. I still can't believe she's here. I'm so tired by now that I can't see straight. '*I think I'm going to have to go to bed. I'm sorry.*'

She nods. '*I'm not tired yet. Do you mind if I stay here for a while, have a last cigarette?*'

'*No, of course not.*' I go towards her but don't know what to do when I get there. She looks up expectantly and I stroke her hair, just briefly. Then I leave her smoking on her own. As I reach the stairs, the record turns itself over. It's the Beach Boys now.

The song that's always been hers starts playing as I reach the landing. 'Good Vibrations'. I sit down heavily on the top step, my hand clutching the banister, and as her cigarette smoke finds me I begin to cry again, harder this time, the sound drowned in the music.

*

The night passes without incident. I try your father again in the morning. To my surprise, he picks up on the third ring.

'Greg. At last.'

I don't know how to say it now I've got him. I glance

through the salon doors. Élodie is making you laugh on the terrace where you've just finished breakfast.

'Sylvie, are you there?'

'Élodie,' I push out the word, my voice cracking on the third syllable. 'She's here.'

He inhales sharply.

'Greg?'

'Élodie?' he says, voice oddly high with disbelief. I can hear him casting around for his cigarettes. 'She's with you at La Rêverie? Now?'

'Yes. She just . . . appeared. We came back from a day out and she was standing on the drive.'

He's silent again for a long moment, then starts speaking in a rush. 'Right, look, I'm on my own with the boys tonight. Nicole's mum has had a small stroke and they're really upset – they were with her when it happened – but I'll set off as soon as she's back. The roads will be clear. I should be with you by dawn.'

'Okay.' My mind has gone blank again. I twist the phone cord around my forefinger, tighter and tighter, watching as the tip turns red.

'Sylvie?'

'I'm still here.'

'How is . . . How does she seem?'

'Different,' I say, as I did to Camille. 'I don't know really. I can barely think straight.'

When I put the phone down, I don't know whether the thought of him coming makes me feel better or not. All I really feel is lightheaded and slightly seasick, which takes me straight back to being pregnant with her. If it were possible, I'd go upstairs and sleep for a couple of days.

'Mum, Élodie says she doesn't have anywhere to be for a while,' you inform me, when I emerge onto the terrace again. 'So she'll be able to stay longer.'

I sit down and pour myself some coffee. 'That's good,' I say carefully, the word so woefully inadequate that I could laugh. Now she's here, I can't imagine wanting her to be anywhere else. But it doesn't make her presence any easier.

Élodie shoots me a dazzling smile. 'You don't mind?'

'Of course she doesn't, do you, Mum?' You smile at both of us. 'This is your home too.'

'Maman?' Élodie says.

I nod. 'It is. It's your home. It never stopped being that.' I take a breath, rub my sore eyes. 'I managed to get hold of your father at last. He's driving down late tonight. He'll be with us by morning.'

'So it'll be all of us?' You can't keep the glee out of your voice.

'We will be four again,' says Élodie. *'En famille.'* She raises her cup and you scramble for your tumbler of juice to clink against it. 'I am very happy to be here with you. I have dreamt of it.'

I've dreamt of it too, so many times. Isn't there a theory that there are infinite parallel universes, a new one created every time we make a decision? I think of those endless alternatives, multiplying like a hall of mirrors: the ones where we hadn't risked coming back to France and the ones where we'd never left at all. I feel like I've slipped into one of the latter, dragging you with me. Soon Greg will be here, the slide into that other reality complete.

*

Martine turns up exactly on time for the viewing, the English couple squeezed into the back of her little Renault. She's tiny, with a sleek cap of dark red hair and black ballet shoes that must be child-sized. The Johnsons – Barbara and Keith – are a nice couple in their late fifties, her soft-spoken and faded, him trim and twinkly. With their old-fashioned manners, they remind me a little of Greg's parents, though these two are much more at ease with each other. I haven't seen Charles and Margaret in years; Greg takes you to visit them once a year, around Christmas.

'Martine said you live in England,' says Barbara, smiling. 'Is that right? Your accent is ever so good.'

'Thank you. And, yes, my daughter and I live in London. Her father is English, although he lives in Paris.'

Barbara looks as though she's going to ask why it worked out that way, but then thinks better of it. 'Isn't it sweltering?' she says instead. 'It was like an oven in that car. I thought I'd faint.'

'They're saying it's the worst heatwave for a decade,' Keith chimes in. 'The whole area's a tinderbox, and that's the parts that haven't caught fire already.'

I follow them as Martine leads the way around the house, just in case she's unsure about anything, though she seems confident enough. They exclaim over something in every room: first the old wallpaper and original shutters, then the wooden floors and high ceilings.

I'm about to go downstairs when Martine pops her head out to say she's going to take some decent photographs of the interior.

'While I do that, do you mind showing them the garden?'

I lead the way downstairs and out onto the terrace. The sun is blinding after the relative dimness of the house and Barbara digs in her handbag for sunglasses.

After they admire the pool, which I'd made you skim the usual leaves and insects off half an hour earlier, Keith asks about the barn.

'I'm after a workshop, see. It doesn't have to be anything fancy, just big enough to keep a couple of cars out of the elements. I restore vintage Jags and sell them on. Not to make money – it's just a hobby really.'

You intercept us on our way round there, smiling at the strangers, which is sweet of you because you don't want the house to be sold.

'How's it going, love?' you murmur to me in the old-man voice. 'Shall I put the kettle on? Make us all a nice cup of tea?'

I cover my mouth with my hand and you grin back at me. Barbara and Keith are not so unlike our pretend couple.

Though I'd rather you didn't, you follow us into the barn. It feels bigger than usual, perhaps because I'm viewing it through strangers' eyes. Although I don't like being in here, it's a relief for the eyes after the intense sunlight. Keith whistles as he takes in the space.

'Blimey, it must be twenty-five, thirty feet high.'

I see him notice the open-sided loft space in the back corner, a ladder leaning against it. 'Anything up there?'

'I doubt it. I haven't gone up in years.'

'Be careful, love,' Barbara calls, as he begins to climb. She rolls her eyes at me. 'He thinks he's thirty-five.'

I glance round for you but you're still hovering on the threshold. Your smile has gone now and you're pale under your new freckles. I was scared this would happen. I'm just about to ask if you're all right when Keith calls down.

'You had someone staying up here?'

'What do you mean?'

'There are clothes. And other bits.'

A wave of anxiety rises in me as he climbs down, Barbara steadying the ladder from the bottom. They want to see the terrace again and I can hardly say no but I want to go up that ladder and see for myself what's there. I look around again for you, but you've gone. There's no sign of you in the garden as we cross it to the steps either. The anxiety roils inside me again.

Martine is waiting for us on the terrace. *'I've got a good feeling about them,'* she says, nodding towards the couple, who are surveying the lawn, Keith making a sweeping gesture and Barbara smiling. *'You wait. I wouldn't be surprised if they're the ones.'*

'We love the house,' he says at the front door, after shaking my hand, 'but we'll need to go away and have a good think.'

'Of course,' I say distractedly, because I'm thinking about the barn loft and you disappearing so fast.

It seems to take for ever to manoeuvre them into Martine's car but then, finally, they're driving away, a cheery toot from the horn as they disappear down the drive.

I stand on the front step, paralysed with indecision. I want to check you're okay but I also want to go back to the barn and climb the ladder, reassure myself Élodie was telling the truth by the pool. That anything left is from when she would hide out there and I would lie awake, wondering if this were the night she'd burn the whole thing down with a careless or not-so-careless cigarette. I developed a fixation with it for a while; almost a phobia. Some nights I found myself padding through the dark house to the only window you could see the barn from, the tiny, net-covered square in the *souillarde*. It was almost as if I knew what would happen.

I give in to the urge to move, hurrying along the overgrown footpath that loops round the side of the house to the barn, quicker than the drive. In the scrub that lines it, the racket of the cicadas is like an assault. Sweat blooms at my hairline and under my arms. A hot runnel slides between my breasts.

It's quiet in the barn, the noises of outside cut off cleanly. I can hear my heart thudding in my ears. The metal of the ladder is cold. I can smell the iron under my clammy hands as I begin to climb, strong enough to taste, like blood from a bitten tongue.

It's dark at the top and I have to squint while my eyes adjust. What there is comes into focus slowly: a mound of clothes heaped on an old mattress, a plastic water bottle on its side and a cigarette packet, its lid ripped off. I scramble on to what is really just a glorified ledge, a glance back to the floor making me falter because, like you, I've never been very good with heights.

I pick through the clothes, looking for signs of recent occupation. But I'm just not sure. I can't be certain if the denim jacket, soft with wear, and a couple of sun-faded T-shirts are old or not, even if they're hers or not. I thought there would be no doubt – something I remember from the past, or else something that is definitively *not* hers – a man's overalls or boots, proof that a stranger had slept rough here for a time. Which is, perversely, a less alarming idea to me than the thought of Élodie hiding out here while we were in the house, unaware that all those uncanny feelings I was having about her being close by weren't so fanciful after all. That they were real. My eyes alight on the foil square of an empty condom wrapper. I snatch it up and turn it to the light to read the expiry date. 1998: five long years away. Surely it must be new.

And then an explanation occurs to me, and I curse myself for not thinking of it before. Perhaps all of it belongs to Luc. That was why I'd caught him hanging around. Maybe he was using this place, or had been, as somewhere to escape his mother's suffocating attentions. He could have been using it for years, filling the pool for himself, not us. I wondered if he'd ever brought those boys on mopeds back here for a party, or maybe a girl.

The denim jacket has something hard in the breast pocket and I slip my finger under the metal button. It's a lighter: the cheap disposable kind, made of clear purple plastic. I push down the wheel with the side of my thumb, and a flame sparks. I wonder who was the last person to do the same, and where they did it. I think about the *souillarde*'s scorched walls.

I find you in the salon, where you're sitting on the very edge of the armchair where Élodie had sat when she arrived, your hands clasped between your bare knees. I perch on the arm and that's when I see you're clutching your inhaler. I reach out to stroke your hair.

'What's set that off? Something in the barn?' I can't tell if my voice sounds natural or not.

I don't know what you've recalled, but I hope it's unformed, unspecific. An aversion to the barn that you don't understand, and may put down to something irrational and harmless. A fear of shadowy corners, of insects or rats.

There's still a wheeze in your chest; I can hear it clearly. You look back at me and your eyes are unfocused. I know it's not me you're seeing.

Before you, we had become a fractious three. Now, despite our best efforts not to, we end up forming two evenly split factions, Greg and I more unable to communicate than ever. It doesn't help that he was hard on you from the start, much stricter than he'd ever been with Élodie. I wonder sometimes if he's punishing you for not having the difficulties Élodie has. The unfairness of this occasionally makes me despise him.

Your wheezing starts when you're almost three, and I take you to the village doctor. It's a new one now, a woman, and she diagnoses you with asthma. She tells me that an attack can be triggered by lots of things: exercise, allergies, hay fever.

'*I wouldn't worry*,' she says briskly, writing a prescription with a gold-nibbed fountain pen that somehow speaks of a calm, ordered life. It briefly makes me want to swap places with her. '*It's probably something in the garden that's set it off, or something blowing over from the fields. You might try a foam pillow too. Feather allergies are common.*'

Back on the street, I take your hand and cross the road to the pharmacy. When I pull out my purse to pay, I see at the bottom of my bag the little notebook I'd intended to show the doctor. I'd changed my mind when she looked at the clock, just like old Dr Bisset would have done. Inside its pages, I've been keeping a log of all the times you get wheezy and I notice that any possible triggers for the attacks – I've looked this up in the library – simply don't correlate to times you've been in the garden. I'd swapped your old feather bolsters for foam pillows months ago; you were still getting wheezy.

What I have read about, but the doctor hasn't said, is that asthma can also be set off by strong emotions, especially in children. Laughter is apparently one of the commonest triggers of this type. With you, it isn't laughing I'm worried about.

Now I have the doctor's official diagnosis, I feel able to show Greg the logbook: my record of all the times your breathing has grown laboured, your little chest heaving, eyes wide and panicked as you look to me for help, unable to get any words out; the terrible rattling wheeze I've started hearing in my nightmares.

He takes one look at it and throws it on the table, where it lands in a ring of spilt wine, red soaking into the cover.

'What do you want me to do with this?' He stands up and shoves his chair back under the table so hard that the cutlery jumps on the plates. 'What do you want me to say?'

'I want you to back me up on this, Greg.'

'To who?'

'I don't know – maybe just to me. Maybe I need you

to actually sit down and listen to me properly for once, so that we can help her. What if we went to see Dr Morel again?'

He's been pacing as though he can't wait to leave the room. Now he strides to the door.

'I'm not discussing this again. You know what I think of his sinister little diagnosis. She's just a child. So she resents her little sister sometimes. What child who's been the only one for so long wouldn't?' His outward denial is almost a reflex now. He's been doing it for so long he doesn't know how else to be. The more I push, the more he resists.

He leaves five minutes later, not returning until dawn, when he comes in and starts packing for his next buying trip without a word.

'Oh, so you're running away again? What a surprise.' I can't help it. Tears and pleading never work with him because they make him feel guilty, which he hates, so I'm now reduced to this kind of bitter jibing. He doesn't reply and is gone by seven, a day earlier than necessary, adolescent wheel-spin on the lane as he drives away.

It's always hurt that Greg won't support me when it comes to Élodie. Now I start doing the same thing to him if he tells you off, and the shaming thing about it isn't my own hypocrisy but the pleasure I get from undermining him just as he has me so many times. A continuous tally of what's unfair click-clicks in my head, an endless cataloguing and calculating of his crimes, Élodie's crimes, the injustices suffered by you, by me. Click, click, click. And because my memory is so much better than

Greg's – because I remember everything, going back years – I begin to win the arguments I've previously lost because I've been too upset by the confrontation to fight back. Now, at least when it comes to our marriage, I find it difficult to care as much as I once did.

'I want us to find our way back to each other, Sylvie,' he says, on the odd occasion he gets maudlin drunk, rather than the passive-aggressive kind I'm more used to. And I look at him, my face no doubt shuttered and unmoved, because I can't fathom how we can ever cross such vast distances to reunite. It feels much too late, and like too enormous an effort. I can feel myself turning cold, closed off to everything but you.

1993

You're drained after all the Ventolin you've taken since the barn and go to lie down in your room. When I put my head round the door half an hour later, you're asleep with your headphones on. On the floor is a half-written postcard to one of your school-friends. I would never normally read something not meant for me, but worry trumps privacy. Who knows what you might admit to a friend rather than your mother? But your looping, aqua-blue script gives nothing away. Surprisingly, it doesn't even mention Élodie. I don't know what to make of that.

To distract myself from puzzling over you, and where Élodie might have gone, I station myself in the smallest bedroom, which became something of a dumping ground in the years after Élodie was born. I make myself start going through the clutter, deciding what to keep and what to hand over to a man whose name Martine has given me: he has a stall at the local *brocante* market. With every item I label, a little voice says, *This is it: the end of an era.* I suppose I shouldn't be surprised: this is the break-up of my family home, where you and I both took our first steps, spoke our first words. Where Élodie did too. I've been at it a while when I hear an engine too high-pitched and whiny to be a car. I go to the window just in time to see a girl clamber off the back of a moped. It's Élodie. She hasn't been wearing a helmet and her hair has been whipped by the dry breeze into long, tangled waves. The man she's with takes off his helmet then, shaking his long fringe into place. It's Luc.

He reaches out to grab her hand but she dances away. She blows him a kiss as she runs up the drive towards the house. I hear the front door open and bang shut but I don't move, watching Luc for a moment longer. As he puts his helmet back on and revs the engine, dejection weighs down his movements – I can see that even from here. I think about the clothes and condom wrapper in the barn.

I expect Élodie to come upstairs but she doesn't, and I force myself to carry on with my task. I've lost concentration now, and soon I'm back at your door, seeing if you've woken up. The bed's empty, the covers pushed back as though you've left in a hurry. I run downstairs but no one's there.

At the top of the terrace steps, I listen for voices, which carry easily in air that is both syrupy and smoky. I don't want to be seen to be so obviously monitoring you both, which would annoy and confuse you. But as I hover there, I can't let it go. I spent four years here in a state of hyper-vigilance over you and anything much less, especially after the barn episode earlier, feels like negligence.

I cross the lawn, still hoping to hear you, but it's quiet;

dead quiet. Today is apparently too hot for the birds. Even the cicadas have fallen silent. I creep closer to the glint of the water, just visible through the trees, ready to retreat if I see movement. But there's nothing when I get there except your damp towel, abandoned on a lounger. The water ripples slightly, as though I've missed you by seconds, which perhaps I have.

Almost without conscious thought, I race round to the barn again but it's empty, the door still standing ajar from earlier. *At least it's not that.* I wipe my forehead with the back of my hand because the sweat's running freely off me now. Where would she have taken you? I go back to the house but it's still empty when I call your name, the echo of my voice too loud.

An hour later I'm ready to ring the police. I've checked Élodie's room and her battered rucksack is still there. Nothing of yours is missing. It doesn't seem irrational to me that I've jumped to abduction but I suppose it would to anyone else so I decide to wait another ten minutes before I raise the alarm. I know you're not a tiny child any more but I can't help it – I keep seeing those awful CCTV images that had haunted the news in February: two boys in a Liverpool shopping centre, the smaller one's hand so trustingly in the other's, as he was led away into oblivion. It had made me shake so hard that I'd had to take one of the pills I'd kept from the last months in France.

The self-imposed time limit is almost up when I hear your voice out on the drive and rush to the front door.

You're talking animatedly to her, turning to check

that she hasn't grown bored. Both of you are holding carrier bags from the small supermarket in the village. Relief washes over me for a blissful second before anger crowds in.

'Where have you been?' I shout from the front step, though it's obvious. I see Élodie glance down at the bag she's holding as if to say as much and it makes me even angrier.

'How dare you take her off to the village without telling me?' I stride up to her. It's strange because I've railed at her so many times in the past and I've always had to look down. This is the first time we've ever been eye to eye in an argument.

'Mum, what are you doing?' You're outraged, dropping your bag to the dusty road. 'We just went to get some stuff to make a cake. A cake for you. It was supposed to be a surprise. Why are you being so mean?'

Élodie doesn't say anything. We're still looking at each other.

'You don't know anything, Emma,' I say, not taking my eyes off your sister. 'You have no idea about anything that went on here when you were little. If you did . . .'

'How can I know?' Your voice is choked and high and I know you're on the verge of tears. 'You've never told me *anything*.'

'I'm sorry, Maman,' Élodie says. *'I –'*

'Why do you keep calling me that? You called me Sylvie in that last year, do you remember? Never Maman. You knew I didn't like it, that it made me look so cold in front of other people.' It's

liberating to slide back into the old language of our fights, the words flying out of me.

'I hate you for being like this,' you cry. 'And stop talking in French as though I'm not even here.' You storm past me into the house, the bag of shopping forgotten. For once, I don't even consider going after you.

'*That man who came to look at the house found some clothes in the barn loft earlier,*' I continue. '*Some other things too. I wondered if they were Luc's. Have you two been hiding up there together? Do you know what I think? I think you've been hanging around for a while, longer than you said by the pool, watching us on the sly before you were ready to announce yourself. I think it was you who set a fire and then put it out in the souillarde. You knew it would bring me back.*'

Still she says nothing. I watch as a single tear rolls down her cheek.

'*You don't want me here, do you?*' she says, so softly that I automatically lean towards her to catch the words. '*You never did.*'

'*But I did!*' I cry, a beat late because now I'm closer she smells of smoke, but it's cigarettes, I tell myself. It must be cigarettes. '*I so wanted you. But then it got impossible to keep you here, to manage your behaviour. Maybe you're sorry for what you did now. Maybe you've changed. But how can I know that? You come here out of the blue and charm Emma, like you've always been able to charm anyone when it suited you, and you know I can't tell her the truth because it will break her heart. How can I ever tell her that you wanted her gone?*'

'*I didn't, I never . . . It was an accident. I never meant . . .*'

'*You think I don't want to believe that? I want it more than*' *anything. You're my daughter, I'm your mother. I love you whatever you did. But you must be able to see how difficult it is for me to take you at your word when, as far as I know, you've never done anything by accident in your life.'*

We continue to stare at each other, faces inches apart. I'm breathing hard, my hands curled into fists, and I look down to see that hers are too, though she unclenches them as soon as I notice. I watch as different expressions cross her face like clouds and I can't honestly say which are real and which have been rehearsed in a mirror: deep, profound sadness or something very like it, then cold fury, then blank exhaustion, which, as the last of my anger ebbs away, looks exactly how I feel.

I don't know how to navigate this and I'm so terrified of making a mistake I won't ever be able to take back – not just in terms of you but Élodie, too. Everything I do and say feels critical, like a surgeon easing a scalpel past arteries ready to bleed out. I can feel how easy it would be to lose you both. I've come so close before.

When I go back inside and into the salon, you're shoving a cassette into the tape deck. And when you turn to me, hovering in the doorway, you look as hostile as I've ever seen you.

1983

I am at the hospital visiting my mother, who has been diagnosed with advanced heart disease. I have been driving back and forth to Toulouse to see her since before Christmas, buckling you into your car seat each and every time because I'm the only person I trust to look after you.

On the way back from taking you to the toilet, Maman's doctor catches my eye and beckons me into a small, overheated room. He tells me she probably won't last much longer. Though he hasn't yet said anything to her, she seems to know this intuitively, asking me when I get back to her bedside if I would mind going to pick up her rosary from the flat she still shares with Aunt Mathilde.

Outside the plate-glass window at the end of the ward, the night is bearing down hard on the day, though it's not yet four o'clock. Machines hum and beep; nurses glide past on rubber-soled shoes. I sit on a plastic chair moulded for someone wider than me and know that I will soon be an orphan. The existence of my own family – Greg, Élodie, you – doesn't make this any less frightening.

Maman regards me anxiously, even apologetically,

and at first I assume it's because of all the driving she knows I'm having to do in order to see her. She never learnt to drive and has always viewed it as an enormous, stressful undertaking. But it's not that.

'*I should have stayed,*' she says. '*I should have been there when you needed me most. I'm sorry, Sylvie.*'

I tell her it doesn't matter, that she has nothing to apologize for, but her hands reach for mine across the starch-stiff sheets, stroking them tremulously. It's such a familiar feeling from childhood, but the bones of her hands feel sharper now, the skin like fine old paper.

'*I knew something was wrong,*' she says, unable to let it go, though I shush her. '*I remember when she was only three, maybe four, and you asked me if I thought she was all right, if I could remember you or Camille being like that. You asked if I thought it was just a stage she was going through, and I said yes.*'

Tears course down her cheeks, and I wipe them away gently.

'*I'm sorry, chérie. I was a coward.*'

'*No, no. You mustn't say that.*'

But she keeps on, and I let her because she's so agitated; because this is an apology stretching back years. She needs to say it before she dies, which she does a few weeks later, just after Élodie turns fourteen. She does it quietly and without fuss, much as she lived.

In the bleak, purposeless days after the funeral, a strange and secret part of me hopes that she will now be returned to La Rêverie and to me – that I will have a sense of her in the kitchen behind me, or in the chair she liked to doze in at the end of the day when Camille and I were growing up. But it isn't like that. It's the very opposite, in fact: a more acute sense of loneliness than I have ever experienced before. You're my great comfort in this, of course – my only comfort, or so it feels.

'If you're not careful you'll suffocate her,' your father says, one sullen day in late March. He's packing to go away again. I lean against the window as I watch him move around the room, opening drawers and picking things up, and I can feel the chill fingers of the mistral at my back. La Rêverie was built to keep out the heat of summer and is never really warm enough when the temperature dips and the wind gets up, the old radiators ticking and trickling like empty stomachs.

'Can't you just be glad that I'm so close to my daughter?'

'*Our* daughter.'

'You take no notice of her. She tried to show you one of her paintings the other day and you barely glanced at it. She looks so like you too, Greg. I'm amazed you're not more interested.'

'What's that supposed to mean?'

I don't bother answering. Apart from the dense pit of anxiety that always yawns at the root of me, I feel entirely flat and numb, as if nothing could penetrate. My mother has been dead for exactly two weeks.

'Sylvie, I'm talking to you.'

'What?'

He sighs. 'You just want me to hurry up and go, don't you?'

It's true. I'm planning to get into bed once he's gone.

I've just put you down for your afternoon nap so I'll have at least an hour to lie in silence and think about my mother, gaze fixed on the dull white sky outside. Élodie is out and hasn't said when she will be back. I'm not entirely sure who she's with and that feels wrong, but it also feels entirely beyond me to do anything about it. Besides, Élodie can take care of herself. She always has.

Greg has not long driven off when Laurent knocks at the kitchen door. I can see the top of his head from the bedroom window. I wonder whether he's been watching from an upstairs window at his own house, waiting for Greg's car to go past.

I hesitate before going downstairs to let him in. I want to be on my own. But then I think how nice it might be to spend some time with a man who isn't waiting to challenge or catch me out. In a peculiar way, and despite our romantic past, Laurent has become the closest I can get to a parent: someone who has known me for almost as long as I've known myself, and who feels something close to unconditional or at least familial love for me.

I lead him into the salon. He's brought a bottle of good red wine with him and opens it to breathe.

'I wanted to check you're all right. She's only been gone a little while.' He lays a large, tentative hand on mine, completely covering it.

I lean my head against his shoulder, knowing that I'm breaking one of our unspoken rules, which I began to enforce when I returned from Paris with Greg and found Laurent engaged to Annette.

As the wine begins to work, the effort of holding myself together finally starts to catch up with me. Laurent puts on some music – something classical: a piano played in a minor chord – and I allow myself to cry as I haven't yet, not even at the funeral. And it's such a relief, and I am so grateful to him, that eventually I sit up, clamber into his lap and begin to kiss him.

I don't really expect him to tell me to stop and he doesn't. It's a nice kiss – a comfortable kiss, the angles and sensations of it completely familiar, as though we never stopped. I remember then what I knew when I applied for university in another country without telling him: that I love him much more than I want him. And that my wanting him – what there is of that – is really about how much he wants me. It's a perverse kind of egotism and suddenly I'm appalled by myself.

I get up and, for a split second before he opens his eyes, his face is naked with longing.

'*I'm so sorry, Laurent. We shouldn't do this.*'

'*Salut.*'

The voice, melodic and rich, makes both of us swing round. Élodie stands in the doorway, a smile playing on her lips. Her hair is loose, like it always is, gold and caramel rippling over her shoulders.

'*How long have you been there?*' I say, voice sharp.

She twirls a length of her hair as her eyes dart between us. Laurent, who is hopeless at deception, looks at his feet. I know the expression on her face so well – I've been familiar with it since she was a tiny child. She's weighing things up, working out how this new situation can best serve her. She's got better at hiding it over the years, but I can still spot it.

'*Élodie? I'm talking to you.*' Being in the wrong makes me sharper than I've a right to be.

A small cry sounds from upstairs. You've woken from your nap and want to come down, your hand reaching up to rattle the handle. I feel for the key in my pocket and, without looking at Laurent or your sister, head for the stairs to unlock the door and let you out.

Laurent has gone by the time I come down with you in my arms, though you're getting too heavy for me to carry you. You're still sleepy, your cheeks hot and pink, your eyes unfocused. I love it when you're like this, curled around me, your head lolling and heavy, like a rose on its stalk. In the kitchen I sit you down on the table and give you some weak grenadine. You swing your legs as you drink.

'I bet you're hungry too, aren't you, *ma petite*?'

You nod and yawn, making me yawn too.

I feel slightly intoxicated from the wine and what just happened with Laurent, as well as Élodie having witnessed it. I move around the kitchen on automatic pilot, peeling a banana to slice, and picking out a couple of the tiny plum tomatoes you love, cutting them lengthways so you can't choke on them.

It's only as I reach for a plate from the draining board that I see her. She's sitting on the stool in the corner. She's been there the whole time, watching me without saying a word.

'*Merde, Élodie, you frightened me.*'

She stretches like a cat, lifting her arms and arching her back. '*Laurent left.*'

'*I gathered that.*'

'*Why were you doing that with him?*'

I carry on slicing fruit. '*Not now.*'

'*Why not now?*'

She hops down from the stool and sidles over. Beneath the perfumed oil she has taken to putting in her hair, she smells of something else. I can't quite disentangle the different scents, but it's something earthy, almost sour.

I'm just about to ask her when she picks up the uncut half of the banana and takes a bite. I watch her wander back to the stool. Your eyes, like saucers, don't move from her because you've been fascinated by Élodie from your earliest days. Even when she makes you cry you never take your eyes off her.

'*Where have you been today?*'

'*Around. Does it matter?*'

'*Yes, it matters because I'm your mother and I'm asking you where you spent the day.*'

'*I went to Marseille.*'

I stop what I'm doing. '*Marseille?*'

'*Oui.*'

'*That's over a hundred kilometres away. Who with?*'

'*No one.*'

I can feel my temper beginning to fray, as it always does. My mother has just died, I want to scream. My mother has just died and you want to play these stupid games.

285

'Did you hitchhike again?'

She shrugs.

'You know your father and I don't like you doing that. It's dangerous. Élodie, are you listening to me?'

I hate the tone I always use with her, flint-hard and shrewish. I'm not like that with anyone else, even Greg. She has the knack of bringing out the worst in me, though I feel guilty even thinking in these terms, as her parent. Still, I can't help believing our relationship and our ages are irrelevant sometimes: a pair of magnets that were always destined to repel. Mother and daughter, adult and child, but also equals, forever pitted against each other.

'Laurent looked like this when he left,' she says, pulling the upside-down mouth she did as a child when she was pretending to be upset. She's moved on to different methods now. These days, if Greg is there, and one of us has crossed her, or refused her something she wants, she weeps – big tears that well up in those mismatched eyes and slide prettily down her cheeks. What is it they say in English? *Don't turn the waterworks on.* That's exactly what it looks like: no more emotion than an opened tap, though Greg is taken in every time. He finds her crying almost unbearable to watch. The first teardrop has scarcely rolled off her chin before he is by her side, his thumb brushing away the tears tenderly, his wallet out if money is what she's after.

'Poor Laurent,' she says now.

I ignore her, popping a tiny tomato half into your mouth. You like holding them on your tongue, waiting until they've warmed up before biting down.

'*Does Papa know about him, Sylvie? Sylvie, Sylvie, Sylvie, Sylvie, Sylvie. Are you listening to me, Sylvie? Tu m'écoutes? Tu m'écoutes?*'

She echoes my own nagging words – *Are you listening, Élodie?* – but the sing-song tone is her own, and it grates on every nerve. '*Tu m'écoutes? Tu m'écoutes? Tu m'écoutes?*'

'For God's sake, shut up!'

Your bottom lip begins to tremble because you hate any conflict, even when it isn't to do with you. In contrast, Élodie always seems invigorated by it. Her goading or defiance makes her hard and bright, like a diamond, cutting through all that hippie lassitude she affects when it pleases her, her eyes suddenly alert, and her mouth twisting as though she's trying not to laugh or cry out. Fighting is the only time the two of us truly engage with each other, to the exclusion of everyone else, even you.

'*Sylvie, Sylvie, Sylvie, Sylvie!*' Her voice grows louder each time.

You put your hands over your ears and begin to cry in earnest.

'*Ça suffit, Élodie!*' I feel myself give in to my own anger in a hot, blissful rush. I storm over and start to pull her off the stool. She's only half a head shorter than me now, and almost as strong. Feeling her resistance makes me pull harder. I've almost prised her off when she goes heavy and limp, and because she's jammed her feet behind the bar, her full weight barrels into me. Both of us crash to the stone floor. You begin to scream with terror as I struggle to get out from under her. The physical intimacy is a shock – it's rare we touch at all.

287

I realize then what it is she smells of. I scramble to my feet and look down at her, still sprawled on the floor.

'*You're stoned.*' I've always hated the heady herbal smell of cannabis.

'*Papa does it sometimes.*'

'*I don't care what he does. You're only fourteen.*'

She stands up and tries to push past me but I get hold of her arm. With my other hand, I start patting the pockets of her jeans.

She stands motionless while I search her, eyes dull now. She's retreated into herself again, spark tamped out.

There's nothing on her but a few coins and one of my lipsticks, which I put into my own pocket.

'*Up to your room,*' I hiss in her ear. '*I don't want to see you again tonight.*'

For once she goes without a fight.

In the morning, when she fails to appear at breakfast, I go upstairs to find her gone, the windows open and creaking in the breeze. She's done this before: clambering out and dropping to the top of the shutter below. It's dangerous but possible, if you've got the nerve, and Élodie always has the nerve. I go over to secure the windows so they won't bang and it's then I notice the scorch marks on the wall, the jungle animals I painted when I was pregnant with her now burnt away in places.

Perhaps the pattern of it is random – Greg certainly thinks so when he comes back and I show him. And it's true that human eyes will find faces in anything. But to me, already uncomfortable in the room – I always feel

I'm trespassing there – I see it immediately: the mouth a howl, the eyes round and staring.

I don't want to think about what it might mean, but I can't help wondering what your sister might have in store for us next.

All I want to do is go downstairs and ring my mother. I know exactly what she would say to calm me down, but when I whisper the same words aloud it isn't the same. It doesn't work at all. I sit on the floor outside Élodie's room and cry in silence so you won't hear me. It only makes me feel worse because, for the first time, I truly understand that I will never be able to speak to her again.

1993

I get into bed that night without bothering to brush my teeth. The tension in the house is palpable though I've apologized to you and Élodie for losing my temper. Your sister hugged me in response, the unexpected physical contact winding me, but you remained aloof and in the salon for the rest of the day, 'Smells Like Teen Spirit' playing over and over.

I don't expect to sleep – I assume I'll replay the exchange that took place on the drive over and over again – but in fact I must drop off immediately. The next thing I know the room is entirely in darkness, the moon gone but dawn still hours away. The music has finally been turned off.

Though the windows are opened wide to catch the smallest sliver of breeze, the air is entirely still, as if the room has been hermetically sealed. The only sign it hasn't been is the faint tang of smoke. I try to hear something, anything – a solitary car out on the road, a mosquito's whine – but there's only the ringing of my own ears. I panic for a moment, in case I've been somehow deafened as I slept, rendered incapable of hearing if you were in trouble, but then I sit up, and along with the internal banging of my heart, I can also hear my own panicky breaths.

Something must have woken me. I'd been fathoms-deep in dreams a minute before. The top sheet is tangled around my legs and I kick it off. The temperature doesn't seem to have dropped even a degree. If anything, the press of darkness makes it feel even hotter. My cotton T-shirt is damp against my skin.

I get up and tiptoe to the door to listen. Still nothing. Then something – instinct or experience – draws me to the window and the gap in the shutters. My eyes have adjusted by now so I see her immediately, ethereal in gauzy white, hair a broad, waving ribbon down her back. She's standing on the terrace, facing the rest of the garden.

I don't know how long I watch her but she remains entirely motionless and the effect is uncanny, as though she is frozen in time, like I'm looking at a photograph. To a degree, we are all unknowable; our most private thoughts and desires would shock the people we're closest to. But Élodie? She had always taken this to another level. There were never any givens. As far as knowing what she's thinking out there, I might as well be a total stranger, learning from scratch.

I'm just about to move away when she begins to descend the steps, her nightdress in the gloom making it seem as though she's gliding, as though there truly is a ghost at La Rêverie.

She walks to the middle of the lawn and lies down on her back, stretching her arms and legs out so that with her head she forms a five-pointed star. A pentacle. I'd forgotten but she went through a phase of this when she was ten or eleven. I'd watched her then as I'm watching now, astonished at her ability to remain still for so long. Sometimes I got close enough to see that even her eyes didn't blink.

Then I remember something else and it makes my stomach turn over, my fingernails pushing into the soft old paint of the windowsill. She used to do it as an adolescent when she was angry, when she'd been refused something, or told off. Before that phase she had raged, slamming drawers and cupboards so hard they would bounce open again. And, of course, in the earliest years she'd screamed in that terrible flat monotone that could draw the whole village square's attention in seconds. It was awful, but when she stopped – when she learnt that these dramatic protests weren't ultimately paying off – she internalized the fury until there was no sign of it on the surface. An incredible feat for a child and, to me, much more sinister than anything that had gone before.

*

Greg arrives when it's still early, about six o'clock, and although I'd witnessed Élodie go to bed from the garden a few hours before, I hadn't managed to get back to sleep.

I run down the stairs, hoping to get there before he knocks and wakes you both, but he's already letting himself in. I forgot he still had a key.

'She hasn't gone?' he says, by way of greeting. 'I haven't missed her?'

I shake my head and point upstairs. 'They're both asleep. Let's go into the kitchen. I'll make coffee.'

Close up, he looks tired but otherwise well: face lightly tanned and hair recently cut. His blue shirt – blue: he'd always worn blue because he knew it suited him – was more expensive than the ones he used to pick up in Monoprix. It was pressed, too.

'What did you tell Nicole and the boys?'

'The truth – well, to Nicole at least. I said my daughter had been found. That I had to go to her. She knows everything.'

'Everything?'

He lights up and takes an irritable drag. 'Christ, Sylvie, I've driven through the night and you're already interrogating me. Haven't we got more important things to discuss? What have you told Emma?'

'She knows some of it. Élodie said it was her fault that we let Emma think she was dead – that that was what she let everyone think. That she was the one to push us away.'

An urge to pour a large drink eddies through me. This is the effect your father had on me in the last years of our marriage. Neither of us seemed able to be anything but the worst of ourselves when the other was around. Divorce is not just what happens when you grow to dislike your husband or wife. It's as much about no longer wanting to spend time with the version of yourself that comes out when you're with them. I can't think now when I was last on my own with him: all my dealings with him are to do with you these days. To be alone with him here seems to double the strangeness. I feel wistful and anxious and irritable all at once.

'I want to see her,' he says.

'Let her sleep for now.'

He sighs and fiddles with the matchbook he used to light his cigarette. I think of the barn, and what I found, but decide not to share my suspicions that Élodie might have been here longer than she's admitting.

'So what has she told you then, about where she's been all this time?'

I rub my eyes. 'She's been living in a commune in Spain. Apparently, she's on a journey of self-actualization.' I raise an eyebrow. *This is your legacy*, the eyebrow says. *You were the one who bought into all that when we were young.* 'Before that, she was travelling around.'

He doesn't say anything as I pour the coffee and fetch milk from the fridge.

'And what about Emma? What does she think about it all? Did she believe Élodie's explanation?'

'She's – I don't know. She's excited, obviously, and still shocked, I think. She watches Élodie like she's expecting her to disappear in a puff of smoke. But she's also quite . . .'

'What?'

'I don't know. Not herself. Distracted, glazed over somehow. Difficult, too. Her asthma's got worse since we've been here. I don't think she's telling me things.'

'What sort of things?'

'Things she's remembered from then. The barn made her anxious yesterday. Why else would it unless she's remembered something?'

I turn to pick up the coffee pot and, as I do, the kitchen around me jumps and judders, like a tape that's been rewound and paused too many times. For a moment, though I know exactly *where* I am, I don't quite know *when*. I look down at my trembling hands, the skin fractionally more crêped now I'm in my forties, and for once I'm glad to be ageing. Anything not to be back then.

*

The reunion between father and daughter is not what I would have expected. The two of you come down together about nine, Greg and I already halfway down a second pot of coffee. You spot him first.

'Dad!' You launch yourself at him and he hugs you tight, but he's already looking over your shoulder. It's how it always was — except that suddenly it's because Élodie is the one hanging back rather than you. He looks surprised and then, as she makes no move to approach or even say anything, increasingly discomfited. She looks to me instead, as if asking for permission, and I find myself nodding. Only then does she go to him, accepting a hug and giving him a peck on each cheek in return. I don't know what to take from this, but then I remember what she said before she went to swim. *He was never there, was he?* Was she demonstrating solidarity?

296

'Élodie,' he breathes, when she stands back. His eyes search her face. 'Look at you, all grown-up now.' His voice wavers on the last word and I see him struggle to contain his emotion. Élodie reaches out, rather stiffly, to pat his hand and I can't help gaping at how odd this is. When she was a girl she would entwine herself around Greg like a cat, her fingers in his hair, her head tucked into the cleft under his chin.

'I thought of you every day,' he says now, his voice steadier. 'When my little boys were born – did Sylvie tell you about them? – I couldn't stop thinking about the fact that their big sister was out there somewhere but I didn't know where. It brought back all the memories of you being born, my beautiful daughter.'

I glance at you, a middle child at a stroke, and your eyes are large and forlorn. I go over to put my arm around you but Élodie is already there, pulling you close.

'I have got my little sister back,' she says, smiling down at you so that your face lights again, her slim finger dancing over the necklace you're wearing: *her* necklace. Of course I haven't told you that the reason you found it behind the chest of drawers is because I threw it across the room at Greg, ten years earlier, on the most frightening day of my life.

'It's amazing to think I have little brothers too,' says Élodie. She beams at Greg and his body relaxes instantly.

By lunchtime, we have entered much more familiar territory. I find myself serving you all, like a mute waitress. It's so hard to fight the old patterns and rhythms. I've even laid out an age-softened, scalloped-edged tablecloth that belonged to my mother, an idea that hadn't occurred to me when it was just the two of us. Perhaps all this effort, this *presentation*, is to create the illusion of control.

As I fetch and carry from the kitchen, you and your father are patently entranced by Élodie. He can't take his eyes off her. He's too eager, too quick to laugh, and bizarrely I find myself feeling sorry for him. As charming as she is, there's still a reserve in her manner towards him.

'We'll go to the village tonight for dinner,' Greg is saying, as I go back outside with a bowl of peaches. He's mopping his plate too thoroughly with a piece of bread and it surprises me to realize that he's nervous. 'Emma, did you say there's a good pizza place now?'

'Yes, they're huge. Mum, it's really nice there, isn't it?'

I lay a hand on your hair as I put down the bowl. You've forgiven me for yesterday, too thrilled with the family reunion to hold a grudge.

*

The afternoon wears on, the temperature rising with the cicadas' chorus. I watch as Élodie continues effortlessly to seduce you and your father. Or perhaps my eyes are so jaundiced I can't tell what's real from what's not. Perhaps there really is no artifice any more. Perhaps she's simply charismatic, with no ulterior motive. I have no idea.

You sit cross-legged in front of her as she plaits your hair into cornrows. There isn't a peep from you as she pulls on your scalp, though I can barely help you put it up into a ponytail for school without you yelping and complaining. You're dressed in something of hers again – a stretchy red bandeau top cut too low – and you're also wearing mascara and something shiny on your lips. It's impossible not to be reminded of the incident with the doll, the felt-tip scribble on your face. It feels like a more sophisticated version of the same game. But when I search your face for signs of strain, like I saw in the barn, a fragment of memory catching the light, there's nothing. You're glowing with pleasure.

'*Tu es très jolie*,' Élodie exclaims, when she's finished, and kisses you on the top of your head. You blush, your eyes shining, and I feel unease flex inside me, like a cramp. My instincts are still telling me to separate the two of you, just in case, but you'll hate me for it if I do.

With Greg there, I take the opportunity to retreat inside and crawl back into bed. I don't know what else to do with myself and the repeated nights of broken sleep are beginning to make me feel spaced-out but no less anxious, my body fried from the relentless pumping of adrenalin.

*

I'm woken a couple of hours later by Olivier ringing. Luckily I'm the one to catch it; the three of you must still be outside. I say luckily, as if I don't have every right to speak to another man. The pull of the past is hard to resist, though, and I've just been dreaming of London in the late sixties, when Greg and I were new. It's a small act of treachery from my unconscious mind when I least need it.

'*Is everything okay?*' Olivier says tentatively. '*I didn't want to disturb you before.*'

'*I'm sorry, I should have rung. I can explain, but I'm not sure I'm up to it right now. My ex-husband is here and I –*'

'*You don't have to explain. It's none of my business. I just wanted to check you were all right.*'

'*Thank you. You always seem to say the right thing. Look, you could come round but . . .*'

'*It's fine . . . It would be good to see you sometime. Just know that I'm here, if you want to talk. There's something else, too.*'

I clutch the receiver tighter, sure he's going to tell me something about Élodie, something I don't want to know.

'*It's good news. The English couple want to make you an offer.*'

I can't think of a reply.

'*Sylvie, are you still there?*'

'*Oui.*'

'*Have you changed your mind about the sale?*' I think he sounds hopeful.

'*No, it's not that. I just didn't expect them to make a decision so quickly.*'

'*Don't you want to know how much they've offered?*'

'*Oh. Yes, of course I do. Sorry, I'm just taken aback.*'

'*It's fine. I didn't expect it to happen so quickly either. But they loved it apparently, the husband particularly. I guess they saw the magic after all. They've offered a hundred thousand francs under the asking price. That's about ten thousand in sterling, more or less. They didn't know about one of the taxes, they said, or they'd have stumped up all of it.'*

I stare out of the salon door to the terrace beyond. I can see the spear-headed parasol pines beyond, motionless in the dense air. They look almost black against the azure sky.

'*I see,*' I say vaguely. '*That seems fair.*'

'*Do you want me to tell Martine you agree or would you rather hold out for more? It might be worth trying.*'

He's speaking carefully, as though to someone slow-witted. I push my thumbnail into the flesh of my bare thigh hard enough to make a deep, sickle-shaped indentation. I imagine leaving La Rêverie behind for good, and even as sadness creeps in, a weight eases off me, the sensation so tangible it feels literal, a great dark bird lifting from my shoulders into the air.

'*No, no. Please tell them yes. And thank you. To Martine too.*'

We say our goodbyes and it's strange because I feel like I haven't seen him in weeks.

I'm just about to hang up when a last question spills out. '*Olivier, before you go, what are people saying in the village?*'

He sighs. '*They're saying that the Durand girl is back from the dead.*' An awkward silence falls between us for the first time.

After that, I feel too unsettled to go back upstairs. I wander down to the pool to find that Luc has turned up and is apparently quite comfortable on a lounger, bottle of beer in hand. He and Greg are in conversation but Luc's eyes don't move from the water, where Élodie is swimming. As she gets out, she gifts him a smile, coquettish and knowing, and he gazes helplessly at her, eyes hungry.

You're watching them from under the oleander tree, your headphones on, gloss smeared on your lips again, and I realize you're old enough now to understand that look between them: halfway to being a promise.

1983

After Élodie catches me and Laurent kissing, I expect her to tell Greg as soon as he gets back. I'm so sure she'll do it that I've already been rehearsing excuses and explanations in my head. None are lies. It's true that Laurent caught me at a vulnerable moment; that I'm missing my mother terribly; that Greg is away too often when I need his support.

But even these reasons added up together aren't the whole truth. There's a part of me that acted quite deliberately. You aside, there are times when I simply want to eject out of my own life, and being caught cheating feels easier than sitting your father down to discuss divorce and custody. I think Laurent is a self-destruct button I've pushed so that Greg ends it for me.

But if subconsciously I want Élodie to open that can of worms for me, then I'll probably be out of luck. I should know that she never does what's predictable, what's expected of her. That has never been her style.

Of course there's also Laurent himself. He arrives the next day to talk about what happened; he, unlike your sister, has always done as I anticipate. We end up kissing a little again, though something in me has cooled off overnight, even as it's apparently grown more intense in him. The day before, when I made the first move, there was always the chance that he would regretfully disentangle himself, reminding me gently that he's a married man. Now that I know for sure he won't object, I find the urge to do anything else melting away.

He doesn't seem to notice my hesitancy and, anyway, to my relief, he can only stay for a few minutes.

'I'll come back tonight,' he says. *'Early evening. Annette's going out. We'll have more time.'* He strokes my cheek tenderly and I think how lovely he is, and how much better suited the two of us might have been, but it still doesn't make me want him.

Élodie comes back that afternoon, the flared hems of her jeans carrying a tidemark of salt, like a pale wave. Maybe it was there yesterday, when we fought, or maybe she's hitched to the coast again. I don't ask this time. I'm too busy thinking that she'll be here when Laurent comes back.

Without meaning to, I drink three glasses of wine over a lunch that consists of little more than your leftovers and a handful of olives. When I put you down for your afternoon nap, benign spring sunlight slanting across the bed, I lie down beside you, intending only to absorb some of the peace of the room. But I must fall asleep because the next thing, I'm emerging from deep inside a dream of childhood, my father and I digging in the garden, and the sun has moved away. It's almost evening.

You're sitting up in the bed next to me, a Richard

Scarry book open on your lap. Greg brought it back for you the last time he went to London and it's become a passion of yours.

'Mummy, I'm hungry. You been asleep.'

I stand up and use your soft little brush to flatten down my hair. My cheeks are flushed from sleep and I go and stand by the open window in the hope of catching a wisp of cooler air. Laurent will come soon.

'Élodie's with a man,' you say, making me turn. You haven't looked up from your book. 'I heard them.'

I feel a shiver of apprehension. I lean out of the window to see if she's on the terrace but there's nothing there, only the remnants of lunch, and two open wine bottles. There was only one when I came upstairs with you. I look again and see, from the shape of one of them, that she's opened one of the expensive bottles we save for birthdays and Christmas.

'You read a bit longer, sweetheart,' I say, taking the key and closing the door behind me. I pause and then lock it. 'Mum, I want to come downstairs too,' you call.

'I won't be long, Em. Just a couple of minutes.' You're witness to enough fights between us.

Élodie is nowhere to be found in the house and at first I think the garden is deserted too. A plane is going over, heading for Nice or Italy, and in the clear air the engine is surprisingly loud. It's only as it fades to nothing that I hear a silken swish of water from the far end of the garden.

She's half in, half out of the pool when I get there, elbows propped on the ledge that runs round it. Her

305

hair ripples down her back, making her skin look paler against the green of the water and the oleander that reaches over to dip its fingers into it. Then she pushes up and climbs out in one easy movement, lean muscles flexing in her shoulders and arms, the water running off her in shining streams. Oh, but she's always so beautiful. That's another reason I can never tear my eyes away from her. Few can.

She raises her arms, points her fingers, then lies down on her back, stretching her legs, lifting one and then the other, wiggling her toes and adjusting her bikini top with a snap of elastic. She still hasn't sensed me there, watching.

Without looking, she reaches down for the glass next to her. It's one of yours – an old Amora mustard jar covered with Disney characters you begged me to buy in the supermarket. Now it's half full of red wine. Her hand knocks against it and wine splashes over the white dress she must've dropped there earlier.

I'm about to approach when she speaks. I freeze, not even daring to breathe.

'Why don't you just sit down? I don't bite, you know.'

I know instantly that she's not talking to me, that flirtatious tone so unlike anything she ever throws my way.

There's a figure standing in the deep shadow of the oleander, only visible through the dense foliage of the pines as he moves and then stops again.

She sits up and pats the lounger. *'Come on. We should talk about things, shouldn't we? After yesterday. Have some of this.*' She holds aloft the glass, which still has some in it, and laughs. '*It's Papa's good stuff. I won't tell him if you don't.*'

But the figure through the trees still hesitates. He's probably only a couple of metres from me and I think I can hear his breathing, louder than it should be for someone so still.

'*Élodie,*' he says, in a low, warning tone, and I know that voice. It makes my insides plummet.

Getting to her feet, she smiles. '*It's nice and warm today,*' she says. '*The mistral's gone, hasn't it?*'

She begins to walk around the pool the long way, past the diving board at the deep end, taking her time, hips swinging slightly. Then she reaches a hand round and unties her bikini top, lifting it over her head and flinging it to the warm stones, where it lands with a small slap.

I haven't seen her naked in years. She's recently blossomed and I'm glad to lose sight of her as she walks out of clear view, reduced to a slip of golden movement behind the trees.

I move fast then, the spell broken now I can't see her.

She's inches from him as I emerge, no hint of self-consciousness as she stands there smiling, head on one side.

'*Élodie!*' I bark, as she reaches up to loop her arms around his neck. '*Get off him.*'

She doesn't flinch but I make him jump so hard it's almost comical. His face as he turns to me is desperate, cheeks and neck flushed, his eyes not quite focused. He reaches up to pull apart her hands, stumbling slightly as he backs away.

'*Salut, Sylvie,*' Élodie singsongs at me. I stride over to the lounger and pick up the stained white dress, throwing it at her as soon as I'm close enough.

'*Put it on,*' I say coldly, because I either have to pretend total self-control or be sick all over the stones.

She goes then, that smile on her face, and I'm glad she does because I want to slap her. I turn to Laurent, pushing at him again and again, until he's right up against the trunk of the oleander. He doesn't resist. He can't even look at me.

'*What the fuck, Laurent? She's fourteen. Has this happened before?*'

He finally meets my eye. '*Of course not. How could you think . . . ?*' He's clearly horrified. '*I came to see you.*'

'*But you bumped into my daughter instead.*'

'*Sylvie, I didn't know she was going to do that. She was in the pool when I got here. She waved me over and I didn't want to be rude. Not after what she saw. I didn't want to antagonize her. Please, Sylvie, I had no idea.*'

'*No idea of what?*'

'*That she had . . . feelings. A crush.*'

I can't help it: I laugh. The sound spills into the garden, high and hard. It reminds me of hers: completely devoid of warmth.

'*A crush, Laurent? You think Élodie has a thing for you? My God.*' I shake my head, wanting to keep going, be cruel to him, humiliate him. What stops me is the realization that, beyond his foolish egotism, this is not really his fault.

I'm not furious because I want Laurent. I'm not jealous of Élodie's potent youth and beauty either – and I interrogate myself about that pretty hard. I think it's simply that with Laurent I've always been able to resurrect the old me. To him, I'm not just Élodie's mother or Greg's wife, I have remained Sylvie Durand from the house across the fields, no more or less. With Laurent, I am the me I'm always trying to get back to, who usually feels like someone else, these days.

Élodie has understood this, somehow, and she has tried to ruin it. I sometimes forget that she is as observant of me as I am of her. Greg would shake his head in disbelief if I were to say it aloud, but in our own way, Élodie and I are closer to each other than anyone else. Everything we do in this house is with the other in mind, like lovers or deadly foes. I don't think there's much difference sometimes.

1993

The pizzeria is busier this time. The holiday season is in full swing now and I see that Olivier was right when he said things were changing. I hadn't noticed before but the café that's been there for ever has invested in new umbrellas, huge square things in tasteful cream, lit from underneath by white lights. I feel a small pang for the old parasols, sun-bleached red and emblazoned with beer logos.

We get the last outside table, almost on the road, and as we sit down, all eyes are on us. I check but most belong to tourists and it occurs to me that they might be looking simply because Élodie is so arresting, dressed in a flared sea-green dress that brings out her tan and the golden lights in her hair, left loose and damp from the shower.

The meal passes without incident. I find myself in the unfamiliar position of being grateful to Greg for maintaining ceaseless conversation about nothing in particular. I have no idea what he's said to Élodie about the years she's been gone. Despite all my misgivings, I'm glad you seem so happy. Élodie is making a fuss of you, which in turn makes your father, who always took his lead from her, indulge you too. You're glowing prettily from all the attention, and from the subtle physical contact Élodie is constantly making with you: her hand on yours, the other smoothing your wildly crimped hair, now loosed from its many plaits. My own hands itch in my lap to stop her, oddly like a jealous partner, but I can see – anyone can see – that you're basking in it. Unconsciously you've angled your body towards her, like a cat curling around its owner's legs.

There are stalls set up in the square again, most of them selling gifts: expensive linens, silver jewellery and wine. After the pizzas, all of us in need of a break before we can contemplate dessert, you ask if you can go and look at them.

'Okay, but don't go too far. We haven't finished yet.'

'Will you come?' she asks Élodie.

An old reflex has me opening my mouth to object but she's already pushing back her chair and holding out her hand to you.

'*We won't be long, Maman,*' she says. '*I'll look after her.*'

'Don't go far,' I can't help saying again. 'Stay where we can see you.'

I catch your tut but then you turn back to your sister, all smiles again.

Greg turns to me with a raised eyebrow. 'Surely even you can't claim this hasn't been a pleasant evening.'

I gesture at a passing waitress for another bottle of wine.

'What do you think, then?' I've been waiting to ask him this all night.

He gives me an uncomprehending look.

'Of Élodie, I mean. Do you . . . Do you think she's different?'

Greg gets out his cigarettes with an exaggerated sigh. 'I take it you don't.'

'I honestly don't know. I keep changing my mind. I think she is and then I remember what Morel told me about the twenty per cent who don't grow out of it. Remembering how she was, I don't know if it's possible for her to truly change. However much she might want to . . . However much *we* might want her to. Besides, if she's grown out of it, why didn't she come back sooner? We can't afford to get this wrong, Greg. For everyone's sake . . .' I tail off.

'Do you really think the way she's being with Emma – the affection, the fuss, all of that – do you really suppose that's for show? She was never like that before, was she? Emma barely existed for her. Apart from when . . .' He doesn't finish.

I watch the two of you, further off now, Élodie a head taller, her arm slung around your narrow shoulders. I'm sitting forward in my chair, as though to stay closer to you, if only by a couple of inches.

'I'm afraid that might be exactly what it is. A show. I know it sounds cold, but someone has to play devil's advocate here. And don't look at me like that. You can't blame me for being so cautious.'

He finishes his wine. 'No, okay. But isn't it possible that some of it might be genuine? She was at the Institut for three years without any incidents. She told me about the ashram.'

'She told me about it, too, and you know what I think about those places. It's not all peace and love. I mean, look at what was going on in Oregon with Osho.'

He doesn't say anything. Greg was always more of a natural hippie than me. I know he still hankers after that sixties idealism he found briefly in Paris, which died a slow death the decade after. The world was a cold and dangerous place, after all, and perhaps his daughter was too. It always made me feel sad for him. Angry with him, as well. Because for as long as he clung to his naivety, I was forced into being the cynical one.

'Don't you want her to have come out the other side?' he says softly now. 'Don't you want her to be okay?'

'Of course I do.'

He nods. He knows that, beneath all the fear, I do want that. Somewhere, a long way down, she's still the baby we took home that day, the tiny girl we loved so much, the child who grew up to be such a painful mystery to us both.

Of course I want her to be better. I want it very badly. I just don't know if it's too much to hope for. And I owe it to you as your mother to be careful, not to let my guard down yet.

Around us people are talking about the fires. *Les feux.* I catch snippets. It makes me realize what I've been too preoccupied to notice – that the smell of smoke is still present, a dark bass note beneath the aromas of food and perfume.

'By the way, we've had an offer on the house,' I say to take my mind off it.

He turns to me in surprise. 'That was quick. God, La Rêverie being sold. I can't quite believe it.' He absently taps a cigarette on the table before lighting it and I wonder how many hundreds of times I've seen that little tic. Unexpectedly, he holds it out to me and I take it gratefully.

'Sylvie, what are we going to do about Élodie when you have to go back to London?'

I sigh. 'I don't know. I haven't a clue how to approach any of this. What about you?'

He shakes his head. 'When you were asleep this afternoon, I rang Nicole. I said I'd tell Élodie she would be welcome to stay at our place for a while, if she wanted to.'

'Oh. What did she say?'

He looks away. 'She said she didn't think it was a very good idea. Not with the boys so young.'

I check you're still in sight. For a second, I can't see either of you but then I spot Élodie. She looks as though she's staring right at us, though it's hard to tell from a distance. I crane to see better but she moves out of sight.

I can't blame Nicole but I'm surprised too. I suppose I never thought he'd tell her everything. After all, he had never sat down with me and had a frank conversation about what had happened. I don't know whether to be gratified, angry, or just sad.

'So what, then?' I say. 'She said northern France didn't feel like home so I don't think she'd want to go to Paris anyway. Let alone London. I can't imagine her somewhere without the sun. Perhaps she'll want to go back to Spain.'

He rubs his temples. 'I never did know what was best when it came to her. I know I left you with it all, Sylvie. I do know that.' He reaches out and briefly squeezes my hand. I nod, not quite able to speak. If he'd only done that more often back then. It would have made so much difference in those last years if he'd reached across the divide.

We lapse into silence and I finish my cigarette before you can come back and catch me smoking.

'I think she might have been sleeping in the barn, you know,' I say, as I stub it out.

He looks up, surprised out of his thoughts. 'Who, Élodie?'

'Yes. There were clothes in the loft. I wasn't sure, and I suppose I'm still not, but I think she was there, maybe with Luc. She used to hide up there all the time in that last year – do you remember? I think Luc's been with her or helping her. I think she's been around a while.'

'Haven't you asked her?'

'She said it was only a couple of days and not at the house, but I've got a feeling. Both of us felt watched here before she came. Emma was beginning to think the house was haunted.'

He remains silent.

'Don't you think that's a bit worrying?'

He shrugs. 'So she was too scared to approach at first. I think I can understand that.'

'You know why I came in the first place, don't you?'

'The damage in the *souillarde*? Surely you can't think . . . Why would anyone start a fire in there? It's hardly more than a cupboard. It barely even got going, did it? I thought it was kids.'

'Perhaps. I thought it might have been a way of getting me to come back here. Maybe it was the only way she could, I don't know.'

'Like she's reeled you in. Jesus, Sylvie. That sounds a bit far-fetched to me.'

'And yet here I am. I'm back and so is she. We're all here together. For the first time in a decade.'

I watch him take that in and wait for the protests, the accusations of paranoia, but they don't come and, for once, I wish they would.

I look for you again and see that you're on your way back, rushing ahead of Élodie to show us something. Behind you, your sister is moving unhurriedly, languidly, hips swaying in time with her hair. As she passes an old couple, locals rather than tourists, I see the woman nudge her husband and nod in Élodie's direction. They watch her progress, mouths pursed, backs stiff with disapproval, and I have no idea if it's the amount of flesh she's showing or because they know who she is. *Brebis galeuse.*

'Look what Élodie bought me.'

You hold out your arm. You've put all your neon bands on one wrist, replacing the ones on the right with a bracelet: a slender silver hoop clasping a small ceramic plate, pale pink with tiny blue flowers dotted in the opposite corners.

'She's got one too.'

You lift her wrist to show me and she meets my gaze

for a moment. I think there's a glint of a challenge in her eyes but then she glances away and I wonder if I'm just looking for it.

Her bracelet is identical to yours, though the silver looks brighter against her butterscotch skin. In the centre of the ceramic plates, between the flowers, and so recently painted by the stallholder that the black lines shine wetly, is a curlicued letter E, just like those she once graffitied on her door handle, just like the one she scratched into my beloved jewellery box. E for Élodie and now E for Emma.

No one wants anything else so Greg pays the bill and we start to cross the square. At the far edge, the boys we saw on the night of the circus are back. Their mopeds are propped up in a ragged line next to the bench they're draped over, smoking and laughing, though without real enjoyment. I catch you scanning their faces for Luc but he's not there. They see us a beat later or, rather, they see Élodie. This has been happening all evening: married fathers, waiters and old men staring, apparently unable to help themselves.

'*Élodie!*' they call. '*Viens ici, Élodie!*' They watch her ignore them as one, and the calls get more frenzied, though they don't quite have the nerve to approach. Greg gives them a look, which makes them laugh again, but it's even more mirthless now. One gestures at you, nudges the boy next to him and says something I don't catch. I pull you towards me.

'*They seem to know you quite well*,' I say to Élodie, as we walk on, but she doesn't reply, which makes Greg frown again. Far off in the distance, I can hear sirens. I look for the glow on the hills, but there's nothing. I can smell the smoke again, stronger now.

*

Although your father could sleep in Camille's old room, or even the cramped little room opposite Élodie's, I decide to give him the blue room, you coming in with me. I feel safer that way.

With you next to me that night, I sleep like I used to back in London, deep and mostly dreamless, released for the time being from perpetual sentry duty. And then it's morning and I wake up refreshed and reasonably calm.

Out on the terrace over breakfast, the temperature is already intense, though it isn't yet nine o'clock. I can feel my skin beginning to burn. I think the smoke is incrementally heavier too. I don't want to mention it in case it frightens you.

After breakfast, you and Élodie go to the pool and Greg shuts himself in the study to make another phone call to Nicole. Suspended between these factions, I decide to do some gardening. There's no real need – the Johnsons have already seen the house – but the possibility of the fires getting worse has rendered me incapable of staying still.

As it is, there is plenty to keep me occupied. Everything in the wide borders needs hacking back and clearing, years of leaves and sap-coated pine needles clogging the beds and stickily carpeting the margins of the pool area. Once I start, I can't stop, the nervous energy that has been trickling back all morning, bolstered by a good night's sleep, seemingly in danger of bubbling over.

I should have worn a hat. I know that by early evening. As the sun slides below the pine trees, I sit shivering in a tepid bath, the tiniest movement of air on my goosepimpled skin as sore as if I've been whipped, my head thumping like it's been in a vice.

I know it's sunstroke because I had it once as a child. I can clearly remember lying on my back in bed, which made me feel marginally less awful than every other position, and thinking it a shame that I was going to die before my ninth birthday. I felt so desperately ill – the relentless nausea, the way the room lurched when I tried to sit up, my heart galloping in my chest, mouth as dry as dust – that I didn't even consider the possibility I might survive.

In fact, people can die from too much sun. When the body's internal temperature exceeds forty degrees centigrade, the organs start to cook. I had read up on it afterwards, in my mother's huge old medical tome. There were three whole pages dedicated to *insolation*.

I stand shakily at my bedroom window. The three of you are out by the pool, and I can see glimmers of movement as the trees move in the wind. The wind. It takes me a moment to absorb that there is definite movement in the air now, and that that's not a good thing when forest fires are already burning. It's not a gentle breeze either, but something quarrelsome, buffeting the trees in spiteful gusts. I wonder if any of you will think to check the *météo* report. If you'll think to check on me.

I don't remember much about the evening or subsequent night. I'm sick a few times, only just managing to crawl to the bathroom in time, freezing sweat giving way to a minute or two of bliss, my skin drying on the cold tiles before the nausea starts to slosh back in. At some point, one of you brings me a bowl so I don't have to leave the bed. Later, I hear a murmured conversation about calling a doctor, silhouettes against the lit doorway, but then I slip out of consciousness again. Sometime in the middle of the night I understand you aren't next to me in the bed but I can't do more than register the fact.

The next morning, I feel almost as bad, but my temperature must have come down a degree or so because my thought processes are more orderly. I realize I must have been delirious in the night. You slip in soon after I wake, your breath smelling sickly-sweet of croissant and chocolate, a glass of what looks like iced tea in your hand.

You smile and put the straw to my lips. 'You've got to drink lots of fluids. It says in the big medical book. Élodie looked it up. She made you a *tisane.*'

You pronounce the word perfectly. She must have taught you that.

I try to sit up but it's too much effort. I slump back down on the pillows.

'Dad says he's going to come up and see you before

he leaves,' you say. It takes me a moment to comprehend the words.

'Before he leaves? What do you mean? He's only just got here.'

You shrug. 'He has to go back to Paris.'

It turns out he's been summoned: Nicole has clearly had second thoughts about him disappearing to the south for an intimate reunion with his ex-wife and daughters; his first family. Even as ill as I am, I can't help feeling a grudging respect for her. He had never done my bidding, had never come back for me, even when I'd begged him.

'What about Élodie?' I say, when he appears at the door a couple of hours later, sheepish and defiant at the same time, like a naughty boy.

'I've told her to ring me tomorrow, so we can arrange to see each other soon. She's got my number.'

'But not your address.'

He can't meet my eye.

'Greg, please, don't go.'

His face softens and he starts to move towards me but then stops. 'You'll be okay now. You're probably through the worst of it already. Élodie and Emma will look after you. Élodie's been checking on you every fifteen minutes. I've been watching her, Sylvie. She's not like the girl from back then. I know she's not.'

'But you don't know that for sure,' I want to say but I can't marshal my words.

He shakes his head slightly, and it makes me think of someone warding off a persistent fly. 'Emma's not a baby any more. You know I wouldn't go if I thought there was even the smallest chance . . . Anyway, you'll be up and about in a few hours. Everything will be fine, Sylvie. Sometimes things are. Usually they are.'

'What about the fires? The wind . . .'

'They're barely getting any closer. I got a paper in the village. The wind should die down later, too. They think the fires'll be under control by the end of the week.'

'But, Greg, please, listen –'

'Look, I've got to go. I'm sorry but I have to.'

And then he's gone. I hear your goodbyes in the hall downstairs and then the front door closes. After that it's quiet.

*

When I next come to, I'm not ready to be 'up and about' at all. Greg had been wrong about that and I wonder what else he might have misjudged. I'm shivering again, and I know I'll be sick soon. I have no idea what time it is. When I swing my feet to the floor to go to the bathroom, I sway, the blood booming in my ears, like water rushing into a cave. I call but no one answers. I feel afraid for you, somewhere alone with your sister, but like a wounded animal too hurt to run, I'm also afraid for myself.

I half crawl downstairs to the phone and ring the emergency doctor's number on Olivier's note, almost weeping at the sound of his calm, capable voice at the other end. He arrives within the hour and prescribes me

323

a tranquillizer to stop the shivering, which is only raising my body temperature. The rest of the day blurs after that, though I have a dim memory of shadows looming over me like the previous night, briefly blocking out the bright light from the hall I don't have the wherewithal to turn off.

I remember your voice, Emma, sounding far away and too young, and I wonder if I've been catapulted back in time. I wake every few minutes, or so it feels like, disembodied except for the crushing weight of fear on my chest – fear that somewhere beyond the bed, something bad is going to happen to you, may be happening to you already.

Hearing music at some point, I stagger in my confusion to the window. The sun has slunk away for another night and the air reeks of hot things: earth, flowers and, most of all, fire, despite what Greg said about it not being close. The music gets louder as I strain to push the windows wide, and I think the doors to the salon must be open, the volume on the old record player turned up, the speakers moved to face outwards. I recognize it then: 'Hotel California'.

I push myself up so I can see down to the terrace, and what is there is such a strange spectacle that I have to blink and blink again. There are three of you dancing. I peer again, my head ringing, and see that Luc is there with you and her. You're spinning on your own, laughing as you do it, your hair flying out and your feet nearly stumbling over each other as you grow dizzier. Élodie and Luc are pressed together, moving more slowly, not an inch of space between them. Dancing to remember, perhaps. Or is it to forget?

The scene makes my stomach churn. I think they must have given you something because I haven't seen you so entirely unselfconscious in years, not since you were a tiny girl.

I decide I must go downstairs. I must somehow get between you and them, and I promise myself that I will in just a few seconds, when I feel less weak and watery. I lie back on the bed, chilly nausea sluicing inside me, and start counting. I'll go when I get to fifty.

1983

Greg and I have been sent to the coast to save our marriage. His parents have paid for us to get away from the house and spend our fifteenth-anniversary weekend in a luxury hotel we would never have contemplated ourselves. I am taking tranquillizers, just a couple a day to get me through, but I'm not used to them yet and their effect is different from the wine I'm trying to give up. It distils Cannes down to just a handful of images: white-jacketed waiters in the hotel restaurant; a green marble bathroom in which my cheap items of make-up look pathetic; skinny old women out on the Croisette with Jackie O sunglasses and tiny dogs at their heels.

Once I would have relished this short foray into glamour but everything seems tinged with melancholy. I feel haunted by other people's lives, even by times I was born too late to know. The beauty of the Martinez sign on the roof, 1930s neon against a rose-coloured sky, makes me cry on the Saturday night. Greg gets angry, thinking me ungrateful for his parents' generosity.

'You don't understand me at all,' I say. 'Not any more.' And he stands and leaves me alone on the terrace.

We leave early on Sunday, neither of us wishing to

dwell on the failure of what was an unspoken last-chance saloon. That's not the only reason I want to go home. I am feeling increasingly jittery about you, even through the soft haze of the pills. A couple of weeks ago Élodie gave you wine sweetened with lemonade while I was at the supermarket. I was out for less than an hour and Greg hadn't heard anything unusual, but then he was ensconced in the study with his headphones on. I only left you with him because Élodie had gone out for the day, or so I thought. You were staggering around the garden by the time I got back, so that for an innocent moment I thought you'd been spinning and were only dizzy. Then you were sick and I smelt the alcohol and I knew.

I didn't bother to say anything to your sister, who was lying on a towel on the grass in a neon-pink bikini. What would have been the point?

After that, I agreed to the hotel only because your grandmother promised me she wouldn't take her eyes off you. She's never said anything to me directly but I have never forgotten her face when she saw those drawings Élodie did all those years ago. Even before that, I think she had her concerns. Women are always better at spotting it than men. Of course she would never have dreamt of taking my side over Greg's, but I believe she and I are in silent agreement over this. It's why we've not seen much of them over the years, I'm sure of it.

If I'd ever doubted Margaret's instincts about her eldest granddaughter's difficulties, the relief in her face when I mentioned that Élodie would be away at a friend's house while we were in Cannes would have chased away any uncertainty. I don't know this friend – one of the older kids Élodie has somehow fallen in with. Greg and I gave her a lift to this girl's house on the way to the coast. I made him wait until I saw her go in. She's hardly ever home at the weekend now.

When we turn into the drive at La Rêverie, it feels wrong immediately. I couldn't have articulated why: some unusual tension in the air, perhaps, or the profound silence of the cicadas and birds? I'm not sure. All I know is that I get out of the car so fast I almost lose my balance.

'Sylvie?' Greg calls after me but I'm already shoving the key into the front door.

His mother is asleep in the salon, her neat grey chignon slipped and her mouth open, making her look years older. One of your Richard Scarry books lies open on the floor.

I shake her awake, not particularly gently, but I'm so full of foreboding I feel I might scream.

'Where is she? Where's Emma?'

She comes to slowly, blinking dumbly at the empty space beside her, now occupied only by your little blue teddy.

'She was just here. We were reading her book together.'

I think back to myself on a beach, waking to find Élodie gone. I know how easily this happens.

'It can only have been for a moment,' she says defensively. 'She must be with Charles. He was upstairs . . .'

I run into the hall just as Greg comes in.

'Charles!' I shout, as I begin to race up the stairs. 'Are you up there? Emma!'

He emerges from the bathroom, his face half covered with shaving foam, an old-fashioned brush in hand.

'Is Emma with you?' I run along the hall, checking the bedrooms. All empty.

'No, she was with Margaret. In the salon.'

Greg has followed me up. 'What's the big panic? She'll be in the garden.' Our eyes meet and I know what he's not saying in front of his father. *It's okay. Élodie isn't here.*

'I need to find her. I'll go outside. You check the house properly.'

I run back downstairs, kicking off the high heels that are slowing me down, and rush out into the garden. The terrace is empty. The lawn is deserted. You're not by the pool or in it, and the huge relief of that, at least, allows me to sink to my knees for a moment, to catch my breath.

And then I smell it, a yellowing of the atmosphere, curling down to this part of the garden, where the air is always caught and held by the tall pines. It's smoke, faint but real. I get to my feet and then I see it for the first time, a spiral of dirt rising from the barn beyond the garden. I cut my foot on the path that's the quickest way round but barely feel it.

The barn door is closed, which it never is, and my blood freezes. There are no flames on the outside and some sensible, adrenalin-drenched part of my brain tells me this is a good thing. The fire can't have been going

330

very long. Apart from the brick back wall, the barn is entirely constructed from old, seasoned wood, which is currently drier than usual because it hasn't rained for weeks. *Once it gets hold it's going to be unstoppable.*

As I wrench the heavy door open, Greg and Charles arrive on the scene, the terror I'm already in the grip of only just registering in their faces. Margaret appears behind them and she looks much more how I feel. I've never seen her so undone, her hair torn from its chignon, eye make-up smeared down her cheeks.

I go in and the heat is a shock, like a physical wall. The fire has been set in the middle of the floor, where a big pile of wood, straw, old newspapers and even books has been heaped up. One book has fallen clear and it's an old one of mine from childhood, a collection of fairy tales I gave to Élodie as a child.

'Emma!' I scream. 'Emma!'

The roar of the fire grows louder, and there's a huge pop as an old log blows apart, sending sparks over our feet and making Margaret shriek. The flames leap higher, closer and closer to the old oak beams. Once the roof catches . . . Charles and Greg begin to search the dark corners at the back, among the old mowers and tools, the dark recesses between shelves stacked with nails and rusted tins of varnish.

I can't move, my eyes scanning the cavernous insides, lit weirdly by the flames so that shapes and shadows shift and move, tricking me into thinking I see you. Margaret is coughing now, a terrible rattling sound and Charles rushes her out. I can feel the smoke in my own lungs and my eyes are already burning. I tear off my blouse to hold over my face.

'She's not here,' Greg shouts, suddenly appearing from behind the wall of fire. 'I don't think she can be in here. Dad's gone to ring the fire brigade.'

And then I look up and, because Charles has left the door open, just enough light is cast on the loft so I can see all the way to the dim back of it. It's nothing more than a glimpse of lemon yellow but it's enough.

'She's up there! I can see her T-shirt. Greg!'

He's already running towards it and I'm just behind him. We both realize the ladder has gone at the same moment. We hadn't noticed but it's there, in the heart of the fire, hacked into pieces.

'Emma! Em, can you hear me?' Greg's voice is much stronger than mine.

'She must be unconscious,' I say, sounding oddly far-away. The sounds of the fire seem to be deepening, spreading. And then you move – I think you move. It's hard to tell but the pale yellow shifts, just an inch or so.

Greg sees it too. 'Emma! Emma! Come here, come to the edge. Now, you've got to come now.'

And you do, so slowly I think I'm going to die, crawling inch by agonizing inch. You're so scared of heights. Dimly, in the long dark spaces between each cogent thought, I marvel at how she got you up there. Finally, you're kneeling up at the edge, eyes huge and dark, your little face stiff and chalk-white with terror.

'You'll have to jump, darling,' Greg shouts, but you don't move.

Behind us, the burning pile of wood shifts, the side nearest us collapsing, like a cliff, so it's closer, and so much hotter.

'Now, Emma,' says Greg, his voice hard with determination. 'You've got to jump now or we're not going to get out of here.'

And you stand, and for a terrible moment I think you're going to turn and walk to the back of the loft and curl into a ball, like a frightened animal cornered by a forest fire. But you straighten up and I can see your small chest heaving because you're so wheezy and then you close your eyes and jump, and I hear the air thumped out of Greg's body as he catches you, and I begin to sob.

The sky, when we get out, is so huge it makes me dizzy. I half fall as I reach out to take you from Greg. You're struggling for breath and so frightened that you've wet yourself. You're almost catatonic. But you're alive, you're intact. I've got you.

1993

When I open my eyes again it's morning. My body finally feels as though it's beginning to right its inner equilibrium, though my head still pulses with pain and my nightdress is wringing with sweat. Then I remember I never made it downstairs to check on you. I stumble to the window but the terrace is deserted, except for a tide of empty bottles and ashtrays. The salon doors are still open. Someone's T-shirt is discarded over the back of one of the chairs.

A presence behind me makes me turn and nearly lose my balance. It's Élodie, hollow-eyed and unkempt but still beautiful.

'*Maman, you shouldn't be up.*'

She helps me back to bed, turning over my pillows so they're cool and dry, then brings me a tall glass of iced tea just like you did the day before, or was it the day before that? I can't work it out.

'*Where's Emma?*'

'*Fast asleep. It's early still. Only just seven.*'

'*Is she all right?*'

She shushes me and produces a cold flannel, pressing it to my temples. It's blissful.

'*What about Luc?*' I manage to say, though the heavy blanket of exhaustion is creeping over me again.

'*Luc? Luc wasn't here.*'

'*But I saw him. I saw the two of you. You were –*'.

She places two cool fingertips on my mouth, and as she leans over, a hank of her long hair falls forward to brush my collarbone, goosebumps rising all over my sore skin in response.

'*Hush, Maman, you must have dreamt it. He was never here. Sleep now.*' She kisses my forehead and then she's gone, closing the door softly behind her. I lie there peacefully for a while, then force myself to get up, get dressed. But the vertigo and nausea swell again, and I lie down, helpless. The hours pass meaninglessly, the sun moving round behind the shutters oddly fast, like someone's time-lapsed the day and is playing it back to me. Soon enough, it's dark again, and Élodie is back with another drink.

You slide into bed with me that night, I don't know when, and relief that you're okay penetrates the fog briefly. There's a strange odour to your skin but I'm still too weak and cotton-headed to work out whether it's perfume or alcohol or something worse. It comes to me just as I drift back into another fathomless sleep: you smell older.

In the morning, I feel weak but purged. Almost like myself again, which in itself seems quite miraculous. We forget to appreciate feeling well until we're ill. We lie on our sick beds and the memory of just feeling ordinary – no sickness, no pain – is like a beautiful shore we've been carried away from, exiles who might never be allowed to return.

I look down at you, asleep beside me, and feel as though the two of us have survived a shipwreck. I can see the remains of make-up around your eyes, mascara clogging your lashes, glitter on your lids, but you're intact. There are no bruises or pinch-marks, there's no awful wheeze as you breathe in.

I creep downstairs, noting that Élodie's door is closed. There has been some sort of attempt to tidy up but the kitchen and salon still carry a soiled air, cushions squashed down into the gaps between chair seats and frames, crumbs and sticky patches on the work surfaces. The wine and beer that were in the fridge have gone, but much of the food looks untouched. I wonder when you last ate.

Out on the terrace, a coffee bowl overflows with cigarette ends, some hand-rolled, others bought. I can smell it on the hot air, distinct from the smoke that doesn't seem quite so strong today – that, and the sourness of spilt beer. It makes my mouth water nauseously and I remember that I need some food. I have no memory of eating anything in two days, swallowing only those drinks, which kept arriving, cold and sweet down my sore throat. As I sit eating stale baguette dipped in milky coffee on the terrace steps, a plane goes over, wings glinting in the sunlight. Though the sky above the house is a sharp, celestial blue, it's one of the Canadair planes, heavy with water pulled from the Mediterranean. Dimly, I think I ought to check the news, see what's happening with the fires.

I don't hear Élodie come up behind me until she's already there and putting a sunhat on my head.

'*Thank you,*' I manage to say, as she sits down next to me. I'm startled by her sudden presence and oddly shy of the intimate way she's helped look after me. I have a vague memory of her changing me into a clean night-dress before you came up to bed, moving me about with a nurse's deftness and ease, as though I was as light as a bird. But perhaps I'd dreamt that too.

'*Maman, I'm so sorry about the mess. I thought I would get up early this morning and clear up but you've beaten me downstairs. I'll replace the wine.*'

I wave my hand. '*It doesn't matter.*' And I think I mean it. She's twenty-four. If she wants to smoke and drink, who am I to stop her?

The day wears on and I stay in the shade. You and Élodie take turns to bring me cold drinks under the ole-ander tree, where Élodie has dragged a lounger and heaped it with pillows. I even venture into the pool in the afternoon, the water silken and soothing to my dry skin and gritty eyes. When I get out, Élodie is standing there with a plate of cheese and grapes.

'*You must eat,*' she says, smiling. '*Your body needs susten-ance after being so ill.*'

I do as I'm told, though I can't manage much. I let Élodie plump my pillows and brush my tangled hair. I'm so bonelessly weak from the sunstroke that I don't even have the energy to feel anxious. Anxiety becomes habitual, adrenalin pumping at the slightest provoca-tion. But the sunstroke has apparently reset me, leaving my system drained but tranquil.

Even as the light fades out of another day, night

seeping in from the darkest corners of the garden, I remain calm. *I am becalmed*, I think: a placid sea. I test the feeling gently, as though inspecting a bruise, but it's real. It holds. Even when I look at the turquoise necklace that's still around your neck, the tremor is only very slight, like thunder that's long moved away. I can remember everything about my old fear. It's just that I'm viewing it through thick glass now. Oh, and it's such a relief to let it go.

All evening and into the next morning, we three are inseparable. Just before noon, Élodie announces that she is going to buy food, before the shop in the village closes for the three-hour lunch tourists always find outrageous.

She comes back with two bags full of the kind of food a child would choose: Petit Écolier biscuits, caramel ice-cream, mini glass bottles of Orangina, a heavy tin cylinder of *sirop* – the same brand of grenadine I always used to buy.

'*Did you buy anything healthy at all?*' I say, marvelling at the ease in my voice, I who could never sound anything but sharp with her.

She pulls a melon out of a paper bag and squeezes it. '*It's perfectly ripe. It'll be like eating sunlight.*'

Melons were always her favourite, especially the ones from Cavaillon. I had always loved them too, that Amaretto sweetness that seems so decadent compared to other fruit. A barbed memory springs up then: I'm trying to wipe her face clean of melon juice with a flannel, and she claws my cheek with her sticky little fingers because she doesn't like it, making it bleed. I push the memory down again and find it recedes, quite easily.

She's also bought fromage frais, which she spoons into the dessert glasses my mother once used for *îles flottantes*. Then she stirs in strawberry jam – the expensive stuff in the squat hexagonal jars – until it marbles, pink and cream. It's delicious: soft, pillowy unctuousness with bursts of intense fruit. I have a small helping before drifting into a light doze, still aware of your voices, kept low so as not to disturb me.

Élodie wakes me a couple of hours later, her breath smelling of grenadine, her tongue and lips dyed an artificial pink. '*I know the sirop is too sweet for you,*' she murmurs. '*I've made you another tisane.*' It's iced tea again and I gulp it down, vaguely wondering if it's Lipton's or whether Élodie made it herself, enjoying the sound of ice clinking against my teeth. From the bottom of the garden, I can hear you splashing about in the pool.

'*Is Emma okay?*'

'*She's fine. Like a little fish in the water.*' She takes my empty glass and stands to rearrange the cushions behind me. Faintly, I can smell her old scent, sweetened into headiness by the grenadine.

'*Maman, do you remember what you said to me the first night you were sick?*' She strokes my hair back from my face and sits down next to me.

'*I – I'm not sure. It's all a bit of a blur.*'

She moves a little closer. Even in the soft light, I can see every minute shading of colour in her amber eye. It looks almost golden. The blue eye is darker, more uniform, the sea after a storm, sand swirling out of sight below the surface.

I try to cast my mind back but it veers away to more scenes of the sea, heaving gently, the sway of Élodie's hair. I can't concentrate. I'm so tired and my head is starting to ache again.

'You said that when I was born you were so full of love you couldn't eat.'

I smile. *'That's true. It's true.'*

As I fall away into unconsciousness again, the ormolu clock tick-ticking, she's smiling back at me.

1983

The *pompiers* have just left. They were fast and this means the barn has been saved. The inside is charred but the flames hadn't quite reached the roof. It's structurally intact. Part of me wishes it had burnt down, the fire razing the place that might have been the scene of your . . . But I can't bear to go near the word.

Margaret has been sedated and put to bed. Greg and Charles are in the salon with you asleep between them, large brandies in hand. The doctor said you were fine, miraculously. Though you'd needed your Ventolin you hadn't inhaled much smoke. Still, when I'd held you close, you'd smelt sharply alien. It was fear.

'You didn't see her?' I say quietly to Charles, when you've fallen asleep, the trembling from your shock finally subsided.

He shakes his head. Greg knocks back his brandy. All three of us know we're talking about Élodie. I leave them then, once Greg has promised he won't let you out of his sight.

When I get outside, smoke hangs in the air above the garden, still shockingly new. I begin to run. I need to burn off some of the fear still swirling inside me. She's nowhere in the garden, though. I knew she wouldn't be but I had to look anyway. I go to the barn next.

The interior is dark and dripping from the water, the walls scorched. The smell of smoke is still acrid enough to catch in the back of my burnt throat. I methodically search every shadowed corner, though of course I can't get up to the loft because the ladder has been reduced to ash. I look and look but there's no sign of her, not until I clamber up on to an old storage cabinet to survey the place from a higher vantage point and see the glint of metal. It's a chain, caught on a large splinter sticking out from the edge of the loft floor. I almost lose my footing in my haste to get down, my heart missing its beat as I catch myself.

I fetch a long pair of garden shears and manage to knock it loose, snatching it up to make absolutely sure. Of course it's what I think it is: a silver necklace strung with tiny turquoise stones, a long golden hair tangled in the broken catch. I think back to when I last saw her, as she got out of the car on Friday afternoon, and, yes, I'm sure she was wearing it. The silver and blue always looked so bright against her caramel skin. It's the only piece of jewellery she never takes off.

I rush out and sit down hard in the dust, the sun and my shock bleaching everything around me to stark, featureless white. The chain feels hot in my hand and I want to throw it as far and hard as I can. But I can't. I need to show it to Greg first. I need to make him understand that the barn is our last warning. I don't think we'll get another chance.

If anyone had told me I would ever consider deliberately

hurting you, even just a little bit, I would have thought them insane. But I have come to understand that the means to an end is not always a straight path: it isn't about easy decisions.

After I find the necklace on the barn floor, I go straight back to the salon.

'Greg, I need to talk to you. Now.'

Charles looks at me fearfully, his eyes sunken, ten years older than when we left for Cannes. You're still fast asleep. 'Stay with her,' I say again. 'Don't take your eyes off her.'

Greg follows me to her room. I don't know why I go there. It seems appropriate, somehow.

I hold up the necklace. 'I just found this. In the barn. It was up there, where Emma was.'

I watch his face blanch. 'But . . . That doesn't mean . . . She could have lost it any time.'

'She was wearing it when we dropped her off. I'm certain she was.'

'How can you possibly remember that? Anyway, if she was here, where is she now?'

When he caught you in his arms in the barn, I loved him more than I ever had. Now I hate him for his cowardice, for not giving voice to his perfect comprehension of what has happened – the awful knowledge I can read in the new lines etched into his face, lines that weren't there this morning.

I throw the necklace at him, as hard as I can. It goes wide, hitting the top of the dressing table behind him, its surface littered with hair-bands and make-up and

345

balled-up receipts from places I've never heard of. It skitters to the back and vanishes. I'm glad. I never want to see it again.

'Why don't we take her back to that doctor, then?' he says weakly, after a long, loaded silence. 'See what he has to say.'

'Morel, you mean? You want to go to him now? Don't you think it's a bit late? I told you what he said years ago. I told you what he said when I went back, after Emma was born.'

He squares his jaw and I want to cross the room and smash my fist into it.

'Shall I remind you?' I say, louder now. 'He said that we had to be vigilant. He said that younger siblings can be vulnerable. That they can be a source of resentment. But that wasn't enough for you, was it? You always said it was alarmist advice, that if we were to ask for proper support, the authorities would surely need some proof, though really you meant you, didn't you? Well, if today is not enough for you, not enough *proof*, then nothing ever will be.'

'I'll ring the friend's house,' he says suddenly. 'Where we took her. I've got the number. She gave it to me months ago when she needed picking up.'

Downstairs, I make him pull the phone cord as far as it will go, out into the hall. I don't want to disturb you. Charles watches us in silence, his expression grim.

It rings for a long time. 'I told you,' I mutter in Greg's ear. 'No one's there.'

But then it connects, a lazy voice answering. '*Oui?*'

'*Is Élodie there?*'

There's a pause. The static is loud while we wait. I can't quite catch my breath.

'*I think so,*' the voice finally says. '*Maybe.*'

Greg looks at me. *See,* his expression says. He's so desperate for her to be there that he's started to shake. I snatch the receiver off him.

'*Can you go and fetch her then, please?*' I say to whoever this girl is at the other end. '*We need to talk to her now. It's important.*'

Another pause. Then the phone in that house, which I'm certain doesn't contain my daughter, is dropped. I can hear voices in the background and the low thud of bass, the odd screech of laughter. After a minute of shouting into the mouthpiece, just when I think no one is ever going to answer, the girl comes back on.

'*Élodie's not here,*' she says. Then she lets out a scream, which twists into laughter. '*Arrête, Thierry! Look, someone said they saw her leave this morning. She got a lift with a couple of guys who were driving north. She said she might be back tonight.*'

I don't bother replying. I hand the phone to Greg and run outside, to begin another search for her – for further clues. My brain whirrs furiously as I scour every inch of the garden and the fields beyond. I'm finally realizing that I will have to act alone. I know I'm running out of time. I need to get her away from you, and I can't afford to wait until she tries something like that again. I've been marking time for so long, waiting to find the proof that Greg has always demanded – the

347

irrefutable proof that Élodie is dangerous. But if a necklace dropped next to the scene of a fire like a sinister calling card isn't enough, I will have to manufacture something myself.

I think of it like a vaccine: a little danger now to protect you from the larger threat that's drawing ever closer. Your older sister has tried to burn a building down with you in it, for God's sake. What else am I supposed to do?

The choice as I see it is stark: one daughter or the other. And though in so many ways it breaks my heart, when it comes down to it, it feels like no choice at all.

Perhaps I'm slightly insane, I don't know. I still believe I'll be saving your life.

1993

I wake early in the light-soaked salon, the shutters left open and the voile curtains no match for the sun. My mouth is so dry I can barely swallow. I finish the dregs of tea in the glass next to me, then stumble into the kitchen to drink straight from the tap.

I'm so unsteady on my feet as I straighten up that I have to grab for the counter. I think I need to eat something. I take a spoon and eat the rest of the fromage frais without closing the fridge door, the chilled air on my legs making me feel slightly more alert.

A noise on the stairs makes me turn. It's Élodie, fresh from the shower. There's something I want to ask her but then it's gone. The *tisane* glass on the counter catches the sunlight from the door to the garden. Even the tiles under my feet are warm today. A runnel of sweat creeps down my spine, though I suddenly feel cold.

'*Shall I make you another tisane, Maman?*' she says. As she passes me, I catch the shampoo scent of artificial fruit and some undertone that's just Élodie. She's suddenly back, her breath on the nape of my neck. '*You're so pale. Come and lie down again. You're taking things too fast. You shouldn't have got up yesterday. You shouldn't be up now.*' I let her lead me back to the salon. A question is beginning to form slowly in my head, and it makes me think of the shiny white square of a blank Polaroid, slowly darkening into something recognizable.

'*Élodie, the tisanes –*'

'*Do you like them? Someone at the ashram showed me how to make them. She knew all about herbs.*'

'*What's in it?*' I'm lying down now and, for the first time in a day – or is it two? – I feel a ripple of nausea.

Élodie covers me with the blanket again, although I can't tell whether I'm hot or cold, goosebumps rising even though my skin is clammy. I open my eyes, although I can't remember closing them, and she's gone. I try to sit up and then I see you sitting there in the corner, reading *Bonjour Tristesse*, Greg's old headphones on, too big for you, and a record on the turntable. She's got you listening to our music – her music – but you're so apparently fine that I allow myself to fall back against the cushions.

'Hey, Mum,' you say, pulling off the headphones. 'How are you feeling?'

'Are *you* all right, darling?' I murmur.

'Yeah, fine. Why wouldn't I be?' The headphones are half back on.

'Where's Élodie?'

'Swimming. She wanted me to stay here and keep an eye on you.' And then you're back in the music, instantly absorbed, just like your father used to be, and I close my eyes again, though I don't sleep. The Polaroid in my mind is beginning to colour in.

1983

I hate the government-run Institut where Élodie is now *receiving treatment*, where your father and I have exiled her by signing our names on a piece of paper. It smells like I've always imagined an old people's home to smell: pine disinfectant and desolation. There are attempts at homeliness, which fall flat and are almost worse than something more openly institutional: asinine watercolours and cheap cushions that haven't worn well. There always seems to be someone shouting or screaming three or four closed doors away, muffled but still loud enough that you can't ignore it.

She sits opposite me on an orange plastic chair. Her beautiful hair is greasy and lank and she has a cluster of spots on her chin. Her eyes look empty and my first instinct – despite everything – is to go to whoever's in charge and get her out of there. But then I think about you, and I know I can't bring her home.

'*You did do it, didn't you?*' I say, like I did the last two times I came. '*I know you did because I found your necklace right there, but I want to hear you say it. I need you to tell me why. I know you hate me but she's just a little girl. How can you feel like that about her?*'

She looks off to the side, out of a window that would be too high in a building that didn't have security built into its fabric, the glass strengthened with criss-crossed wire. It reminds me of the little *souillarde* window. *Such a bad mother*, a voice says. *But how much better would you have done?* says another.

'*And the campsite up in the hills,*' I continue, when she doesn't answer, determination and the ever-present anxiety making my voice shake. '*That was you too, wasn't it? Who were you trying to hurt then? Tell me, Élodie, because I don't know when I'm next going to see you. Your psychiatrist says family visits can set patients back, that it would be better if we didn't come at all for a while.*'

I watch her profile, blue eye glinting darkly, and then she turns back to me so suddenly that I rear back in my seat.

'*I like it. I like fire. It's pretty. I like the way things go up. Whoosh, like that.*' She slaps the table between us. '*You must have been so glad when he said you shouldn't come any more, if he even did. Was it actually you who came up with that idea and he went along with it? Like Papa letting you go and live in England?*'

I shake my head. '*You can ask the doctor yourself if you don't believe me. How many other mothers do you see here?*'

She takes that in and I watch her face flatten again, the fire fading from her eyes. We sit in silence. I watch the second hand on the clock at the end of the room glide round twelve times, and then she speaks again.

'*What about you, then? If I've confessed, then you must too, Maman.*'

1993

I open my eyes and, for once, hardly any time seems to have passed. I wander into the hall, wondering where you and Élodie are. The kitchen door is ajar, and I grip the jamb because I'm still not quite steady on my feet. Élodie is in there, caught in the late-afternoon light, wet hair from the pool dripping on the tiles. She's making me another *tisane* and I watch as she fetches ice from the freezer drawer, banging the tray on the counter to loosen a couple of cubes. She spoons in the tea, and water, and six sugar cubes, and then squeezes half a lemon into the mixture, stirring it so it swirls goldenly round.

Then she reaches into the back pocket of her cut-off denim shorts, and my heart stops dead in my chest as she brings out a handful of dark green leaves, which she throws into my mother's old marble mortar and begins to crush. A pinch and then another is swept into the glass, and it's the same colour as the swimming-pool water in a storm.

As she picks up the glass and begins to walk towards the door, I find I can't move quickly enough, my legs not obeying me. When she finds me there, she doesn't flinch. She never did.

She smiles instead. '*What are you doing up? I was just bringing you this.*' She holds the glass aloft, the green gone now, disappeared into the gold.

I push past her clumsily and go to the mortar, bracing against the counter as I bend down to smell the contents.

'*What is it?*' she says, from behind me. '*What are you looking for? It's mint from the garden.*'

And it is. I sniff it. It's only mint. I turn to her and she has every right to say it – *just because you did it* – but she doesn't. She only takes my arm gently and leads me back to the sofa.

1983

It's two days since the fire in the barn, two days since we almost lost you. I'm convinced the air around the house still smells of smoke, though Greg says that's impossible.

It's almost four o'clock. You'll be getting hungry for your *goûter*, the afternoon snack you love so much: three squares of good chocolate pressed into a length of baguette. On hot days like this, when the sunlight turns molten, the chocolate softens and spreads into the cloud-soft insides of the bread before you can finish it.

I'm not going to need it today.

You're sitting on the terrace, under the shade of a parasol. Earlier, I laid out a blanket and helped you carry your miniature tea set down from your room, along with a selection of your beloved teddies. You still look for Maurice, the little monkey that was ripped apart, but you never mention him.

I glance towards the lawn to check that Élodie is still there, sunbathing on her front, and she is, bikini straps untied so she won't get a tan line. Her hair is fanned out around her head, gold against grass. I haven't spoken to her since before Cannes.

In the china teapot, you're making a potion. We've lately read a book together about schoolgirl witches and you're obsessed with spells and broomsticks and cauldrons. From my position at the salon doors, I watch you add a dripping slice of ripe pear to the watered-down *sirop* I've already mixed for you. A handful of raisins follows, then a crumbled *langue de chat* biscuit sparkling with sugar, and finally a splash of milk from the little jug. You stir it round with a tiny spoon and look inside. You sigh, not happy with it, and my heart begins to flutter wildly as I watch you cast around for more ingredients. *I need to stop this,* I think. *I need to stop it now.* I don't move.

As I'd known it would, your eye alights on the vivid pink flowers I picked for you earlier, arranging them on the china plates, one each for the three teddies at the tea party. You pick one up and rub the petals between your fingers. As you drop it into the mixture, then do the same with the rest of them, I cover my mouth with my hand.

The spoon goes round and round, mushing up the contents to combine them thoroughly. You inspect it again and, apparently deciding it's ready, pick up a cup and pour the brackish liquid. At first you take only a small sip, but it can't taste too bad because you raise the cup to your lips again. This time you drink it all and pour another cup.

Nearly twenty minutes pass before it takes effect, every one of them stretching out as long as a year for me, still stationed at the salon doors. Élodie hasn't moved and she doesn't move when you get to your feet and cry out. I call your name and you turn to me, your hands clutching your stomach, your face pale and waxen. I scoop you up and rush you inside and up the stairs. Catching my reflection in the hall mirror for a brief second, I see my face is haggard with shame.

It happened to me once. I was only a little older than you, maybe five. I ate the same flowers from the garden because I thought something so silken and pretty would taste good. The poisoning came on dramatically: the garden tipping on its side, my stomach starting to twist and writhe. When Maman found me, a strange holy light surrounded her head, like the priest talked about in church.

I was horribly sick that night and into the next day, but then I was fine.

No harm done.

When I was better, Maman took me down to the oleander tree.

She knelt next to me. '*You must never touch this tree, Sylvie. The leaves and flowers – all of it is poisonous. If you have too much, you can die. Tu comprends, chérie?*' She gripped my arm so hard I whimpered. '*Tu comprends?*'

I sit up with you through the night, rubbing your back when the cramps come. You're not as bad as I was, but the guilt is still terrible. I try to keep the same image from the barn at the front of my mind: your dirty lemon T-shirt out of reach as the flames crept higher.

Downstairs in the salon, I hear the ormolu clock chime four times. It's twelve hours since you drank it; you're probably halfway through the sickness now. I

357

think of what's also in the salon: Maman's big old medical dictionary. Attention hasn't been drawn to it yet but there's a particular page marked with a slim packet of cigarette papers. Greg smokes Gitanes; these papers are the kind Élodie uses. I took them from her room when she went outside to sunbathe.

There's a single word at the top of that page, printed in bold black type. *Empoisonnement*. I planted another clue – an afterthought, really. A single long hair, caramel-coloured when held up to the light, as it will be tomorrow. I'll show Greg and then I'll phone the police.

1993

The next day I feel like myself for the first time in what seems an age. My stomach is flat but there's no ache, no nausea.

As I step into the hall, I can hear you singing in the shower. It's 'Good Vibrations'.

When I get downstairs, Élodie is outside on the terrace drinking coffee, her tanned feet on the table, her hair pinned loosely on top of her head for once, showing her delicate neck. She jumps up when she sees me and there's no accusation in her eyes. She puts me to shame.

'*You look so much better today*,' she exclaims. '*Sit down. I bought croissants. There's one in the oven for you, keeping warm.*' She goes inside and I do as I'm told. The sun is blinding and I close my eyes against it. Every muscle aches, as though I've been running all night. The sunstroke has left me but I'm still weak.

Élodie puts a plate down in front of me. '*I went to the good bakery. The other one was always a rip-off.*' She smiles conspiratorially. '*Do you think you'll be up to the party tonight?*'

'*Party?*'

'*At the Martins'. I won't go but you and Emma should.*'

I'd completely forgotten about it. *'Why not you?'*

She shakes her head and looks down at her bare feet. She's painted her toenails the colour of raspberries, and they shine wetly where the sun hits them. *'They won't want me there. Annette won't anyway.'*

I've never known if Laurent confessed anything to her about kissing me that time, or about that night by the pool. There was only one thing Annette and I had ever agreed on, and that was that Luc didn't fall into the pool by accident. I also know what the local women thought of Élodie once she blossomed so suddenly into a woman: the village's very own siren. She had become dangerous in a new way then, and they hated her for it, even more than when she threatened their little ones. The memories feel different now, as I hold them up in my mind. There's a different kind of sadness. For Élodie, for a young girl hated by grown women. It wasn't her fault she was beautiful. I thought of Morel, telling me the first time that she couldn't help it, that it wasn't anyone's fault, even mine.

'I don't think I'll go tonight either,' I say now. *'I'm not up to it.'*

'Oh, but Emma will want to see Luc. You can't deny her that.' She laughs softly and glances up at me. It's the amber eye I can see as she looks away again, framed by long lashes. From nowhere, I feel the urge to cry. I look down at my hand and wonder if I dare cover hers, just inches away. Mentally I check myself over again but the fear feels far off. I'm not afraid of her, not in this moment at least. Briefly, I have the urge to search her for identifying marks, but what imposter could ever fake those mismatched eyes?

The possibility steals into my head: perhaps nothing bad is going to happen after all. The past has never felt so distant at La Rêverie. I sit there, looking at my first-born, and the memories fail to rush in. I glance down the garden towards the oleander tree, but it doesn't seem to signify anything any more. It's just a tree.

By seven that evening I'm showered and deciding what to wear. There's a soft knock at the door and Élodie comes in.

'*Can I help you choose?*' she asks.

You sidle in behind her, slipping your headphones off, a biscuit in your mouth. 'Let Élodie do your hair,' you say. 'She's really good. We can do your make-up too. *Maquillage*. That's right, isn't it?' Élodie and I nod at the same time.

I submit to it, though I expect to feel more self-conscious as she first dries and then twists my hair into waves like hers. When she does my eye make-up, lean-ing right in with the kohl pencil, our faces are so close that I can feel the warmth of her breath. I can smell her skin. Her touch is deft but gentle and when I look in the mirror, once she's finished, I smile at her reflection, which, in its perfect symmetry, looks exactly the same. I take in the three of us – her, me and you perched on the bed behind – and it's somehow easier to comprehend as an image reversed, this miracle of a normal family scene.

We lay out all my dresses. I feel leaner than I have in years; the silver lining that a short illness offers to the diet-conscious. Still, I shake my head when Élodie points to the bright yellow cotton dress I always take on holiday but never wear: with its full skirt and nipped-in waist, it's the sort of thing I would've worn before I was a mother, when I wanted to draw attention. Perhaps I bought it for that reason.

'That one,' Élodie says mock-sternly. You nod from behind her. *'If I'd seen it before, I'd have borrowed it.'*

I laugh at this reference to the way she always stole my things, often ruining them in the process. Somehow it's been recast as a harmless joke. A family in-joke, even. Is this how it could be? I ask myself cautiously. Is it possible for us to be that kind of mother and daughter? Hope shimmers in my peripheral vision.

'Are you sure you won't come?' I say, when we're downstairs. *'Luc did invite all of us.'*

'No, thanks. I'd be shy in front of all those people. Like an . . . exhibit at a museum. I've been so nervous when I've gone to the village, though no one has said anything. I don't want to push my luck.'

'You didn't seem nervous when we went out for dinner. I still can't imagine you getting nervous. You never did as a little girl.'

'I was a strange one, wasn't I? It must have been so hard for you. I felt all of it inside but I didn't show it. I don't know why. I look back and it's like watching a different person with my face. I'm open now, open to everything. Except maybe Annette Martin's anniversary party.' She smiles bewitchingly and pushes a lock of hair behind her ear. *'I'm going to have a nice peaceful evening instead. Have a bath, try the television again, perhaps.'*

'Oh, the news. I meant to check earlier about the fires.'

I go through to the salon but the television is no longer tuned in at all, nothing but static as I turn the dial. I can't get closer than distant voices, which roll away, like the sea, when I chase them. I think the smoke might be stronger as I walk back outside, but perhaps I'm just imagining it now, nothing but a ghost scent. I don't recall any more Canadair planes having gone over and that's surely a good sign.

'Perhaps we're just getting used to it,' I say aloud, because there's still something unsettling about the thought of a fire burning on somewhere, out of sight. I can't entirely grasp it, though, the concept fogged and distant, my mind strangely blank when I try to search it.

'Are you ready, Mum?'

I've been lost in thought for a moment and suddenly it's time to go. You stand before me, back in Élodie's white dress, though it's been washed now, the wine stain bleached away. You're wearing make-up again, but it looks pretty in the glow of early evening and I find I don't really mind. You're fourteen. Didn't I try out make-up at that age? I can't remember. I'm sure my father wouldn't have let me go out in it, but I'm not my father.

*

When we get to the Martins', it feels as though we're late, though we aren't. Everyone is talking about the fires – I keep hearing snatches of excited conversation as I drift through the crowd that has already gathered. It occurs to me that the need to discuss the shared threat is probably what got them all here so promptly in the first place.

We greet Annette, whose eyes skim over your dress and then mine, mouth thinning as she smiles coldly in our general direction. *'No Élodie?'* she asks.

'She's back at the house. She wasn't sure she would be welcome,' I find myself saying.

'And when would that ever have stopped her?'

She moves away, and you ask me in whispers what she said. I shake my head. 'It's not worth it. She's just an old cow.' You giggle and it makes me laugh too. I wonder if Annette is watching us but don't bother looking back to check. At the drinks table, I pour you a Coke and pick up a glass of champagne for me.

'There's Luc,' you murmur in my ear, your sweet breath tickling me. I look over. He seems to be marshalling a gaggle of children younger than you, organizing them into some sort of game. He looks tired, drained. One of his hands is bandaged.

'Can I go over?' you say, and I haven't the heart to say I'd rather you stayed with me.

There's a small jazz band setting up in one corner of the garden and I see Laurent nearby, talking to a couple of men I don't know. When I reach them, they're talking about the fires. Of course.

'Sylvie,' Laurent says softly. He leans over to kiss me, warm hand heavy on my shoulder.

'What's the latest about the fires?' I ask when the introductions have been made. *'I've been in bed with sunstroke and now the television's broken so I have no idea what's going on. I thought they were almost under control?'* I smile round at the men. Someone has refilled my glass.

364

One of the men, introduced to me as Nicolas, shakes his head censoriously.

'Things are serious, like nothing we've seen for years. There's a new fire just north of the Pelletier farm. If the wind gets up again, I think they're going to have to evacuate the whole village. The pompiers have been going door-to-door. Didn't they come to you?'

Unease begins to penetrate. I try to remember hearing a knock at the door. *'Evacuate this village? Really?'* I can hardly believe it. He's right, this man who is regarding me as though I'm an idiot. Nothing like that has happened for years and years. Not for decades. In my childhood, old people had talked about a fire that burnt down a couple of farms on the edge of the village, but I don't think that was even in their lifetimes.

Laurent gives Nicolas a look. *'Well, they're not near enough to panic quite yet.'*

'Didn't you see the flames in the dark last night?' the other man says. I can't remember his name already. The champagne has gone to my head. *'They turned the moon red.'*

Laurent puffs out his cheeks. *'Actually, Luc had a near miss with his friends. Someone dropped a cigarette and the place is such a tinderbox it went up immediately. He said they put it out, but he burnt his hand, had to get it dressed.'*

'I'm telling you,' says Nicolas, *'we might all have to go. They said on the news that it can jump if it's intense enough. It can outrun a car.'*

The hairs rise on my arms and I automatically glance around for you. But even as I do, I try to tell myself that this is a clean sort of anxiety I'm feeling, not personal but elemental. We are all in this together, you, me, everyone crammed into the Martins' garden to drink and listen to the band, like we're aboard the *Titanic*. Élodie too.

Something about this strange, slightly apocalyptic atmosphere is making the wine flow fast. I allow my glass to be topped up again. I don't feel drunk exactly, just pleasingly blanketed from reality. The champagne, the laughter in the garden, the warm scented air – that's what feels solid, not the fires.

It's Nicolas who wakes me up from this daze. I happen to pass him as he's repeating to others what he told us earlier, clearly gratified by their murmurs of horror. *It can jump if it's intense enough. It can outrun a car.* The second hearing penetrates properly, and a delayed warning bell goes off in my mind.

Moving entirely by instinct, I hurry to the edge of the garden that adjoins the one-hectare field that once belonged to La Rêverie. The parasol pines that guard the pool have grown since I last saw them from this angle, tall enough now to obscure even the tops of the chimneys. Now, next to them, rising even taller, as if pointing a finger to the heavens, is a thick plume of smoke. I look behind me but I can't see you or Laurent or Luc and I can't wait either.

I wrench the gate open and begin to run.

I have to stop to get my breath when I'm halfway across the field. The smoke catches in my lungs and the news about the fires comes back to me again, amplified and etched in horror.

As I cross the part of the stream that always dries to

a trickle by June, I see through the ranks of pines what is alight. The oleander tree. As I run towards it, I can see the heavy heads of the deep pink flowers crisping and curling into nothing, swiftly as a match thrown on celluloid.

'*Élodie!*' I cry, and I don't know for sure until the sound comes out of me, more of a howl than a shout, that I'm terrified. And it's not *of* her, but *for* her. There's something so right and pure about that that it makes my voice ring out stronger.

'*Élodie, please!*'

But there's no answer, only the roar of the fire, the pop and hiss of old wood giving in to its own destruction. I run part way across the lawn but she isn't in the house. I know it at a glance because although the windows and doors stand open, there are no lights on inside, giving the place a look of stupefaction.

I turn back to the tree, trying desperately to decide what I should do next. Ring the *pompiers*. Try to put it out myself. Run back to Laurent's for help. And then: *it's so dry, it will undoubtedly spread. It will burn La Rêverie to the ground.*

I cover my face with my hands, rooted to the spot while all these thoughts trample over each other. Where is she?

When I lower them, my eye is snagged by something in the pool that's been turned orange by the fire reflected in it.

For a moment I think she's floating, her singular eyes fixed on the heavens, body cradled and lifted by the water, hair spread out saint-like. But as I run to the edge, avoiding the molten missiles now exploding off the tree, I see it's all wrong this time, that where her face should be there is only hair. She's floating face down.

I try to call her name again, but it doesn't come out or I don't hear it over the fire. In that moment, the moment I understand that she's dead – not missing, not disappeared, but truly gone – I feel something black crawl into the heart of me and it's grief, deep and true.

When I lost her on the beach that time I felt the gossamer brush of relief, and I was ashamed. Now I know, for the first time since she was a few months old, that the rest of it is irrelevant. Élodie is my child and I cannot bear for her not to be alive. I love her and it's uncomplicated and infinite – just as it always was for you, Emma. As I kick off my shoes and jump into the water, I have the clear thought – crystalline blue among the raining fire and ash – that even if Élodie isn't cured then I am.

I launch myself towards her, my arms thrashing through the water, but I can't quite touch the bottom where she's floating. She is heavy, so unbelievably heavy, and I have nothing solid to brace against. I pull aside the heavy hanks of her hair to get to her face and there is so much of it, endless weeds that tangle around my clumsy fingers. Her face, when I find it, is so perfectly made. I turn it towards me and lift it clear before I go under myself. Struggling back to the surface, I try again and manage to turn her properly but her eyes are still closed, as I knew they would be. It's impossible when I'm also kicking to try to keep myself afloat so I loop one of her arms, chilled and leaden, and push out towards the shallow end, dragging her with me.

And then I feel her move. As I twist to take her face in my hands, a raw joy punching through me, her arms go around my neck and I'm pushed under. *No, no,* I say in my head. *It's me, Maman. I've got you. Let go or . . .*

But she doesn't let go and her body feels different now, not slack but tense with life. With cool determination. My eyes open wide, the water stinging them, but she's behind me and I can't see any part of her except her arms pinned around me, one round my neck and the other braced against my shoulders. As my chest begins to burn, disbelief turning to terror, I start fighting her, twisting back and forth to try to free myself. Precious air bubbles foam around us and I hear my own distorted cries. But she clings on, like she's part of me, like we're joined again, as we haven't been since the day she was born. The truth barrels hard into me. You've always been incidental. It's me she really wants to hurt.

In a featureless place beyond the panic and certainty that I will die, there's a deep, gnawing sadness. For those seconds that I simply loved her, and wanted her to be all right more than anything, I felt freer than I have for twenty-four years. But that's gone now and there is no exultation in being right that I should never have trusted her, to have known from when she was tiny that she wasn't made like other people, that where her heart should have been there was nothing but muscle and sinew.

I keep fighting because somewhere across a field, where the world isn't just fire and water, is you. And you need me. But though I keep kicking and writhing as hard as I can, even though there's no breath left inside me, I do allow myself to close my eyes.

I open them again when my hip meets something solid and unyielding – the bottom of the pool. There's still a struggle going on and I can't work it out because I don't seem to be part of it. Everything I have left is resisting the animal urge to breathe in.

Hands grip me under my arms and I think Élodie has changed her position, but the hands are pulling me up and up, and then I'm at the surface and I open my mouth and suck in as much air as I can, and it's no less sweet for being as much smoke as oxygen. The same hands push me towards the edge and I use my last bit of strength to haul myself out. I roll on to the stones and lie there splayed and spent, chest heaving.

'Élodie,' I say, no louder than a whisper. With a huge effort, I turn my head towards the water. There's movement among the reflections of fire and it takes me long seconds to untangle the limbs in my head. The realization when it comes hits me like a brick. It's you, Emma, your still-pale legs kicking so strongly out in the middle of the pool. It's you who pulled me back out from under. All those lessons in a London pool and now you've saved me.

You break the surface. 'I can't, Mum,' you cry, and I

can't distinguish the tears from the pool water streaming down your cheeks. 'I can't get her. She's stuck.'

I don't have time to answer before you fill your lungs and go down again. I stand on shaky legs and try to make out the shapes at the bottom of the pool but you're obscuring her.

'It's her hair,' you scream when you come up again. 'It's caught in the filter.'

I stand there dumbly.

'Go,' you shout, the adult to my child. 'Go to the house and get scissors. Now.'

I run, frantically pulling out drawers in the kitchen until I find my mother's old pair. I race them back to you, and you go down again, frog-kicking to the bottom. I can see her, held there by that beautiful stream of hair. And then she's suddenly free and you have your arms around her chest, bringing her to the surface.

You're so brave, Emma. So sure. You couldn't have done any better. But I know before you break the surface that it's too late for her. I know this because something has gone out of the world and I felt it go: a lost charge, a light dimmed; the exact reverse of when she had fluttered inside me for the first time. The fear has gone, but so has some essential part of myself.

Afterwards

The letter is there when I get home from work, in our metal box in the communal hallway. I know it's French immediately, not from the postmark, which has been smudged during its journey from the place of my birth. It's not because of the handwritten number '7' in the postcode either. It's the handwriting, strong and sure, black ink on decent paper. Olivier's.

> *I don't have your telephone number in London and it seems that you are ex-directory. So forgive me for writing with this news, when it might have been better to speak on the telephone. I chose not to contact Camille because she would have wondered why I needed to get in touch with you, and you only, so urgently. I thought you should know first.*

I scan on down the page and then read it again, from top to bottom, more slowly this time.

> *When you've had time to digest this, please would you call me, Sylvie? Please will you do that? Let me help you sort this out. Remember I am here. I still think of you.*
>
> *Olivier*

Initially, the Spanish authorities had got in touch with the corresponding French departments. Through Élodie's old records from the facility, they acquired her registered home address, which was Greg's old apartment. No one knew him there, but then they noticed a reference to the family solicitor; found Olivier.

It seems that when the commune was disbanded, no one knew what to do with her. She was left with the old woman who'd rented them the land in the first place. She was apparently dirty and slightly underfed but was — and is — otherwise healthy. The woman, who had been under the impression that somebody would be returning, waited for a couple of weeks and then contacted the police. She said she was too old to bring up a young child on her own, especially one who had been allowed to run so wild.

She has been examined and is thought to be about three years old. There is no record of an Élodie Durand or Élodie Winters having a caesarian section at the right time in Spain or France, as far as anyone has been able to trace. The old woman had no idea who the father might be. Besides, as you'll see from the photograph I've included, her mother's genes dominated. I have never seen a picture of Élodie when she was a little girl, but if I can see the adult woman so strongly in the child, I can only imagine how powerful the resemblance might be for you.

Perhaps you have guessed by now that I'm not just writing to inform you of her existence. You, Emma and your ex-husband are her nearest living relatives. Unless you were to refuse, which of course is your right, she is yours. Though, as I've said, there appear to be no official documents, she says her name is Sylvie.

373

I take the Polaroid to the window, where the London sky is already lowering, though it's not yet November. She stares back at me through the camera lens, heart-shaped face, the sharp chin lifted, gaze defiant and little fists clenched. She isn't smiling but, then, it isn't that sort of photo. It was probably taken by a policeman or a social worker. She must be looking into a bright light because she's squinting slightly, inadvertently showing off long sooty lashes. You can still make out the colour of her eyes through them, and they're amber, flecked with gold.

I found out what that tattoo of Élodie's meant. I went to a tattoo parlour in Camden Town and sketched the three black swirls for a woman with orange carp and cherry blossom twisting around her arms.

'Yeah, I can do that,' she said, when I finished. 'Where do you want it?'

'Oh no, I don't want – Sorry, it's just that my daughter had one like it. I saw it before . . . before she died. I wondered what it meant. If it stood for anything.'

She looked at me, her face softening into thoughtfulness. 'It's one of those really old symbols. It means motherhood. Maybe she had it done for you.'

I glance up as I hear the latch of the front door click, the tinny beat of your music spilling into the silent flat. You're home from school. And I turn, ready to show you the picture of your niece, a last piece of my first daughter found: a glint of something precious I might be able to pluck from the wreckage. Another chance.

Acknowledgements

My biggest thanks must go to my wonderful editors, Jillian Taylor in the UK and Seema Mahanian in the US, who helped me make *The Heatwave's* central relationships much more complex, interesting and real. Thank you, both, for pushing me without ever being pushy. I'm so grateful to the rest of the brilliant team at Michael Joseph, too – especially Ella Watkins, Grace Long, Sophie Shaw, Hazel Orme and Emma Henderson.

Another huge thank you goes to my amazing agent Rebecca Ritchie at AM Heath, who was not only a cheerleader for this book from its very first lines but so supportive of me writing a more contemporary novel.

I would also like to thank Marie-Laure Pierson and Jacqueline Priou, long-standing family friends I have spent many a happy childhood holiday with *en France*. Fortunately for me, they possess between them excellent English and experience in child psychology – an invaluable combination for this book. On the British side of the Channel, my step-mum Joan Reardon advised on French terms and also played a crucial role in establishing France as a sort of beloved second home for me. (And yes, you were right that I should have done GCSE

French instead of Drama. I don't know what I was think-ing.) Any mistakes are mine and not theirs.

My early readers are also owed a big debt of thanks for being so encouraging, helpful and kind. Thank you to Darren Loftus, Emma Stonex, Emylia Hall, Amanda Reynolds, Hayley Hoskins, Helen Hockenhull and my mum, Meryl Parker. All my friends and family, in fact, have been fantastic. I couldn't do it without you.